Welcome to Heron House
An Eastport Beach Romance

Tara Ryan

Above Average Press

ISBN 978-1-967758-02-9 (Paperback) 978-1-967758-01-2 (eBook)

For my mom, who always encouraged my love of books. Love you, Mom.

Chapter One

People wear white to weddings and black to funerals, so what color should you wear to the death of your marriage?

Riley smoothed her hands down her best skirt and confronted her image in the mirror. Who was she kidding? It was her only skirt. She'd spent the last ten years wearing her work uniform of jeans and polo shirt embroidered with Big Larry's Collision & Body on the chest. Which left her with little need for an iron either, and was why the collar of her button-down shirt refused to lay flat. At least her hair was semi-cooperating today. Her curls gave her blonde locks a little body and hid the split ends that were another casualty of the upheaval of the last few months.

She dabbed another dot of concealer on the evil little pimple that chose today of all days to rear its ugly pink head. She'd made it through her teens and twenties with surprisingly little acne, but apparently now that the big 3-0 was looming, her normally smooth, blemish-free skin was yet another thing of the past.

Giving up the coverup, she brushed some loose powder over her face to set the makeup—attempting to conceal the bags under her eyes, the new worry line etched on her forehead and the nasty little pink demon.

The peal of the doorbell startled her, and the makeup brush flew out of her hand. It clattered against the counter before skittering to the tile floor. Holding her hand to her chest, she took a couple deep breaths and counted to eight. Her therapist had told her ten, but she'd found eight usually did the trick. Fourteen, fifteen...eight wasn't going to cut it today. The doorbell rang again. She grabbed her phone, checking the time as she reached the door.

The man on the other side looked a little warped through the peephole, but she could see he was dressed nicely and was more well-groomed than anyone she'd ever seen in her low-rent apartment complex, which immediately put her on high alert.

"Can I help you?" She made no move to unlatch either of the locks on the front door.

"I'm looking for Riley Kirkwood."

"She's not here." It wasn't a complete lie.

"Will you be seeing her?" The man appeared to be squinting at the peephole as if he could see the hazel eye glued to the other side.

Riley stepped back from the door trying to figure out his angle. She paced the small foyer, checking her phone again for the time. She had to leave soon, or she'd be late. "I'm not sure." On tiptoes, she pressed her eye back to the hole. "Who's asking?"

The man's brown head disappeared, and she heard a scratching noise. She glanced down to see a business card slide under the door. "I'm an attorney. I need to speak to Ms. Kirkwood."

There it was again. Guess she'd have to get used to it.

Retrieving the card from the floor, she tried counting again. At twelve, she opened her eyes and stared at the simple beige card. Benjamin Ward, estate attorney. "Who died?"

"I'm afraid I can only speak to Ms. Kirkwood about this matter." The attorney looked harmless enough. Unless he had a tommy gun in his briefcase.

Leaving the chain on, she undid the deadbolt and cracked the door. "I'm Riley. But it's Taylor. My maiden name is Kirkwood."

He bowed his head slightly. "Mrs. Taylor, then. May I come in?"

After some deliberation, Riley closed the door and took the chain off. When she opened it again, she found that Benjamin Ward was pretty damn good looking when he wasn't distorted by a funhouse peephole. She swung the door wider and gestured toward the living room. "Please, call me Riley."

He brushed past her in the small foyer and, once in the more open space of the living room, turned to face her again. "I didn't mean to catch you off guard, Riley, but I've been unable to find a phone number for you. Probably because I didn't realize you were married."

Unable to meet his eyes, she stared down at her phone. "I won't be in one hour and seventeen minutes." She raised her head slowly, trying to blink back tears. "Sorry, the last guy in a suit that came looking for me served me divorce papers."

The sophisticated attorney face slipped, and for a moment, Benjamin Ward looked downright devastated.

"It's okay, I mean, I'll be okay, really." Now she was outright lying to this perfectly nice gentleman. How was she going to be ok? In a matter of months, she'd lost her husband, her job, and the one thing she'd wanted as long as she could remember. Riley sucked her bottom lip in and bit down to stop the tears from spilling out. She would not cry in front of this stranger. And she certainly wouldn't cry in front of her ex.

Who she had to face in one hour and fifteen minutes.

"Mrs. Ms. Uh, Riley." He reached out and placed his hand on her forearm. The warmth from his skin permeated her thin shirt and spread up her arm. She blinked back the tears, and as her vision cleared, his hand came into focus. "I'm so sorry. This is obviously the worst possible timing. Perhaps we can set up a better time."

She couldn't stop staring at the gold band circling his ring finger. And as she had too many times to count lately, her thumb stroked over the smooth flesh of her own ring finger. She finally raised her head and met his eyes. They were huge and deep brown, like her neighbor's Basset Hound, Wylie. They were so full of compassion and empathy that Riley knew he had to leave. Now. Or she was going to lose it. And that was not an option. Not today.

"There's a coffee shop down the street. The Green Mug. I can meet you there tomorrow at ten." But right now, he had to leave. *Would it be rude to shove him out the door?* She had to get him out of here before the dam burst inside her head.

"It's a date, um, I mean, that works." He ducked his head, raking his hand through his hair.

Was it possible that this man that seemed so put together was nervous? It didn't matter. Riley wasn't falling for another cheater.

***

The courthouse loomed tall over Riley, a tower of sandstone reaching to the Carolina blue sky. Her last visit here had been a happy one, full of hope and excitement. A beginning.

This was a beginning too, she supposed. An end and a beginning.

"I swear, if that man even thinks about speaking to you, I'm going to smack him into next week." Kelsey stepped beside her and craned her neck upwards. "What are we looking at?"

Riley threaded her fingers through her sister's and squeezed. "I told you not to come." She rolled her eyes further up and blinked several times in quick succession. She wouldn't give Larry the satisfaction of her tears. It was why she told her sister not to make the three-and-a-half-hour drive with a newborn. Having her family with her today would make her too emotional.

"Active labor wouldn't have kept me away." She turned to face Riley, not letting go of her hand. "Luckily, this fella popped out in a jiffy, and here we are."

Riley could just make out the smushed pink face of her new nephew, tucked safely in a complicated shawl/straight jacket/baby carrying contraption. "Liam, you should know right off the bat that your mother never listens to anyone." She stroked his velvety soft head and felt a little of her tension melt away. "Thanks, Kelsey."

Her sister shrugged. "You're my baby sister. Of course, I'd be here."

Kelsey had been a kindergartener when Riley came along, and she'd been taking care of her little sister ever since. Now she had two kids, the perfect marriage, and a beautiful house in the suburbs. It was nice to have her here, but the comparison was almost enough to make Riley's avocado toast reappear.

The obnoxious roar of a too-loud engine shattered the peace of the morning. Riley's stomach roiled again. Worst breakfast decision ever.

A giant white truck with jacked up wheels and a custom exhaust system careened into a parking spot down the block. Obnoxious truck with an obnoxious driver.

"You know, my attorney said I don't technically have to be here." She turned and headed for the crosswalk.

"Oh, no." Kelsey grabbed the back of Riley's shirt, bringing her to a halt and thwarting her escape. "You are going to march into that courtroom and show that big dumb buffoon that you are a strong, independent woman with your shit together."

Riley couldn't very well fight off her sister on a public sidewalk. There was law enforcement everywhere she looked, and Kelsey was literally *wearing* a baby. "But I don't have my stuff together."

Her sister rolled her eyes, whether at her lack of confidence or her choice not to cuss, she couldn't be sure. "Fake it 'til you make it, babe." She wrapped her arm around Riley's shoulders and pulled her toward the building, but suddenly stopped short. "You have got to be kidding me."

Riley followed her sister's gaze in the direction her soon-to-be-ex-husband had parked his gargantuan truck. There he was, Larry Taylor, of Big Larry's Auto Body and Collision, the first boy she kissed—hell, the only boy she'd ever kissed—helping his big-boobed, big-haired, home-wrecking mistress out of the truck.

Leave it to Larry to bring a date to their divorce.

***

"I still say he has a secret bank account in the Caymans." Kelsey shifted Liam in his carrier and kissed the top of his head.

"Shh!" The elevator doors slid shut, and they were finally alone. "I seriously doubt Larry knows anything about secret Cayman's accounts." Riley sagged against the wall, a barrage of emotions threatening to overcome her. Facing her ex in the courtroom had been harder than she imagined. *I just need to make it to the car.*

Kelsey rolled her eyes. "Then he stuffed the extra money down Miss Big Hair's cleavage. There is no way that business isn't making money."

Big Larry's had always done well in the years Riley had run the office. Larry had either run it into the ground in the last year, or Kelsey was right, and he'd stashed his money somewhere.

Riley hated it when her sister was right.

"I told you not to marry that loser. You were always too good for him."

Right again.

The elevator lurched with a ding and the doors slid open. "I'm just glad it's over." *And as soon as I get to the car, I can get rid of this alien-getting-ready-to-burst-out-of-my-chest pressure.*

Kelsey harrumphed. "You got a raw deal. If I ever run into that bast—"

Riley slapped a hand over her sister's mouth and pulled her into an alcove as her ex-husband and the silicone queen stepped out of the other elevator. "Hush, I don't want to make a scene." *I just want to get in my car and drive away from this day.*

As soon as the couple exited the lobby and were out of sight, Riley released her grip on Kelsey's big mouth.

"—ard, I'm going to give him a piece of my mind and a kick to the nuts." She started toward the door, likely trying to catch up to Larry and deliver her threat.

"Kelsey, please just leave it alone. I'll be fine. I'll figure it out." Figure out how to afford to go back to school now that she got exactly zero from her divorce settlement. Figure out how to quit her job at the mini-mart and find something less soul-sucking. Figure out what to do with her life now that she'd failed so spectacularly at marriage.

Chapter Two

Ben thought about the last time he traveled down this winding road hugging the side of a mountain. But he had promised himself no melancholy today. This was meant to be a happy reunion, not a rehashing of the worst day of his life.

The canopy of trees thinned, he rounded the last curve, and the large red farmhouse appeared, looking exactly as it had two years ago.

He pulled his car beside the old Volvo station wagon that brought back memories of making out in the backseat. Clinging to the good times, he grabbed a bouquet of dahlias and leapt up the porch steps.

His knock on the door went unanswered for long minutes. He raised his hand to knock again, but stopped when he heard shuffling on the other side of the door. The curtain moved to the side and Genny appeared, the same, yet so very different. Her blue eyes widened, and a giant grin filled her face. She disappeared and then the door swept open.

"As I live and breathe. Benji!" She held out her arms, and he walked into her familiar embrace, savoring the smell of peppermint that always seemed to cling to her.

"Hey, Genny." He held her tightly, reigning in his emotions. When he was confident he could speak without losing it, he let her go and stepped back to study one of his favorite people.

Long, dark hair flowed over her shoulders and down her back, same as always, although the streaks of gray were new. Her skirt dusted the ground, layers of brightly colored fabric competing for attention, much like her paintings. The cane was also new, and not altogether unexpected, yet still seemed so incongruent to the vivacious woman he knew. Belatedly, he thrust the flowers at her. "These are for you."

She took the bouquet, bringing them up to her face to smell the blooms. "You always were the sweetest. Can't believe you remembered my favorite flowers." She stepped back and gestured inside. "Come in, come in. Let's put these in some water."

As he stepped over the threshold of the old home, more memories rushed at him. Everywhere he looked, there were paintings—on the walls, leaning against furniture, piled on the sofa. So much like Sarah.

Ben shoved his hand in his pocket, pressing the penny between his fingers, putting all his emotions into that disc of copper. He'd gotten the idea from a podcast about dealing with grief. He could no longer discern which president's face was on the coin.

Genny hobbled along in front of him, making her way to the kitchen, rambling about how long it had been.

Two years, one month, six days.

As he passed the dining room, he stopped short, his breath leaving his lungs. Over the fireplace hung the piece Sarah had painted for her aunt's fiftieth birthday. It was this very house, surrounded by massive trees adorned in all their fall glory. Just as always, his wife's work moved him—literally took his breath away.

"Benji? Are you coming? I'm slow as molasses, so if you can't keep up with me, you're in trouble!"

He filled his lungs again, took one last look at the painting, and forced his feet to move him to the kitchen. "Sorry, just admiring your work. You've been busy." The kitchen was just as cluttered with art as the other rooms on the main floor—and likely upstairs. Geniveve Wilder was as prolific as she was renowned. Her primitives were known the world over and hung in famous galleries, museums and even Buckingham Palace. Ben had no doubt Sarah's work would have gotten the same attention if given the chance.

"If you don't stay busy, you die." Genny filled a vase with water, then began attacking the stems with a pair of shears.

Cancer will do it too.

But he didn't begrudge her the statement. She had always been straight to the point, no fluff, no cushion. A bum knee might slow her down, but it'd take more than a creaky joint to stop the force that is Geniveve Wilder.

"Now, tell me. What brings you to my side of the state?"

"Well, I finally tracked down Archie's niece. She lives in Ashford."

"I hate that I missed the memorial. This stupid knee makes traveling nearly impossible. I had to cancel a West Coast tour this summer. But I've got surgery scheduled for next month and then I'll be good as new." She arranged the flowers in the blown glass vase, fussing over the placement. An artist in every regard.

"So many people came out to honor Archie, but you were definitely missed." With Archie and Sarah both gone, his circle had shrunk considerably. "I hate that you're so far away. When I realized I was traveling to Ashford, I had to see you."

She stepped closer and patted his cheek. "You are always welcome here, Benji. I love you like a son. Even though I'm not nearly old enough to be your mother." She winked and went back to arranging her blooms.

He wasn't about to tell her she was older than his mother. Genny lived in a beautiful bubble of her own making here in the countryside surrounded by majestic mountains. She thrived as a working artist, sharing her creativity and talent with the world. But she preferred a solitary life. Painting took priority over everything—and as much as she loved her nieces and Ben, she wasn't the best at staying in touch with the outside world.

"So Archie had a niece, huh? He mentioned his brother once or twice, but it was rare for him to discuss family. Stubborn man. I wonder if she has an artistic streak?"

"I literally met her for about five minutes this morning. She was on her way out." A stab of regret hit him as he remembered her beautiful hazel eyes welling up with tears. "All I know about her is that she's probably divorced by now."

"Five minutes and she's getting a divorce? Haven't lost your touch, I see."

Ben shook his head and laughed. "You're the worst."

"If I recall, you had Sarah under your spell in a week flat."

"That was most definitely the other way around." He'd fallen hard and fast for the vibrant artist-in-training who lived in paint-splattered overalls.

Genny rolled her eyes. "One minute I was painting a beautiful coastal scene, and the next I was helping plan a wedding."

He settled on a stool at the counter, realizing that it felt good to talk about Sarah. It felt good to remember all the happy parts. "That was the happiest time of my life."

"You have lots of life left, Benji." She sat beside him and leaned against the counter, a serious look on her face. "Are you keeping your promise?"

Of course, Sarah told her aunt about their deal. The one where she promised not to haunt him as long as he promised to move on after she was gone. The one he agreed to just to make his dying wife happy.

He squirmed under Genny's intense scrutiny, knowing full well he wouldn't pass inspection. "Archie was sick for a while and there's the estate to settle..." He trailed off, averting his eyes, praying she'd let it drop.

"Archie wouldn't stand for being used as an excuse. Your wife died. You didn't. There are a lot of years ahead of you and she didn't want you to be alone. Or wallow."

They sat in silence for a few minutes, Ben focused on a pastoral scene above the sink.

Then Genny eased off the stool and hobbled over to the pantry, using the island for support. "Divorce is hard too. I bet Archie's niece is feeling pretty alone right now. Maybe you could be alone together." She pulled a bottle from a rack and slid it across the counter to where Ben sat. "Wine makes everything more bearable."

He stared at the Pinot Grigio, organizing an argument in his head. He was a lawyer, after all. He basically argued for a living.

"Ben, look at me."

Slowly, he raised his eyes from the bottle to Genny's face. A face of wisdom, laughter, and right now, empathy.

"I'm a loner. It suits me and gives me time for my art. You weren't meant to be alone. You loved Sarah with all your heart. You are meant to love someone like that again." She put her hand up, as if she knew the defense he'd planned. "Take the girl the wine. And maybe something sweet. You don't have to marry her."

He closed his eyes, and instead of Sarah, he saw Riley there. She'd been a little cagey, but who could blame her? A strange man showing up at her door, just minutes before a life-altering event. That would shake anyone. She kept twisting the strawberry blonde hair that fell in waves around her face, her expressive eyes giving away her trepidation. He couldn't compound an already hard day with the heavy news he had to deliver.

They'd agreed to meet up for coffee the next morning, but maybe she would appreciate a little comfort after a morning in court.

When he opened his eyes, Genny was standing next to him, holding out a reusable bag. "You can make it there by one if you leave now."

He wasn't sure how the wine got into the bag or how Genny made it to his side when he had only closed his eyes for a moment. But now she was pushing him toward the door, cane forgotten. "Genny, I came here to visit you."

"I'll let you buy me dinner. I have work to do, anyway. Seven o'clock. Stoney Knob. You remember?"

"I remember." What he had forgotten was what a steamroller the woman could be. At the door, he turned around. "It's hard to let go."

She pulled him into a hug. "I know, Benji, but easy things aren't worth as much as hard things."

***

Ben stopped at a grocery store for a sandwich and, on a whim, grabbed some cookies from the bakery. He didn't know Riley's preferences, but who doesn't like chocolate chip cookies?

Traffic was heavy, everyone scrambling to grab a meal before their lunch break expired. If the court here was anything like at home, they would break for lunch between twelve-thirty and one. That was assuming Riley's case wrapped before lunch. There really was no way to know.

He arrived at her apartment, and when his knocks went unanswered, he figured he had beaten her back. He settled at a picnic table in the courtyard with a view of her door and unwrapped his sub.

An hour later, he was worried her case had been extended into the afternoon docket and she might not be home until after five. People would start to wonder about the strange man stalking a run-down jungle gym. He was debating the merits of staying or leaving when Riley appeared, dragging her feet along the walkway, her head hanging, like the weight of a thousand problems was preventing her from standing upright.

He grabbed the bag Genny had given him and jogged across the courtyard. "Riley, wait up."

She halted mere steps from her apartment, looking between him and the door like she was considering making a break for it. Her expression was wary, whether about him or the result of a hard day, he couldn't be sure.

"Hey, I know we agreed to meet up tomorrow, but I had a feeling today might be rough, so I brought you..."

She pitched to the side, crumpling like someone had turned the blower off on one of those inflatable Santas.

His arms shot out on instinct, grabbing her before she hit the ground. She was so limp, he feared she had fainted, but a loud sniffle made it clear she was still conscious. He tried to keep her upright, but she was dead weight, and her tears were intensifying by the second.

She mumbled something incoherent and buried her face in his chest. Her hair smelled like pineapple.

Without another thought, he swept his arm under her legs and lifted her off the ground. For a moment, it looked like she would protest, but she was clearly too distraught to argue. "Did you eat today?"

Through her sobs, she muttered, "Avocado roast."

He'd never heard of anyone roasting an avocado, but Ashford was a little bougie, so who knew? He shook his head and sighed. "Where are your keys?"

She fumbled with a small purse that was stretched across her torso, making it hard to maintain his grip on her. She wasn't a big person, but she was a grown ass woman, and he hadn't lifted weights since college.

Somehow, he managed not to drop her or the bag of comfort food. It took several long minutes to get the door open and both of them inside.

"Larry didn't even try to marry me over the stresshold."

Ben didn't speak crying woman, so he was at a complete loss. He weaved between half-filled boxes and settled Riley on the sofa. He couldn't tell if she was packing or unpacking.

She grabbed a throw pillow and curled her body around it.

Unsure what to do, he crossed into the small kitchen. He emptied the bag, setting the wine and cookies on the counter. An opened pack of bottled water sat beside the fridge, so he grabbed one and headed back into the living room.

He sat on the ottoman in front of the couch, waiting for Riley to unfurrow long enough to notice that he was still there. His jacket was damp from her tears, so he removed it, shook it out, and laid it over a chair. He checked his watch, wondering if he'd make his dinner with Genny. He was eager to tell her what a bad idea this was. Riley obviously wanted to be left alone.

After Sarah died, Ben had isolated himself whenever he wasn't at work, wanting to hide away from the world and wallow. Archie would come down to the boat and drag him out from down below, feed him and just sit with him. They'd stare out over the river in silence for hours.

So, maybe this wasn't the worst idea ever. It helped him to know he wasn't alone. Maybe just knowing he was there would comfort Riley.

Eventually, her tears slowed, and she peeked her head out of the pillow.

He snapped the cap off the water and extended the bottle to her. "You should drink."

She just stared at him.

"I brought wine, but you have to drink the water first."

Sighing, she reached for the bottle and took a few sips.

"There's cookies too."

She chugged the rest of the bottle, then dragged her hand across her mouth. "Why are you being so nice? You don't even know me."

"I went through a hard time a few years back and someone was there for me. I'm just paying it forward." She was in no state to be told about an uncle she probably didn't know existed.

Riley locked eyes with him. Hers were rimmed in smudged black, and the whites were red from crying, but she was beautiful. Her gaze drifted down to his hand, where he was spinning the bottle cap between his fingers. When she looked back up, her mouth was set in a grim line. "Thanks for your help, but as you can see, I have a lot of packing to do. I promise I'll be less of a mess tomorrow."

"You're not a mess, you've just had a hard day." Her shirt was untucked on one side, her hair was tangled, and her mascara had left streaks across her cheeks, but he was guessing she cleaned up rather well.

She rose from the couch and started throwing magazines in a box. "I really appreciate the food and scraping me off the sidewalk, and all, but..." She wouldn't look him in the eye as she emptied the drawer under the TV stand.

He got it. "I'll see you tomorrow. You need anything, you've got my number." If he had to guess, she'd make a beeline for the wine as soon as he was out the door. "Be sure to eat something—even if it's just cookies."

Ben wasn't certain, but he thought he saw Riley crack a smile as he backed out the front door.

Chapter Three

Riley pushed through the door of the coffee shop down the street, her eyes scanning the small space for the man who had witnessed a true low point in her life just last night. She was dreading this meeting, and it had very little to do with the fact someone must have died and everything to do with the wreck she had been in front of the very put together, handsome, married attorney. Even in her distraught state of mind, she'd noticed the gold band on his left hand. Then she'd spent the evening calling everyone she loved, and they were all very much alive, so she had no clue why she was here.

Benjamin Ward was seated at a corner table, a steaming mug in front of him, and his attention focused on his open laptop. She stepped up to the counter and ordered a hot chocolate with extra whipped cream. She had to work that night, and coffee would mess up her before-work nap.

It was mid-morning, so while most of the tables were full, the barista made her drink quickly and handed it over the counter. Riley wrapped her hands around the wide green mug, soaking in its warmth. The spring day was a little on the chilly side, but the birds were in full song, and she'd even seen some daffodils poking through the dirt outside.

Spring was about new beginnings and that's what she wanted more than anything. With a broken marriage behind her, her plans to return to school on hold, and an apartment full of moving boxes, she needed to figure out what to do with her life. And she hoped like hell it didn't involve working at the mini mart much longer.

Holding her cup in front of her and her head high, she walked over to the small round table. "Hey."

Apparently engrossed in whatever he was doing on his laptop, her greeting startled Ben and he jumped, his knee knocking into the table and his drink sloshing over the side of the cup. "Oh, crap. Sorry." He grabbed a pile of napkins and blotted at the table. The spill crept toward his laptop and in his haste to move it out of the path, he knocked it onto the floor. The computer landed with a crash and Riley watched in horror as the screen went dark.

"I'm so sorry, I didn't mean to startle you." She bent to retrieve the laptop, and her right breast dipped right into the whipped cream piled high on top of her mug. Whipped cream with a chocolate drizzle around it.

She looked down in horror as the white and brown concoction bled into her white shirt. *Why the hell did I wear white? I never wear white. Because I spill things! And apparently dip my boob in them.* "Crap on a cracker."

She plunked the mug onto the table that was already streaked with brown liquid and more whipped cream. Ben stood opposite her, holding the dripping napkins, his mouth agape. Yeah, this seemed par for the course for her interactions so far with this mysterious stranger. She spun around without another word and rushed to the bathroom. So much for trying to appear normal.

Locking the door to the single stall bathroom, she backed up against it and bent at the waist. She tried to take deep breaths and not completely freak out, but the blotch around her breast was distracting. Standing up, she turned to face the mirror over the sink. She'd spun her hair up into a messy bun this morning and it had looked decent, but now half of it hung down limply on the side of her face, her shirt was ruined, and her eyes were shining with tears.

So much for new beginnings. Her life was still the same complete disaster it had been the last year and a half.

Riley yanked some paper towels out of the dispenser and ran them under cold water. She was blotting at her boob when her cell phone chimed with a message. She continued to work at the stain, but instead of helping the situation, now she looked like a pathetic participant in a wet t-shirt contest. If you looked really hard, you could even make out the hole in her bra. Another chime called out from her purse. Chucking the wad of paper towels in the trash, she dug through her purse and pulled out her phone.

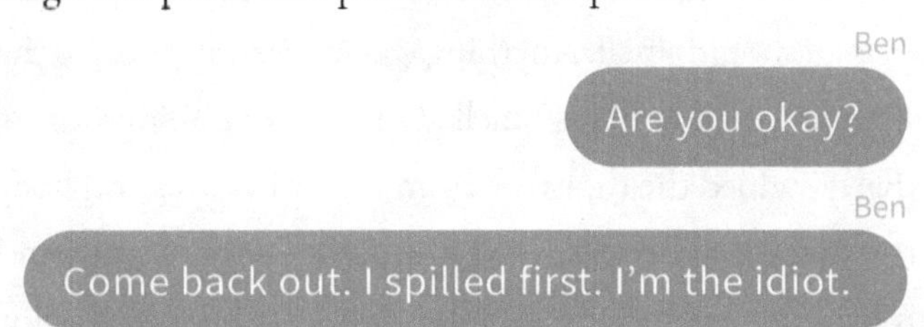

The words blurred on the screen. She'd been to this coffee shop enough times to know she'd have to pass his table to get out the door. Looking in the mirror again, she tried to pull her wet shirt away from her breast. She looked around for a hand dryer. Stained and dry was better than peep show with a ratty bra. But the bathroom was small and only had a paper towel dispenser. Someone knocked on the door. And her phone chimed again.

She'd have to face him eventually. Might as well get it over with. Maybe she could talk him into leaving first. Then she could run through the café to her car with her purse in front of her chest. Why didn't she carry a bigger purse?

She dropped her phone into her tiny purse and turned the lock on the door, peeking her head around it. "Hey." Yeah, completely normal. Casual even.

He didn't say anything, just thrust something at her and turned back toward the café.

She closed the door and relocked it, then looked down at the fabric in her hands. It was a hoodie. A simple grey hoodie with a small Carolina blue Tarheel on the front. It was the most beautiful piece of clothing she'd ever seen.

Riley pulled it on and zipped up the front all the way to her neck. The sleeves were a little on the long side, so she rolled them up a couple times and then looked in the mirror. And smiled. Just a little one.

She took the clip out of her hair and shook her head. Gathering the curls back up, she redid her bun. She tucked her head into her shoulder to fix a stray strand of hair, and that was when she smelled it. A woodsy, but sophisticated scent. Like a man should smell. Anything was more sophisticated than Larry's off-brand Obsession, which honestly smelled more like rubbing alcohol than cologne.

Riley swiped the moisture from under her eyes and nodded at herself in the mirror. She could do this. Twenty minutes tops. Then Ben Ward would vanish from her life, and she could figure out what her new beginning would be. She spun the lock on the door and headed back down the hall to the front part of the coffee shop.

Ben was at the same table, but it was now clear of any evidence of the disaster. He had a new drink and across from him was a fresh mug of hot chocolate. With extra whipped cream. Riley slipped into the chair and attempted a smile. "Thanks for the sweatshirt." She kept her hands in her lap, not trusting them near any beverage at this point.

"Of course, sorry I'm such a klutz."

Maybe this man isn't quite as put together as he seems.

"Is your computer ok?" She dared to move her hand toward the mug because she needed a little chocolate fortitude.

He gestured toward the bag on his chair. "Yeah, I think it will survive. I got the extended warranty in case it doesn't. Last time the coffee landed on the keyboard—fried the whole thing. Learned my lesson." He chuckled and then sipped his drink, getting a dab of whipped cream on his nose.

Riley felt the smile spread across her face. "You've got a little..." She pointed to her nose.

He set his mug down and grabbed a napkin from the new stack standing by for emergencies. Swiping at his nose, he grinned. "Did I get it?"

"Yeah, all good." Feeling bolder, she dared to sip her cocoa. This wasn't so bad. Maybe she could stand twenty minutes sharing a beverage with this charming man. Even if she wouldn't see him again. And he was married.

They sipped their drinks in silence for a few minutes, then Ben reached into his bag and pulled out a folder. "Riley, the reason I wanted to meet with you is because I represent the estate of Archibald Kirkwood."

"I don't know anyone named Archibald." That name would be a hard one to forget. This was likely a mistake. Same last name but no relation.

"He was your uncle."

Riley slowly shook her head. Her only uncle was George, who married her mom's sister last year. "No, I don't have an uncle on my dad's side."

Ben looked downright uncomfortable, then slid his hand across the table and over Riley's. "It's my understanding Archie was estranged from his family. Since his early twenties."

"My dad has a brother he's never told me about?" Riley searched her memory banks for any mention of a brother. She tried to visualize the pictures in her late grandparents' house. Surely there would have been some evidence of a second son.

He squeezed her hand lightly. "Had. Archie passed away two weeks ago."

"Does my dad know?" Riley was so confused. How could she not know about Archie? How could her grandparents never talk about him? Why had she never had a chance to meet him? Their family was small, and she was always jealous of her friends with big extended families. "Do I have any cousins?"

"Your father wasn't at the memorial service, so I doubt he knows. Archie explicitly asked me to reach out to you."

"The memorial service? It's already happened?" How could she feel such a deep sensation of loss when she never even knew the man existed? And now it felt like she had missed her opportunity to grieve.

Ben withdrew his hand and pulled a pamphlet from the folder. He slid it across the table. "There was a small service last Saturday. Just his close friends, other artists."

Riley looked down at the man pictured on the front of the booklet. The resemblance was remarkable. He shared her dad's light gray eyes and even the shape of his face. His skin was wrinkled and leathery, like he had spent his years in the sun. Her finger traced the dates below his picture. "He was nine years older than my dad."

"Yeah, I've seen a few pictures of them as kids. There was a significant age gap."

She flipped the pamphlet open and read a few lines. She looked up at Ben. "You said he was an artist?"

"Riley, your uncle was an amazing artist." His eyes lit up and his smile stretched toward his ears. "He was a sculptor and a painter, but his primary passion was encouraging other artists. He spent most of his life teaching and fostering talent. Giving young artists a boost into the art world." He reached across the table and flipped the booklet over. "This was one of his most well-known pieces. And what I came here to talk to you about." He pointed to a picture of a bronze statue of a graceful blue heron perched atop a fountain in front of a large house. "This is Heron House. It's your uncle's legacy. And he left it to you."

"I inherited a house?"

Ben leaned forward; his eyes bright. "It's so much more than just a house, Riley. Heron House is an artists' retreat, a place for inspiration, a haven." He shifted in his chair and sat back a little. "Well, it was. Your uncle was sick for the last couple of years, and the house has fallen into disrepair. But I have an idea of how you could restore it to its former glory." He gestured to the picture on the back of the memorial brochure.

Riley rubbed her hands over her face. "Restore it? I don't know anything about fixing up a house. And I have zero money." She shook her head. "Eastport Beach is clear across the state. I can't just up and move." Her whole life was here. Her miserable job, her ex-husband, the crappy sublease that was up in a month. Ok, moving wasn't the worst idea ever. "How bad is it?" She peeked between her fingers in time to see another grin spread across Ben's face.

"Just a little run down. Needs some TLC. All the basics are solid. Archie had the plumbing and electrical redone a few years back and the roof was replaced less than ten years ago. Once he got sick, he stopped letting artists stay there so the rooms upstairs are stuffy and dusty. There's some peeling wallpaper, and I'd probably rip out the carpeting, but it's mostly cosmetic." He must have noticed the terrified look on Riley's face, because he slipped his large hand over hers again. "There's a plot of land behind the house. Archie thought about adding on or building a separate studio space, but he never got around to it. You could sell that land and use the money to fix the house up. Open it back up to artists. Archie made a tidy profit every year he allowed guests."

She stared at the hand covering hers. It was a strong hand, one that could probably rip a carpet out. But the closest Riley had ever gotten to a renovation was when she oversaw the painting of the service lobby at Big Larry's. It had taken her a week to choose which shade of white to paint it.

Her mind was spinning with all the information she'd had thrown at her in the last thirty minutes.

An uncle she didn't know existed had died and left her a house. But not just a house, apparently. Could she really make something of it? Could she make something of her life?

"What happens now?"

Chapter Four

The clay beneath his feet was baked to extra crispy under the high noon sun. It was shaping up to be an unbearable summer if it was this hot in late spring. The ball hit with a thud, the bounce low, as Ben scooped his racket underneath and lobbed it back to the other side. Sweat was streaming into his eyes, but he was playing singles and didn't have time to reach up and wipe it away. The ball whizzed at his head with alarming speed, and he stepped to the side to attack it with a backhand. It planted right inside the line, and despite Chesnee's dive, bounced to the back of the court and wedged along the bottom of the chain link.

"Damn. You've been working on your backhand. That was brutal." The younger man brushed off his navy shorts and approached the net with his hand extended. "Good match, old man."

Ben narrowed his eyes, but shook Chesnee's hand firmly. "Way to keep me on my toes, son."

His assistant and friend raked his hand through his damp hair, and Ben was pleased to know he wasn't the only one who had worked up a sweat during their game. They both turned and walked to the bench where they grabbed matching water bottles—a perk from playing in a charity event last fall. Chesnee gulped a long stream of water before speaking. "How was the trip to Ashford? Was it weird being back there?"

Tilting his head back, Ben drained the bottle, stalling for a few moments. Sarah's voice echoed through his mind. "Promise." He swallowed the thick lump in his throat with the last gulp of water and gripped the back of his neck. "A little, but in the long run, it was a relief to get the first visit over with."

"First visit? Do you mean Sarah or Archie's niece?"

"The cemetery, of course. Meeting Archie's niece was fine."

Chesnee shifted his feet, uncomfortable with the talk of death, when he was a shining example of a full life ahead of him. Ben hoped he'd never have to experience a loss that brought him to his knees.

Clapping him on the shoulder, Ben cleared his throat and tried to lighten the mood. "You wore this old guy out. How about loser buys lunch?"

"Sure, but I get to pick where we eat. I'm more of a beer guy than a tea and crumpets guy."

Ben felt his mood lightening as a chuckle escaped. "That was a business lunch. Mrs. Rosilyn expects white glove service. You know I prefer greasy fries and a bucket of beer."

Eyebrows raised, Chesnee cocked his head toward his boss. "Um hmm, I saw your pinky up. I'm not convinced."

Throwing his tennis bag over his shoulder, Ben led the way to the parking lot. "Got the account, didn't I? Pay attention, young man, and I'll show you how to woo them all—from old Manny down at the bait shop to the freaking King of England."

Chesnee threw his head back and laughed. "I doubt the King of England will be showing up in Eastport Beach, North Carolina, looking for an estate attorney."

"I know this is a steppingstone for you, Chesnee. You're going places and one day, you might need the King on the hook."

***

"So did the niece freak when she found out?" Chesnee dipped a fried shrimp into cocktail sauce and popped it in his mouth.

Ben thought back to Riley's face when he told her about Archie. He could practically see the wheels grinding as she tried to comprehend what he was telling her. It'd be a shock to anyone—finding out about a close relative dying—but an uncle you didn't know existed, he couldn't imagine how it must feel. He'd implored Archie to reach out to his family when he became ill, but the man was stubborn and said it didn't matter at that point.

"She handled it pretty well, considering it came right on the back after another life-changing event."

"What do you mean?"

"The day I met her, she'd just come from the hearing for her divorce."

Chesnee took a swig of his beer and shook his head. "Damn, that's rough. How old is she?"

"I don't know, maybe late twenties."

His eyebrows arched, and he tilted his head to the side. "Hot?"

Ben sighed. "Chesnee, she doesn't need someone hitting on her the moment she gets into town. She just got divorced."

Chesnee leaned back in his chair. "Already staking your claim, huh?"

"No. Not at all. But she's vulnerable."

"Um hmm. Sure."

Gripping the edge of the table, Ben leaned forward, looking Chesnee straight in the eye. "I had my one."

"Who says you only get one?" Chesnee challenged his gaze, not backing down.

Promise.

Ben broke the stare down first and leaned back in his chair. He remembered how it felt to have a whole life in front of him, to not feel beaten and broken. He saw himself as a mentor to Chesnee and didn't have the heart to break his spirit. He finished off his drink and rose from the table. "Thanks for the match and for lunch. I'll see you Monday."

Chapter Five

Rain pelted against the windshield, making it nearly impossible to see the pavement ahead of her. Marshes lined the two-lane road, and Riley did not want to end up as alligator food if she drove off the asphalt.

Are there alligators in eastern North Carolina? She'd need to bone up on her ecology of the area. It was important to know about the predators where you lived. Back in Ashford, the only wildlife she had to fear was the pack of raccoons that ate out of the dumpster behind her building. Occasionally a black bear would wander out of the woods, but she'd only seen those on the news, never in person.

Her GPS beeped, and the navigation announced her turn was six hundred feet ahead on the right. Thank goodness. She could get off this road and maybe find civilization.

She slowed at the sight of a blurry red light flashing in an intersection. She looked in both directions. The rain was so thick, she couldn't see a foot in front of her, so she'd have to turn on faith and hope if there were other cars around, they would stop on red. As she regained her land speed record of 25 mph, the GPS showed she needed to proceed another fifteen miles. Fifteen miles in this rain? In the flattest land she'd ever driven through? If she drove off the road at home, she'd likely plummet to her death, but at least it was an interesting drive.

If she didn't have GPS, how would she ever find this place? Turn left at the clump of marsh grasses, then right at the rock shaped like a UFO. Maybe this was a bad idea.

Blowing out a sigh, she turned up the radio and tapped her fingers while humming along to an Elton John tune. She'd chosen her classics station for the drive, hoping it would keep her awake. It was late, and dark, and Ben wasn't expecting her until tomorrow, but she'd decided to drive straight through. Her most recent pathetic job was the night shift after all, so being awake after midnight was normal for her.

She was beginning to regret her decision, however, because she hadn't seen a hotel since she left I-95.

She'd packed up her car after lunch with her mom, who still refused to discuss "your father's personal business."

How sad was it that her life fit in the back of a twenty-year-old Honda Accord? After the split with Larry, Riley had moved home for a little bit and then found a sublease in a crappy furnished apartment, so basically all she owned was a couple suitcases full of clothes, a box of old records, her mystery novels and this car. She didn't even have a turntable to play her records on. Larry had claimed the "sound equipment" in the living room was his and produced receipts to prove it. The bastard didn't even own any vinyl.

But she wasn't about to fight him. She wanted to move on. Like he so clearly had.

A bolt of lightning briefly lit the sky and confirmed her suspicions. Yup, not a speck of civilization in sight. What was she getting herself into? The boom of thunder that followed made her jump, and she swerved briefly into the other lane. "Jiminy Cricket. I'm gonna die and no one will find my body. Just a fat alligator lounging in a Honda Accord." She slowed a bit more and regained control of the car. *This mind-blowing speed is going to make those miles roll by...*

***

The rain finally let up a bit and Riley had even driven through a small town that was either closed up for the night or inhabited by the ghosts of other alligator victims. She couldn't believe her eyes when she saw lights up ahead. She had never been so happy to see a home improvement store in her life. Not that she had a dire need for screws or that it was even open, but it meant she wasn't the last person in a post-apocalyptic world.

It was possible her imagination had taken over on the most boring drive of her life. She really hoped the trip wasn't an omen for her fresh start.

Continuing down the now four-lane road, she saw other encouraging signs of human life. Fast-food restaurants, other cars, and even an all-night drugstore. She swung into the parking lot and bolted out of the car. She'd needed to pee for the last hour and there hadn't even been a bush to go behind, not that she would have ventured out into the alligator-filled darkness.

Bladder emptied and a bag full of junk food clutched in her fist, Riley hopped back in the car and looked at the navigation. Only twelve minutes to her destination. She was finally going to see where she'd be spending the next chapter in her story.

After a wrong turn and fifteen minutes of "recalculating," Riley pulled down a long gravel driveway. The night was dark, the moon barely peeking from behind a cloud. While only a few miles out of town, her uncle's house might as well have been on a deserted island. There wasn't another house in sight, or any sort of light, save a few stars twinkling through the lingering clouds. Her headlights illuminated the rutted path—driveway was a term too generous for the patch of earth her car bumped down—and nothing else. She followed the bend in the gravel around to the left and her lights swung over a large fountain. She immediately recognized the heron perched on top from the picture Ben had shown her.

The fountain wasn't functional from what she could tell, but it was full of water, possibly from the torrential rains. She continued in a slow circle around the water feature and stopped in front of a flight of steps. She couldn't make out the top of stairs in the darkness and the folly of her last-minute decision to drive through the night dawned on her.

Lowering her forehead to the steering wheel, Riley wondered where her brain was residing these days, because it most definitely was not in her head. Pete Townsend and his background singers tormented her from the speakers. Her music was not helping. She didn't have any love to open the door, or any keys, for that matter. Ben was meeting her here tomorrow at lunchtime. Well, technically today. Not a great start to this new "adventure."

She turned off the car and pushed open the door. Grabbing her phone, she switched on the flashlight and illuminated the rocks under her feet. She rounded the front of the car and made her way up a set of rickety stairs. *Just a little run down my ass.* She reached the top of the steps and shined her light around a large, covered porch. Here was a little potential, at least. A couple hanging ferns and some rocking chairs would spruce it up, make it feel homey, like a Cracker Barrel.

From the small beam of light, all she could make out was a bench beside the front door and a hanging swing swaying in the light breeze. And then she smelled it. She inhaled deeply, the crisp air filling her lungs. The smell of the ocean, freshly cut grass, and rain all rolled into a dreamy, best-selling candle scent. She must be really close to the water. If only she could see it. And any alligators that might creep out of it...

Not exactly clear on her actual plan, she pulled at the screen door and said a brief prayer before trying the doorknob. Not surprisingly, the door remained locked up tight. She briefly considered breaking the glass and letting herself in, but from the little bit she could see, she had enough to fix without adding a window to the list. She glanced down at her phone. It was after one, so she didn't dare call Ben. What would his wife think about a strange woman calling her husband out in the middle of the night? She sighed and plopped down on the bench, not noticing the small pot until it was lying in pieces on the wooden floor of the porch. She sighed heavily and bent to pick up the pieces. Luckily, it was a regular red clay pot, not some priceless heirloom. She fumbled with her phone, trying to put all the pieces up on the bench—and then she saw the glint of metal. No way. She couldn't be that lucky. Not after her night.

She shined the light on the end of the bench and sure enough, in the middle of a ring of soil and water lay a brass key. It was almost as pretty as the hoodie Ben had given her after the whipped cream incident.

Rubbing the metal between her fingers, she shifted the light to illuminate the lock and prayed the key fit. It took a few wiggles, and holding her mouth exactly right, but then the lock clicked, and the door swung into the darkness of the house.

The night outside was eerily silent, save the gentle lapping of water and an occasional cricket, but the quiet inside the old house settled over Riley like a cold, damp blanket. The thin beam of light from her phone did little to penetrate the darkness past the door. She hesitated on the threshold, looking back at her car, then into the desolate interior of the house.

She'd come all this way. There was nothing left for her in Ashford. The only direction to go was forward.

She gingerly reached her arm through the opening and felt the wall to the right of the door. When her fingers found a switch, she felt an ounce of relief and when the light flashed on, she let out the breath she hadn't realized she'd been holding.

Light from a crystal chandelier filled the large foyer, illuminating the base of a grand staircase, a wooden bench, and a smaller version of the heron statue outside. Emboldened by the brightness, she stepped into the space. Into *her* house. That'd take some getting used to.

Off to her left, an arched entry led into another room sheathed in darkness. Feeling lucky now, she leaned through the opening and found another switch. Several lamps flickered on, revealing two couches and several upholstered chairs facing a massive fireplace. She walked through the space, her fingers tracing along the back of a deep green velvet sofa. The furniture was definitely old, but in decent shape, and very fitting of the vibe of the room. Antique with an artistic flair.

It was a far cry from the overstuffed sectional Larry insisted on buying for their living room. She would bet there weren't hidden recliners in these couches. Feeling the side of her mouth quirk into a grin, Riley spun slowly around the room. Her night was looking up. Maybe this wasn't the disaster she'd been dreading on the excruciating drive down here. Maybe this *was* the exciting new adventure her sister had tried to sell.

She continued around the downstairs, turning on lights and finding the kitchen, a generous butler's pantry, a study and a large dining room. The home was beautiful despite the peeling wallpaper, water-stained ceilings and scuffed linoleum. Every room had a fireplace and the art throughout was breathtaking. She wondered how much of it was her uncle's, because the pieces varied wildly in style. Maybe Ben would know more about it.

She was examining a painting of a lighthouse in the study when she heard a creak. From walking around, she had discovered, like a lot of older homes, the ancient hardwoods had settled and made distinct noises with the smallest movement. Was someone in the house with her?

She crept over to the French doors and peered down the long hallway that ran under the stairs and back to the foyer. The ground floor of the house was lit up like Vegas at this point (not that she would know what Vegas looked like). Surely no one could hide with all these lights on?

"Hello? Is anyone there?"

The old house didn't answer her.

For the first time in her life, she wished she'd paid more attention when Larry tried to teach her how to shoot a gun. Not that she was packing, so it probably wouldn't help her present situation.

"Ben?" The lawyer wasn't due for another ten hours, but a girl could hope.

Two choices lingered in her mind. She could close and lock the French doors and cower in the study until Ben showed up, or whoever was in the house simply broke the glass and let themselves in to murder her, or she could pull up her hipsters and be brave. It was likely just the sounds of an old house in the middle of nowhere.

"I'm coming out." She looked wildly around the room and spotted a brass shovel on the hearth. She grabbed it and raised it up against her shoulder, looking out into the hallway again. "I'm armed, so if you're planning on murdering me, I'm not going down without a fight." She crept down the hall, hugging the wall that ran under the stairs. The front door was still closed, but she couldn't be certain if she had locked it. "Seriously, I am not to be trifled with. Everyone tells me I'm surprisingly strong for a girl." *Yeah, that'll scare them.*

At the end of the hall, she swung to the left into the dining room, wielding her decorative shovel. "Ahhhh!"

And her murderous serial killer revealed itself.

Sitting smack dab in the middle of the twelve-person dining table sat the fluffiest grey cat she'd ever seen. The feline stared at her apathetically, not the least bit intimidated by her show of bravery. Its tail twitched against a lace tablecloth yellowed with age. Green eyes appraised her, then the cat stood up, stretched its back legs out, leapt from the table and wandered into the kitchen without giving Riley a second look.

Feeling a tad ridiculous, Riley slowly lowered the shovel and leaned against the wall. *Yeah, a cat. I totally knew that. Ha ha. Joke's on you.* After catching her breath, she followed the cat into the kitchen.

The room was as empty as her first pass through it. She glanced behind the fridge, under the island, and even opened a few cupboards. An old box of crackers, some pots and pans, and a few distinctive small brown pellets. Apparently, the cat wasn't performing its duties.

She poked her head into the butler's pantry. There weren't many hiding places in the narrow space, but she opened a few cabinet doors, anyway. On her fourth try, she hit the jackpot. Still no cat, but she found Archibald's stash. It appeared her uncle was something of a connoisseur. At least a hundred bottles of wine filled the lower cabinet, most covered in a thick coating of grime. She selected a 1982 Chardonnay. Her typical wine was aged by months, not decades, but she wasn't a snob—she'd give it a try.

"Don't mind if I do, Archie."

She went back into the kitchen on the hunt for a wine glass. Hell, a plastic tumbler would suffice at this point. All thoughts of locating the resident feline fled as she searched the upper cabinets for any vessel that would hold wine. It had been a long day, and a glass of grape juice was exactly what she needed to help her wind down and get some sleep.

It was hard to imagine how anyone had lived here without the basics—where the devil were the plates and cups hiding? She leaned against the island, tapping her finger to her temple, trying to figure out this mystery. Someone who owned that much wine must have wine glasses.

Her fridge was always stocked with the finest box of vino money could buy and she had two wine glasses, but they were packed in a box in her backseat. No way was she going back into the dark night full of axe murderers and rabid alligators. Her eyes traveled around the space and finally lit on the doorway to the pantry.

Of course! Fancy people with butler's pantries. All the dishes were probably in there. She went back into the room and looked at the upper cabinets this time. Eureka! Beautiful china and crystal filled the shelves, sparkling despite their coating of dust. She selected a goblet—okay, the biggest one—and took it into the kitchen and turned the faucet on. Her luck was holding out. She had electricity *and* water.

She washed and dried the glass and then grabbed the bottle off the island. She gripped her hand around the top of the bottle and turned. Apparently, they hadn't invented screw tops by 1982. And this definitely wasn't a spigot. Throwing open the nearest drawer, Riley began digging through it for a corkscrew. She was on her third drawer when she stopped with her hand on a melon baller. Was that a door opening? She swung towards the dining room, clutching her latest weapon. This one didn't even have a sharp edge.

"Riley? Is that you?" Ben's deep voice came from the front of the house, stilling her racing heart.

"Ben, I'm in the kitchen." She was so relieved to hear his voice that it took her a minute to wonder why he was here in the middle of the night. When he walked into the kitchen, he looked like he had, in fact, rolled straight out of bed and showed up at her door. His hair was rumpled, his cheeks covered in scruff, his joggers and t-shirt were wrinkled, and the pair of sneakers on his feet looked like they'd run thousands of miles.

He looked delicious.

Riley mentally chided herself. *Married, married, married.* "You're a little early for our meeting." She was going straight to hell for flirting with a married man in the middle of the night.

"Yeah, well, so are you." He rubbed his eyes and then squinted at her. "Are you balling a melon?"

She looked down at the utensil she was clutching to her chest. "Ha ha, funny story." She lowered the utensil back to the drawer and reached for the bottle of wine. "Trying to find something to open this baby. Uncle Archie didn't believe in screw tops. And the cat scared the bejesus out of me. You didn't tell me there would be a cat. And then I thought I heard the door and well, you know, axe murderers and all." She had to stop rambling. Now. The wine wasn't even open yet.

The corner of Ben's mouth hitched up, and he stepped further into the room, opening a drawer next to the fridge. He pulled out some fancy device and took the bottle from her hand. After performing a legit magic trick, he filled the glass she had washed and handed it to her. "Here you go."

She gratefully took a swig of the wine. Damn, *that's smooth. Not too shabby for old wine.*

Ben leaned against the counter, his arms crossed across his chest, one ankle in front of the other. Grinning.

After a few more sips, coherent thoughts began to form in her brain. The clearing phase that came before the tipsy phase. "It's," she said as her eyes flicked to the clock on the microwave, "two a.m. What exactly are you doing here?" Not that she wasn't supremely grateful, because she never would have been able to open the bottle with whatever that thing was. Heck, she wouldn't have even known what it was for. "Pretty sure most attorneys don't make house calls in the middle of the night. Does opening a bottle of wine count as billable time? Because I don't really have any money, but I'm happy to share." *And the rambling continues.*

She started toward the pantry to get another goblet when he reached out and grabbed her forearm. "None for me, thanks. Even though I'm not on the clock." Then he winked at her.

Winked!

Riley raised the glass to her mouth and took another gulp. *Holy hell.* This was so bad. So very bad. She had to work with this man—at least until the estate was straightened out. *Man, it's hot in here. The wine probably isn't helping.*

Her laugh was awkward and slightly screechy. "Ha, yeah, good one. Thanks for the wine assist. Long day. I'll let you get back to your bed, um, you know, your wife in your bed." Why did she always get so flustered around this man? Her face flamed—between the wine and her embarrassment—she feared it would melt off.

Ben's expression was a mixture of confusion and sadness. "Riley, I'm not married."

Her eyes slid down to his hand. *Yup, still there.*

He followed her gaze. "Anymore." He pulled his hand back and twisted the ring. After a few moments, he met her eyes, his glistening. "I lost my wife almost two years ago."

"Oh, I'm so sorry." Riley wracked her brain. Had she ranted to him about how awful marriage was? She'd been a little bitter the last few months and had given a few people her "perspective." Tilting the wine glass up, she finished it off. She really hoped she hadn't been insensitive to him.

"I appreciate that." He continued to work the ring around his finger. "I haven't been able to take it off."

The air between them felt dense, heady. A man still mourning the loss of his wife and a woman who felt free after a failed marriage. Neither moved for what seemed like an eternity, Ben staring at his ring and Riley staring at her empty wine glass, wondering what the etiquette was on a refill.

There was a click, and the cat appeared in the kitchen, winding around Ben's feet. Breaking the spell.

"Ansel, hey." Ben reached down and ran his hand along the cat's back to the tip of his tail. The cat turned around and rubbed his body back along the same path. Ben looked up at her. "Sorry, I forgot to tell you about him."

"Is he named after that photographer?" Riley had noticed some black and white pictures in the study.

Ben's eyes lit on hers briefly, then back down to the cat. "Yeah, Ansel Adams. Your uncle studied under him for a few years. He considered him a friend and mentor."

Riley's knowledge of the art world would fit in a thimble, but even she had heard of the famous photographer. "Wow, that's amazing. Archibald was a photographer too?"

"He dabbled in all sorts of mediums throughout the years. He always said if he had stuck with one thing, he might have had a different career. But mentoring was the most important thing to him." He raised his hand to cover a yawn.

"Oh crap, it's the middle of the night." Riley palmed her forehead. "I'm keeping you up with all my questions. Sorry, night shift." It would take a while for her system to readjust to regular hours. She looked Ben over again, from his hastily tied shoes to his rumpled clothes. "Remind me why you're here in the middle of the night."

He ran his hand through his hair, and she felt a foreign yearning in the pit of her stomach. Well, at least she wasn't lusting after a married man. She was lusting after a widower. Was that better or worse? It would take another glass, hell, bottle, to figure that one out.

"I live next door. Woke up to get a drink and saw the place lit up like Christmas, so I came over to make sure no one had broken in."

"Ha, just me." She raised her hand sheepishly. "I decided to drive straight through and then luckily I found the hidden key."

Another grin graced his handsome face. "Yeah, I saw the broken pot on the porch."

Riley scrunched up her nose. Next door? She hadn't seen a house for miles when driving in. "I don't remember seeing any other houses."

"Come with me." He gripped her elbow and led her down the hall and out onto the front porch. Pointing off into the darkness, he slipped his arm around her back. "See that light down there?"

It was hard to see since she had squeezed her eyes shut and held her breath the moment his hand touched her back. She tried to discreetly release her breath, but it came out as a wheeze. She forced her eyes open and leaned against the railing, looking in the direction he pointed. The clouds were gone, and the moon was out, lending a soft glow to the landscape. She could make out trees, a gazebo, water, and off in the distance, a light. Was it moving? She gripped the railing. How much wine had she had? "I think so."

"That's my boat."

"You live on a boat?"

"Yeah. I own the next lot over. We were building a house when my wife passed." He stared past the fountain and down to the water. His voice dropped. "I couldn't." He cleared his throat. "I haven't finished the house. So, I live on my boat." His hand dropped from her back.

Her heart hurt for him. Her husband had found a replacement as soon as things got hard and here this man was still visibly mourning the loss of his wife.

"So, I'm close by if you ever need me."

Riley snuck a look at him out of the corner of her eye. He was still staring straight ahead. At the tree line above his docked boat. "Well, at least I know my neighbor isn't a weirdo."

She hoped to lighten the mood. It was getting dense between them again. And the wine sinking in. She pushed away from the railing. "Thanks for checking on things. No cat burglar. Just me and a cat. Ha." *Could I be more awkward?* "I guess I'll go explore the upstairs now and find a place to bunk. The drive is starting to hit me."

Ben turned back toward her and the house, leaning against the railing. "I opened some windows up a few days ago to air things out, but with the rain today, I had to close them, so hopefully it's not too musty. I changed the sheets in the bedroom at the top of the stairs. It has an attached bath, so I figured it might be a good spot for you for now."

"You didn't have to do all that, but I sure am grateful."

His hand gripped the back of his neck. "Well, I guess I'll see you in a few hours. Give you a proper introduction to Heron House. Night." He jogged down the steps to the driveway.

She didn't see another car. "How did you get here?" That light was a ways off.

"I ran over. Used to all the time when Archie was still living here. Could probably do it in my sleep."

The moon had lit up the night considerably, but it was still dark, especially down by the water. "Well, don't let the alligators eat you. I need you to teach me how to use the wine opener."

Chapter Six

Sleep was elusive when Ben got back to his boat. Normally, the gentle rocking motion did the trick, but after a couple hours of listening to the lapping waves, he accepted he might as well start his day.

He dressed in the same clothes he had worn to Heron House last night and laced up his running shoes. The first hint of dawn was lighting the sky when he came on deck and stopped to do a few stretches. He gazed out over the river, savoring the quiet.

Morning was his favorite time, and he itched to go below and grab his camera, but his tired mind told him running would be a better way to shake off the lack of sleep.

A splash was followed by the flapping of wings as a graceful blue heron took flight from the reeds downriver. He watched in amazement as the massive bird glided on the air, extending his black-tipped wings to their full breadth. He'd never tire of watching the shorebirds that shared his home on this river. It was one of the many reasons he had bought the waterfront lot and planned to build a home here. The other was Archie.

The heron landed on a spit of land on the other side of the river and blended into the grasses. Ben stared until he could no longer make out the bird. Then he turned, hopped onto the dock, and started an easy jog up through the site where only a foundation had been erected.

He thought about the grand house Sarah had planned—had drawn with her own hand. Double-decker porches that would offer sweeping views of the river. An outdoor kitchen where they could make a low-country boil without stinking up the house. The widow's walk she insisted upon for the romanticism.

Only she wasn't the one left behind, longing for the one she loved.

Life rarely went as planned. Ben didn't plan to meet Archie and take up photography. He was a lawyer, a black-and-white profession that didn't lend itself to creativity and inspiration. He grew up in a city with little opportunity to experience nature. Moving to Eastport Beach, and especially meeting Archie, opened his eyes to the beauty all around. Made him want to capture those feelings in a tangible way and preserve them for all time.

He didn't plan to meet Sarah when she came to Heron House on a sabbatical. He never imagined he'd fall for a woman who perpetually had paint on her face, only ate fruit while she worked, and believed there were actual mermaids living in the sea.

And he certainly didn't plan to lose her four years after they married.

He broke through the trees along the road and turned right. Normally, he'd go to the left and run into town and back, but as he crested the small hill and saw the top of Heron House, Ben felt the weight in his chest lessen. Archie would be so happy to know this place would get a fresh start.

The house sat majestic against a backdrop of mangroves and live oaks. Spanish moss draped over the branches like someone had left the Halloween decorations up too long. The lawn sloped gently down to the water, reeds and grasses lining the shore. A small gazebo sat on the crest of the hill, offering the perfect vantage point for artists to sit with easel or pad and capture the beauty of the scene before them.

A small dock stuck out into the river, a simple rowboat tied alongside, but Ben knew the boat hadn't been used in years, and he certainly wouldn't trust its seaworthiness.

This place had provided a haven for so many, and Archie's last wish had been that it would become that once again.

The sun made its appearance beyond the river and outshone the last of the night's stars. The sky brightened and light reflected off the rippling water.

Ben came even with the house and noticed an older sedan parked beside the fountain.

He'd been shocked to glance up last night and see all the lights on inside the house. His first thought had been that Archie was on a creative streak and working through the night, but once fully awake, Ben remembered that wasn't possible. The only other thing that made sense was Riley coming early, and he felt a pull to check on her and make sure she was okay. They were in an isolated area, so the likelihood of a stranger wandering into the house was low, but he felt the need for an excuse to show up in the middle of the night.

Seeing her again had an unexpected effect on him. He felt comfortable with her. It made him decidedly uneasy. The way she rambled on about wine, and cat burglars, and house calls—combined with the speed at which she finished off her glass—she was obviously nervous around him as well. It was hard to forget the breast in the whipped cream incident. Under different circumstances, those two things paired well.

But when she brought up his wife, while staring at his wedding ring—it was enough to choke the levity right out of the moment.

What an immense contradiction that he could feel like a single man noticing an attractive woman one minute, and the next, feel 100% married. It was one reason he hadn't even considered dating since Sarah died. That, and the fact that most of the time, it felt like she was right there with him. But he hadn't felt her last night.

As he circled the mangroves behind Heron House, he thought about the last thing Archie said to him.

"Ben, don't drown in your sorrows. Find the beauty in every day and love will find you again. It's what Sarah wanted."

His feet pounded down the path that traced along the river back toward his floating home. What if he didn't want to love again? What if he couldn't handle losing anyone else?

Chapter Seven

The nine-foot beast stalked toward her, but Riley was rooted to the ground, unable to convince her feet to get her the hell out of there. It flicked its massive tail, snapped deadly jaws in her direction, and sneered at its prey.

She might have survived a decade of marriage to Larry and the subsequent divorce, but this ten-foot gator was going to be the end of her. She'd be dragged into the marsh, never to be heard from again. Her sister would mourn, her niece and nephew would hardly remember their aunt. And she'd never know why her father had hidden the existence of a brother.

Riley squeezed her eyes shut and waited for razors to pierce her skin.

The sun seared her eyelids, and she turned her head to avoid the pain. Buried her face in something soft. Waited for the first rip of flesh.

When nothing happened, she pried her eyes open and turned her head back toward the gator that stretched a clear twelve-foot span.

Instead of a prehistoric reptile, Riley opened her eyes to sunlight streaming through sheer curtains and the smell of coffee. She took in the bedroom, with its toile wallpaper, tiled fireplace and upholstered side chair. Her jeans from the day before were slung over the arm of the chair, and her shirt was hanging from a brass sconce. Her head pounded and her mouth was dry like the snakes that probably resided in the forested area outside her new home.

When did she become so scared of reptiles?

Her wine goblet sat on the bedside table mocking her, explaining her current and dream state. The coffee smelled real, but her brain couldn't fathom how that could be.

She pulled back the comforter to find she had slept in her bra and panties. She slid out of bed and grabbed her shirt off the sconce. The tacky brass light fixture was old enough the style had come back around, but she doubted the wallpaper would be so lucky. She ran her hand over the carved footboard of the bed. At least the furniture was timeless and well-built. Her uncle had excellent taste.

Pulling her shirt over her head, she stepped out into the hall where the coffee smell grew stronger, and she heard clinking sounds from the floor below.

Riley gripped the railing of the grand staircase, not trusting her legs to fully support her. Old wine must have a higher alcohol content than the $9.99 carton she usually picked up at the grocery store. She stepped off the last stair and her bare feet met the worn hardwoods. Shuffling along the wall, she followed the smell of morning's nectar and clear thoughts. She must have been smart enough to set a timer on the coffee pot. Damn, she was a genius.

Once in the kitchen, she made a beeline for the coffeemaker and was delighted to see her foresight in also setting out a mug for her convenience. She poured the inky liquid into the mug and raised the steaming cup to her face. One sip and she'd have the energy to find some creamer.

"Good morning."

Ben's voice penetrated her sleepy haze, and she froze with the cup almost to her mouth. She processed, slowly, the circumstances. Hungover, barely dressed, probable bedhead, coffee not yet in the bloodstream. She slid her foot to the left and spun in his direction. He was coming out of the butler's pantry, wearing a suit, no tie, top button open, hair perfectly styled, canister in his hand, smile gracing his clean-shaven face.

The hand not holding her mug slid up and through her hair, snagging almost immediately. She was not one of those women who rolled out of bed, hair slightly rumpled, skin glowing from a good night's sleep, ready to conquer the world. She was drool on the pillow, vermin building nests on her head, barely functioning after two cups of coffee. *God help me.*

"Hi." She yanked her hand out of her hair, taking valuable strands with it, and attempted to smooth it back from her face. She slouched, hoping her shirt would cover up her nether bits and hot pink undies. "I didn't expect you until lunch."

He moved past her and set the canister on the counter. "Yeah, but I knew there wasn't any food in the house, so I brought over some coffee and pastries. Hope that's ok."

Riley spun back toward him, leaning forward, willing her shirt to hang down farther. "It's great. Thanks so much." She noticed the pink box sitting in the middle of the island. He really was thoughtful. And had a bad habit of finding her at her worst. She backed toward the hallway. "I'm going to go freshen up. Be right back."

Ben lifted a mug to his lips, but did a poor job of concealing his smirk. "Take your time."

As soon as she cleared the end of the hallway, she turned and raced up the stairs. *It's amazing what a healthy dose of mortification will do to wake a girl up.*

Riley vacillated between a quick fix and a full attack. She didn't want to keep Ben waiting, but he was the one who was early for their meeting. She settled on a happy medium, dragging a brush ruthlessly through her hair while the shower warmed up.

After she cleaned off the funk of a long drive, a lot of wine and a night of alligator-induced terror, she dug through her suitcase for the appropriate garb for her meeting with the handsome man in the suit downstairs. Realizing she would need someone else's wardrobe to choose from, she settled on a pair of jeans and a tee heralding a "Cruel Summer." She really needed to buy some new clothes.

She really needed some money to buy some new clothes.

Riley threw her hair up into a ponytail, brushed some mascara across her lashes, and slid on a pair of flip-flops. She did live on the coast now.

Eleven minutes from horror show to semi-respectable single gal. Not too bad.

She headed downstairs and toward the kitchen at the back of the house. "Ok, I'm ready. Pants and everything." Stepping into the large room, she discovered she was talking to herself. Correction, she was talking to Ansel, as the cat had appeared and taken up residence on the counter next to the sink. His fluffy grey tail swished back and forth as he peered at her with striking lime green eyes. "Ben?" She poked her head in the pantry, which was empty.

Grabbing a bear claw from the pink box on the island, she dumped her lukewarm coffee out and refilled the mug. She added sugar from the canister Ben had set next to the coffeemaker and found a small container of creamer in the fridge. She took a fortifying bite of the delicious pastry and headed back down the hallway to the foyer.

Ben wasn't in the parlor or the dining room, but the front door stood open, so she pushed through the screen door and stepped onto the porch.

"There you are." She found the lawyer sitting on the swing at the end of a covered porch that spanned the full width of the home. Other than the bench beside the front door, the swing was the only place to sit, so she crossed the wooden planks to join him.

He scooted over to make room for her, and they swung in silence for a few minutes as she sipped her coffee, and he stared out over the lawn toward the waterfront.

"Archie sat out here for hours every morning. He'd read the entire newspaper, front to back, and drink an entire pot of coffee. Said it was his thinkin' time." Ben finished his coffee and slowed the swing long enough to set his mug on the porch railing.

"Eastport Beach has a newspaper?"

Laughter rumbled out of him, low and smooth. "Not anymore. But we can get Wilmington's paper the next day. Stale news in this age of technology, but Archie didn't care. He was old school. Didn't own a computer or a smart phone." Ben shifted his gaze to the bead board covering the ceiling of the porch.

Riley followed his attention and found another project she'd have to add to the list. Paint the ceiling. "How did people even find Heron House if it wasn't on the Internet?"

"I built him a simple website a few years back. People would contact us through the site, and I would print out the emails and give them to Archie. I've got all the passwords and info written down for you."

Riley's pocket vibrated. She pulled her phone out and checked the screen. *Why would someone be calling from the body shop?* She hadn't worked there in over a year. "Excuse me." She stepped off the swing abruptly, causing it to rock off kilter. "Sorry." She sent an apologetic look to Ben and then stepped back into the house to answer the phone.

Chapter Eight

Leaded glass windows lined the porch of the old home. Through a prismatic effect from the angled glass, Ben watched Riley pace the parlor. At one point, she threw her arm up in the air and then gestured at her chest. She was riled up about something.

Her strawberry blonde ponytail bopped along with her motions, the ends brushing against her neck when she shook her head with an emphatic "no." He found himself staring at the graceful curve where her neck met her collarbone. His pulse ticked up, his trousers felt tight, and heat penetrated his entire body. It had been a long time since he'd had that reaction to a woman. He looked down at the band circling his finger, twisting it around and around, but it felt like a vise cutting off the circulation to the rest of his hand.

He looked back up and Riley was slouched on one of the green couches, her shoulders slumped in defeat, listening to whoever was on the other end of the phone.

The look on her face gutted him. He wanted to run to her, wrap her in his embrace and assure her everything would be okay.

The screen door slammed shut, and he blinked away the image of Riley tucked in his arms.

Riley stood at the top of the steps leading to the wrap-around drive, staring out across the expanse of green leading down to the river.

Ben rose from the swing and crept across the porch. She looked like a fawn that would bolt for the tree line if he came on too fast. When he was only a few steps away, she turned toward him, her eyes glistening with tears. He wanted to throttle whoever had made this beautiful woman cry. He reached out a hand toward her.

She turned her head, swiping at her eyes.

"Riley, what is it?"

Facing him again, she shook her head slightly, but her lip trembled as a tear breached her eyelid and slid down her cheek.

Without a second thought, Ben took a step forward and swept Riley into his arms. He curled one hand against her neck, stroking tiny circles there, while the other found her lower back and held her securely.

She fit perfectly in his embrace, almost burrowing her head into his chest, close enough a legal file wouldn't fit between them. He reveled in her softness, absorbed the feel of a woman against him, and attempted to bury the anger vibrating off his body at whoever had caused her sadness.

They stood that way for some time, Riley's tears soaking through his dress shirt, and Ben somehow managed to pull her closer.

The ruffle of feathers shattered the stillness, and a heron landed on the fountain in the roundabout. He stretched his wings out briefly, then settled into the standard shorebird pose, wings folded, one leg tucked under his body.

The bird broke the spell between them, and Riley backed away, running her fingers under her eyes and sniffling. "I'm sorry." She gestured between them. "I'm sorry I'm such a mess."

"No, don't be sorry." He extended his hand, and she took another step back. "Riley, it's okay. Something obviously upset you. Tell me how I can help." She bumped into the porch railing and her eyes flicked from him to the ground. She seemed almost scared. *Had that bastard hit her?* Maybe that was why she was so upset the day of her divorce, not because she was sad about the marriage ending, but because she had to face him in court?

She shook her head "no" again, raked her hands over her face, and sighed. "I'll be fine, really. It's just stupid divorce drama." She stood up straighter and pulled her t-shirt down. "I know you need to get on with your day. Let's get the tour over with."

Ben had cleared his schedule to spend the day sharing Heron House with Riley. He'd met with a client first thing to sign some papers but then had popped into The Coastal Coffeehouse to pick up pastries and a medium roast blend for breakfast. He figured it'd take a couple hours to show her the entire property and then they could grab lunch at The Landing. But now she wanted to get it over with.

"We can do the tour another day. When you're in a better headspace." He stepped toward the stairs, thinking about calling Chesnee for a match. Pounding it out on the court would be good to dispel the anger he felt toward a man he had never met.

"Please don't leave."

The words floated like a whisper on the breeze and Ben wasn't 100% certain she had said them at all.

He turned back to her. She stepped closer and held her hand slightly in front of her, as if afraid to reach for him. Combined with the look of pleading in her eyes, he assured himself she had, in fact, asked him to stay. He reached for her hand and gripped it tightly. "We'll start out here. The property is beautiful and has an incredibly rich history."

He led her down the steps and past the foundation, where they turned around to face the house. The heron flew away upon their approach and disappeared over the roof.

"How did you meet my uncle?" She stared up at Ben, one hand shielding her eyes from the bright sunlight. "It seems like you knew him well."

"I moved to Eastport Beach fresh out of law school, certain I knew all I needed to open a practice of my own. I rented a small space downtown, bought a desk and hung out a sign. And waited. Six months and no clients later, I closed up shop and took a job in Wilmington." He chuckled, remembering how embarrassed he was to break his lease and admit defeat.

"One day, Archie walked into the office, threw his hat on my desk and asked if I knew anything about art. I admitted I knew very little about it, but had a great appreciation for people with artistic talent. He appraised me for a few moments, and I was terrified I had answered incorrectly and would lose a potential client, but he rose from the chair, put his hat back on, and said, 'Come with me.'"

The two started walking toward the gazebo, still hand in hand. It felt natural to hold her hand. "I didn't have any clue where this man was taking me, it was the middle of the workday, and I was due for a reading in an hour. But there was something about Archie that captivated everyone he met. He drew you into his universe." They reached the gazebo and sat on the bench overlooking the river.

"We started walking down the street, going several blocks before he stopped in front of a modern building I had never been in before. It was the Cape Fear Museum. We stepped inside and walked right past the ticket desk, no one asking who we were or why we were there. He led me into a small gallery featuring an exhibit of oil paintings, mostly landscapes. There was one piece that showed a river snaking through the reeds, with a small boat moored to a dock and a white egret wading along the shore. He asked, 'How does this make you feel?'"

Riley bent her knee on the surface of the bench and turned to face him. "Like a test?"

Ben mimicked her posture and nodded. "That's what I assumed, and let me tell you, I was nervous as hell. I kept trying to get a read off his face for the correct thing to say, but he just stared at the painting, not saying a word. So, I stared too. And the piece started to affect me. My heart rate slowed, my breathing evened out, and I felt captivated by the simplicity of the scene."

She looked back out over the river. "Like here?"

"Yeah, exactly. It made me feel like I do when I look out over this river."

They stared at the water for a few more minutes, then she turned back to him. "What did you say?"

"I told him it made me feel calm, at peace. He nodded his head, and gestured around the room, then said, 'This is what I do.' I said, 'You're an artist.' To which he replied, 'Yes, but mostly I help others create peace.'"

Ben didn't completely understand then what Archie meant, but once he handed Ben a camera, he got it. He found peace through that lens.

"I can't ever remember feeling that way." She gazed at her hands in her lap, twisting a silver ring around the pointer finger on her right hand.

He reached out, stilling her hands. "You'll find it here."

Chapter Nine

They spent the next hour wandering the grounds. Ben told her about the birds that came every year to nest on the banks of the river, and why the live oak trees all bent away from the water. He explained the property had originally been over twenty acres, but bits and pieces had been sold off over the years, including the lot next door her uncle sold to Ben when he married Sarah.

Now four acres remained, and the one-and-a-half-acre plot behind the house could easily be sold. Riley knew it was necessary, but the trees covering that land were haunting and beautiful. The graceful Spanish moss that hung from gnarled branches and the twisted roots of the mangrove trees—it was like something from a dark fairy tale. Riley had always preferred *Into the Woods* over stories like *Cinderella*.

She had only traveled across her state, but this area was so different from where she had grown up, it may as well have been on a different planet.

Back home, the forests were filled with evergreens and elms, sycamores and rhododendron, the ground covered in ferns and mosses.

Here, sand and shrubs stretched between the trees, until you reached the shore of the river, where the ground got spongy, and reeds poked up through the brackish water.

And the river—the Cape Fear River, wide enough you could barely see the other shore, with fingers extending from it, winding through marsh and sea grasses. So different from the Broad River that ran through Ashford, with its greenways and tubing companies every few miles.

Knowing that a few miles downstream, this massive river dumped into an endless ocean gave it an immense power and energy.

They stood side by side on the shore, watching a pair of snowy egrets gliding close to the surface, and it was like reality had been suspended and it was only the two of them in the world.

Riley caught movement out of the corner of her eye and redirected her gaze to the water directly below them. There wasn't much of a drop there, maybe three feet, the bank of the river sloping gradually up toward them. A ripple spread out from a log as it slowly made its way down the river.

"It's funny. That log almost looks like an alligator." She flashed back to her silly dream from that morning and, despite knowing it was only her overactive imagination, a twinge of fear crept up her neck.

"Oh, that's definitely a gator." Ben said nonchalantly. Like it was every day that an alligator was three feet away.

Holy crap. Was it going to be every day that an alligator was three feet away?

Riley took a massive step back from the edge. Then another. "Ha. I was wondering if there were alligators here." She willed her voice to remain steady. "But it's probably not something you see very often, right?"

Ben shrugged, then squatted, almost like he was trying to get closer. To the reptile that was likely to eat him. "They're pretty common." He looked back over his shoulder at her. "This looks like a pretty big one. Maybe eight feet."

She backed away some more, bumping into a live oak. She scanned the tree for a foothold. *Eight feet? Could gators climb trees? How fast do they run?* She hadn't run since PE in high school. She was guessing a gator could beat her nine-minute mile. "Ben, do you really think you should be that close? I mean, I can see you have muscles under that dress shirt and all, but wrestling a gator? It seems a bit un-lawyerly."

As the day heated up, he had shed his suit jacket and rolled his sleeves up to his elbows. Before the alligator had distracted Riley, she might have noticed how nice his arms were.

He turned to face her (which meant turning his back on the beast) and smiled widely. "Riley, here in Eastport Beach, we wrestle gators most every day of the week, well, except Sunday, of course, because of the potluck and hoedown." He plucked a piece of grass off the bank and stuck it between his teeth.

Riley narrowed her eyes at him. "Are you teasing me? Do you know how strong the jaws of an alligator are?"

"Come here."

"No." She stepped behind the trunk of the tree, using it as a shield.

He laughed and held out his hand. "Riley, it's fine. Come here."

She shook her head.

Ben walked to where she was and pulled her arms from around the tree, dragging her back to the shore. "It's a log, Riley."

She peered over the bank of the river at the brown something bobbing in the water. A dragonfly circled it and landed briefly on its surface. Okay. Probably a log. Which meant Ben was messing with her the whole time. "Argh!" She pressed both hands against his chest and pushed him back.

He was laughing so hard he could barely keep his footing.

"I can't believe you did that! My heart was racing. I was trying to figure out if I should climb the tree or try to make it back to the house. I was worried about how to contact your next of kin after the alligator ate you!"

Having regained his balance and his composure (mostly), Ben hooked his arm around Riley's shoulders and led her back toward the house. "You don't have to worry about gators, honest. I've seen maybe two the whole time I've lived here, and they were on the opposite shore of the river. They aren't big fans of human activity, so just make a lot of noise and jump around when you're outside."

"So, you're an attorney and a comedian?" She wasn't thrilled with his teasing, but she was a fan of his strong embrace. Maybe she'd let it slide for now.

"Okay, I've had my fun. No more teasing, promise." He squeezed her shoulder tighter and shot her a bone-melting grin. The man was well aware of his charms.

As they mounted the steps to the porch, Ben slid his phone out of his pocket and checked the screen. Riley watched as a range of emotions crossed his face, and the expression that finally seemed to settle there was a determined set of his jaw.

He typed a response to the text and sighed. "Looks like I've got to go into work after all."

"Of course. I didn't expect for you to entertain me all day." Although she was certainly enjoying his company.

He backed down the steps and upon reaching the driveway, looked back up at the old house, his gaze directed to the upper floors. "I had planned to give you the whole tour." His eyes dropped to the ground, where he shuffled his feet like he was suddenly a shy little boy. "And take you to lunch."

Heat rushed to Riley's cheeks. Did he mean like a date? Or did all estate attorneys take their clients' nieces out for a meal? She really didn't know the etiquette here. "I really appreciate that, but I'll manage. I've got the essentials in the car." The box in the back of her car held the meager offerings from her apartment cleanout. Bread, peanut butter, an almost empty jar of honey and an array of spices. Okay, maybe not all the essentials. "I'll run over to the grocery store later, too."

"There's a market near where River Road meets Main Street, which is great for fresh produce and stuff, but if you drive back over toward Bluffville, you'll hit a nice, big twenty-four-hour place."

"Thanks for the tip." She pulled the screen door open, then threw one last glance over her shoulder and caught Ben standing near his car, watching her walk into the house. It had been a long time since a man looked at her like that, and she felt the compliment all the way down to her toes.

Chapter Ten

Ben had been waiting for Judge Collins' schedule to open for weeks. But why did it have to be tomorrow? Pulling into the gravel parking lot behind the historic home housing his office, he mentally began to shift gears. The Kirby estate had been in probate for going on three years now and he knew the family was ready for the matter to be settled, but it would take the rest of the afternoon to prepare for the last-minute hearing.

Not how he envisioned spending his day.

He scaled the short staircase to the back door, stepping into a small kitchen that was mostly original, save for the fancy espresso machine his assistant had insisted on and a refrigerator from the twenty-first century. Grabbing a green juice from the fridge, Ben headed toward his office, veering off at the last minute to lean in Chesnee's doorway.

"Order me a pastrami on rye from The Spicy Mermaid, will ya?"

The younger man looked up from his computer, his too-long hair flopping into his eyes.

"And when are you getting a haircut?"

"You're awfully cranky for the middle of the day. Did you not get your beauty rest?"

Ben refused to acknowledge that his assistant was correct—the kid's head barely fit through the nineteenth-century doorways as it was. But it wasn't merely the lack of sleep making him bark out orders. And he'd be even less likely to tell the town gossip he was upset he didn't get to spend the day with Riley. Chesnee had already jumped to the wrong conclusions where she was concerned. Ben wasn't going to give him any additional ammunition.

"Order yourself something, too. And be sure to tip Gina well, I know you're sweet on her."

Chesnee narrowed his eyes at his boss and flipped his hair back. "You know Gina and I are just friends. But since it's your money, I'll make sure she feels real appreciated."

Despite his ornery mood, Ben barked out a laugh. It was one of the many reasons he kept Chesnee around. The younger man kept him on his toes for sure. "Have you already pulled the Kirby file?"

"It's on your desk." He started to pick up the phone, then paused, the receiver midair. "Should I have something sent to Riley as well?"

The heat rushing to Ben's cheeks made him wish he hadn't shaven, because the scruff would have hidden his tell.

"Or I could run it down there to her myself."

Now Chesnee was playing with fire, and from the cocky grin on his face, he knew it. Ben knew his game, and he wasn't ready to play it. He wasn't sure if he would ever be. "Get lunch and get back here. It'll be a miracle if we're ready by tomorrow morning."

He headed back to his office, willing himself not to stomp. The old wood floors of the house were loud enough without him banging around because Chesnee had gotten under his skin. He twisted the cap off his drink and tossed half the bottle back. The stuff was nasty, but he needed fuel to get him through the towering file in the center of his desk.

***

Six hours later, lunch had worn off and there were mountains of paper strewn across every surface in the office.

"If Harold Kirby hadn't been such a stubborn SOB, we could be hitting some balls right now instead of chasing down DNA reports and family lineage dating back to the Mayflower." Chesnee mimed serving a tennis ball.

He wasn't too far off the mark. Old Man Kirby, as all the locals called him, had left a string of fatherless children across three counties and properties valued in the millions. Which had resulted in so many claims, the court assigned Ben's firm (i.e. Ben) to sort it all out and present it to Judge Collins. It was the equivalent of a public defender if the defendant was a pack of unkempt, jobless miscreants who had spent their lives milking the government and now wanted to milk their absentee father's estate.

From what he could tell, Harold Kirby didn't much like anyone, let alone his children, and it was basically his final F-you to kick the bucket without detailing his intentions.

"The money would be put to better use if it was donated in one lump sum to the foster care system, or a food bank." Ben rarely thought ill of anyone, especially the dead, but he'd been dealing with this disaster for years. And now, instead of taking Riley down to The Landing for a nice lunch and showing her around Eastport Beach on a sunny afternoon, he was holed up with Chesnee, pouring over letters from supposed heirs and reports better suited for an episode of Jerry Springer than a courtroom.

"What, you don't think Earline Hayes, high school dropout, shoplifting expert, and worst employee of the month down at Kip's Treasure Chest deserves 2.7 million dollars?" Chesnee waved a letter through the air. "Man, I wish we still had some beer in the fridge."

"If I kept the fridge stocked with beer, I'd never get any work out of you. That was a onetime thing for St. Patrick's Day." And boy had Ben regretted that decision. Chesnee ended up running down the street hollering about his Irish roots. No more beer at work. Green or otherwise.

His phone beeped multiple times, and he turned it over to read the texts. The screen and his heart lit up when he saw who they were from.

Riley

Wondering if you were home yet? I was hoping you could show me your magic bottle opening trick. It's been a long day and all that wine is goading me from the pantry.

Riley

Nevermind.

Riley

Bad idea.

Riley

Shut up, wine.

Riley

Sorry to bug you.

Before he could catch himself, he was laughing. *She even rambles on text. And that's without wine.*

Chesnee was on him like a seagull on a French fry. "Ooh, let me read it. Someone's got you laughing. Can I assume it's your new neighbor?" He reached across the desk for the phone, but Ben pressed it to his chest.

"We are not teenage girls at a slumber party. You aren't reading my texts."

"Aww, come on. I can help. I've got game."

Ben knew exactly the kind of game Chesnee had, especially when their small town filled up with spring breakers. "I don't need help with Riley. I need help with this case."

"So, it is the hot neighbor!"

Pretty sure I never told him she was hot. Not that she isn't. But I would definitely not tell the young, strapping stud who could charm the pants off the old Bob's Big Boy statue in Mildred Grimer's back garden. And now I'm the one rambling. Maybe I'm lightheaded from lack of food. "I think we should take a dinner break."

"Nice try. Subject change rejected. Have you made a move yet?"

Ben narrowed his eyes at his assistant, who was apparently hallucinating. "There are no moves happening. Let's order a pizza or something."

"See, this is why you need my help. It's been too long. You've lost all your moves."

"I haven't lost anything. If there are moves to be made, I can full well make them." He slid open his desk drawer and tossed the phone inside, closing it with an emphatic shove. "But there aren't going to be any moves. I told you. I had my one."

Chesnee had his phone out and was tapping at the screen. "And I told you, just because your wife died, doesn't mean you have to become a monk. Pepperoni and ham?" He glanced up at Ben. "Pineapple?"

"Pineapple is for fruity drinks and luaus. This isn't Hawaii. Any kind of meat will do."

"It'll be here in twenty. I'm gonna run to the market and grab a six-pack. If I have to work after the sun goes down, you're buying the beer." He held his hand out.

Ben closed his eyes briefly, letting out an exasperated sigh that was mostly for show. Once Chesnee left, he could respond to Riley's texts in private. He dug into his back pocket, drew out his wallet, and slapped a couple bills into the younger man's hand. "Get something decent. That watered down shit tastes like piss and gives me a headache."

Chapter Eleven

Slowly spinning around the parlor, Riley assessed her progress. She'd pulled all the furniture into the middle of the room and covered it with a canvas drop cloth she'd found in an upstairs closet. The material was covered with bright splashes of paint in every color of the rainbow, and she wondered if her uncle had used it, or if it was from one of the artists that had stayed at Heron House.

There was so much she didn't know. She'd love to quiz Ben on all the questions she'd encountered today while exploring the house, but her text about the wine had gone unanswered thus far, and besides, it was mildly embarrassing how she could even ramble in a text.

The lawyer probably had a life outside of rescuing helpless neighbors from stubborn bottles of wine.

She'd taken everything off the walls and carefully stacked it on the huge dining room table.

She couldn't believe the volume of art in the house.

It felt wrong to sell the pieces off, but some of it seemed very good to her and the money would help with the renovation. She'd tried to do a little research on her phone, but it was tedious. Eventually, she'd have to break down and buy a laptop, since she'd also lost that in the divorce. Her technologically illiterate ex-husband probably couldn't even turn the thing on, but since it had the accounting software for the business, he claimed he "needed it."

One last line of bullshit from Big Larry.

Your car will be done in two days.

It may look like just a scratch, but if we don't take care of it the right way, rust will take over and your car will rot away.

I can try to get that part for you, but since it's after market, it's going to be a tad more expensive.

She still couldn't believe Marlene had called from the shop today asking for her help.

Like it was her problem Brittani had left, and Larry was in a foul mood.

According to the older woman, Riley's ex had gone on a rampage, tearing posters off the walls, chucking parts across the stockroom, and spewing hateful words at anyone who dared to get in his path. No way was she getting caught up in his drama.

As much as she liked the people who worked at Big Larry's, she had no intention of getting dragged back into that world. She'd stood firm and refused to talk him off the (metaphorical) ledge.

More than anything, she was mad at herself for letting it upset her.

He'd never cared enough to throw things when they fought.

Maybe she could figure out that bottle opener on her own. She trailed her hands along the bare walls on her way to the kitchen. Well, not bare, per se. In fact, they were covered in vintage (read: old), sophisticated (read: gag), red and beige damask wallpaper. The hideous wallpaper was so desperate to get off the wall it hung in strips in some places and bubbled up in others. The bubbles worried her. Was there water damage hiding behind that God-awful print? More importantly, why did her uncle wallpaper the parlor to look like a bordello?

Before she could travel too far down the rabbit hole of inheriting a possible brothel, her phone beeped.

Ben

I'm stuck at work prepping for a case. I'll have to teach you my wine bottle magic another time. Sounds like way more fun than I'm having.

Riley

Tell me the truth. Did I inherit a house of ill repute?

Ben

I just spat out green juice all over my papers. Why do you ask? Did you find sex toys?

Riley

Um, no, but I'll be checking the closets more closely now.

Riley

Is there a secret BDSM dungeon I need to know about? Because I don't do dark or spiders or whips.

Ben

I can't speak to the whips, but I imagine there are spiders in the basement. And it's definitely dark. You may want to wait for me to accompany you.

Riley

I have so many questions.

Riley

> Seriously, did Archie choose this wallpaper? Was he secretly a madam? And do you even call a man a madam? Or is it master? Or pimp? That doesn't seem right. There's no Wi-Fi here so my Google abilities are limited.

Riley

> I can't even pull up a YouTube video for how to use this bottle opener.

Riley

> What scared you off? Was it the S&M or the prostitution talk?

Riley

> Please don't abandon me or I'll never be able to drink all this wine. I promise I'll keep it purely professional from now on. Contracts and depositions and briefs.

Riley

> I really need to upgrade my phone so I can unsend texts.

He hadn't responded for forty-two minutes. She'd gone and rambled her way into turning off the only person she knew in Eastport Beach. *And the only one who knows how to operate this damn wine opener!*

She chucked the offensive device in the sink and grabbed a knife from the block on the counter. She jabbed it into the cork and twisted. It popped out, the bottom half crumbling into the wine, the top half stuck to the knife. "Aha! There's more than one way to skin a cat!"

There was a click, and Ansel appeared.

"Just kidding, buddy. No one's skinning anyone." She grabbed a strainer from off the wall and held it over her goblet, pouring the wine through.

"Where did you come from?" Her glass filled, she dumped the pieces of cork left in the strainer into the trash, pretty impressed with her ingenuity. Taking a giant sip of the pinot, she looked around the kitchen. There was a door leading outside, but last time she checked, cats couldn't operate doorknobs. All the windows appeared to be shut and after some yanking, even she couldn't open them.

"I inherited a brothel with a magic freaking cat, a pantry full of wine, and enough art to fill ten galleries." She took another giant swig of the wine. "And I scared away my only friend with my stupid stream of consciousness texting." *Must learn to self-edit.*

Her phone beeped again.

Ben

> Sorry, my assistant came back with dinner and he's nosy AF.

Ben

> I'm not scared off.

She couldn't be sure if the heat rushing to her face was from the text or the wine.

Chapter Twelve

The hearing for the Kirby case had run past lunch, so by the time Ben got out of court, he was tired from staying up all night, starving, and felt like he'd gone ten rounds in the ring with an ornery gator. Better not mention that metaphor to Riley.

In reality, every toothless, shoeless, possible relative of Harold Kirby had shown up to court laying claim to his healthy estate. So many, in fact, the case had been continued again, pending more DNA test results. How many women had been desperate enough to sleep with the man? At last count, there were over twenty supposed heirs.

Ben trudged up the back steps to his office, raking his fingers through his hair and loosening his tie. He needed food, a run, and maybe a nap. Instead, he had an afternoon of appointments.

Chesnee greeted him in the kitchen, holding out a chicken ranch wrap from The Spicy Mermaid. "Figured you'd be starving by now."

Okay, Ben had to admit, even though he was sophomoric at times, the kid was an excellent assistant. "I take back all the mean things I said to you."

"You didn't say anything mean to me."

"Then every mean thing I thought about you." He took a giant bite of the wrap and grabbed a root beer from the fridge. Normally, he didn't drink soda, but he needed a sugar boost to get through the rest of the day.

Chesnee clutched his chest, straight up Vivien Leigh-style. "I'm deeply offended."

Ben swallowed his mammoth bite and took a swig of the drink. "I've heard the things your friends call you when you're out drinking. You don't know how to be offended."

The younger man grinned and shrugged. "Thick skin."

"Give me five minutes to eat and then send my next appointment in."

"I rescheduled your two o'clock to next week, so you have ten minutes to eat. You're welcome." Chesnee bowed and went back to his desk.

The slight reprieve allowed Ben to chew his lunch and actually taste it. He wasn't sure what Earl over at the diner marinated his chicken in, but it was as addictive as crack.

He had a tiny galley on the boat, but living there definitely limited his cooking ability, so he often commented that he kept his three favorite eateries in business.

A sudden flash of a memory popped in uninvited. Sarah had sketched out her design plan for a gourmet kitchen in the house they were building. Then she dragged him to Wilmington to pick out samples for the cabinets, backsplash and countertops. They'd had such fun exploring builders' warehouses and offering crazy suggestions, like a pink and purple granite. She'd gotten her diagnosis two days later.

There was a rap on the door, and he shook his head to clear it of the memory. He crumpled up the foil sheet from his lunch and tossed it in the waste bin under his desk. Swallowing the remainder of his root beer, he cleared his throat. "Come in."

Ben spent the next three hours speaking to clients about wills and settlements—all the while, the lingering memory of a fun afternoon just before the end flickered through his mind—keeping him from fully focusing. It was hard not to think about death when it was your entire business.

Chapter Thirteen

Riley had spent much of the day fighting with the wallpaper in the parlor. Funny how parts of it fell off of its own accord and other bits refused to be removed without a wrecking ball.

A quick search on her phone had yielded a plethora of useless and ridiculous ideas. One blog suggested she simply wet the paper down and scrape it off. If water worked so well at removal, then how was it the areas with brown water stains and bubbles were the most stubborn parts?

Finally, she'd had enough, and her arms ached from reaching overhead. She was starting to doubt she could tackle this on her own.

In the kitchen, she cracked ice from trays into a tall glass and ran the faucet until the water was good and cold. Another thing to add to her wish list—a new fridge with an icemaker and filtered water. But it would have to be way down the list, past niceties like replacing the toilet upstairs that only flushed on the fourth try.

She took her water out onto the porch and stood for a minute, staring down at the river. She had a sudden vision of racing down the lawn and launching off the dock into the sparkling water. And then promptly being devoured by an alligator.

Sighing, she sat on the porch swing and pushed her feet against the worn floorboards. Between scraping off decades-old wallpaper and the humidity of the early summer, she felt sticky and hot. Soon, the swing was moving at a clip that generated a subtle breeze.

She'd almost lulled herself to sleep when she heard the crunch of gravel. Startling, she sloshed her water down the front of her tank top. As refreshing as the cool water felt, she had a pretty good idea who her visitor was since she only knew one person in town. One really hot man, to be specific. Not that she noticed things like that.

Ben's car came into view, bumping slowly down the rutted drive. Mentally adding gravel to her list, Riley pulled her soaked shirt away from her body, shaking it like she wasn't having her own personal wet t-shirt contest. *I really can't ever see him when I'm put together and looking nice, can I?* She couldn't remember the last time she'd felt put together, though.

She rose from the swing and walked to the steps, draping her arm around one of the posts in an ineffectual effort to hide her pebbled nipples straining against the thin fabric of her shirt—that were most certainly a result of the cold water, not the man getting out of his car and heading her way with a sexy grin on his face.

"I know I'm a day late, but I took a chance you'd still want wine." He held up a bottle of red, some label she didn't recognize.

"I won't say no, but good ol' Uncle Archie has enough wine to last me the rest of my life. If I can figure out that fancy opener."

He stopped on the steps next to where she hugged the pillar. "Getting attached to this old house?" He quirked an eyebrow at her apparent (and literal) attachment to the house.

"Ha, yeah, love this place." She patted the post while wishing she could disappear between the floorboards of the porch. *Why am I so freaking awkward around this man? I swear I was normal—boring even—before Ben Ward walked into my life.*

He hesitated, likely wondering what he had gotten himself into with his new neighbor. "You want to come inside, and I'll give you a lesson?"

Riley's brain flashed to all the things he might be able to teach her before she realized he was talking about opening the wine. *I also swear I wasn't this fixated on sex before I met him.* "Yeah, that'd be great. You go on ahead. I need to run upstairs real quick." She waited until he stepped inside the house before unwrapping herself from the pillar, crossing her arms over her chest, and hightailing it up the stairs.

Ten minutes, a dry shirt, and a swipe of mascara later, Riley entered the kitchen to find Ben talking to Ansel. Apparently, it was a private conversation, because the cat jumped off the counter and scurried out of the room.

"I don't think he likes me. Every time I come into the room, he disappears. Like, literally. Poof. Magic freaking cat." She propped her hip against the island, feeling less conspicuous in her Nirvana t-shirt that didn't highlight the effect Ben had on her nipples.

He laughed, a slow chuckle she felt down to the soles of her bare feet. "Ansel takes a little time to warm up, but once he does, he won't leave you alone." Bracing his arms against the counter opposite her, he seemed relaxed, like he might stay awhile. "Pretty sure he's not magic, though."

She fidgeted with the pieces of cork littering the counter—a result of her ingenuity from the night before. "But, luckily for me, you are magic." His eyes widened, but she continued before he could refute her statement. "With that wine opener." Gesturing at the sink, where she had tossed the ineffective device the night before, she realized she was flirting. In person. With her hot neighbor/attorney. The widower.

He smiled, grabbed the opener, and stepped closer to her. "Well, I'm happy to share my secret trick with you."

And he might be flirting back.

He reached past her, snagging the bottle he brought with him, and secured it on the island. Positioning the opener over the cork, he demonstrated how to use the high-tech device—including the physics behind its design. Nerdy hot. Which was new for Riley. Her ex was a jock in high school, leading in tackles, not IQ points.

The cork popped up with a little hiss and she looked up to find Ben staring down at her, so close she could reach out and fist her hands in his shirt. Not that she would do that.

She snuck a peek at his left hand. Yup. Still there.

Backing away from the temptation, she headed for the butler's pantry to grab two glasses. "Yup, pure magic. Ben, the wine wizard. Saving the day yet again." Once out of his sight, she braced her hands on a shelf and took a calming breath. It was obvious he wasn't over his wife. Besides, she couldn't have cared less about sex the last year or so. What an inopportune time for her drive to come raging back.

"Everything okay in there?"

How long had she been hiding out in the pantry, waiting for her lust to subside? "Yeah, a okay. Perfect." She emerged, raising the glasses high, praying her cheeks weren't as red as they felt. "Wine delivery apparatus secured." Sometimes even she couldn't believe the things that came out of her mouth. She really needed to work on filtering.

Ben took the glasses from her, his hand grazing hers and sending electricity all the way up her arm. Not helpful.

"This probably isn't as high quality as Archie's stash, but it wasn't the cheapest option at Murray's, so it should be decent." He poured the wine, acting like lightning hadn't struck when their hands touched.

Shaking off the one-sided effect, Riley gratefully took the wine. "I'm sure it will be great. Better than having to strain the cork out of it." She took a giant gulp, barely even tasting it, just willing it to start working and take the edge off.

He chuckled and brandished a steak knife with a piece of cork stuck to the end. "Guess that explains this."

She slid her gaze down to the rough-hewn hardwoods. "Desperate times and all." *He's gonna think I'm a wino.* "This week"—hell, year—"has been rough. You know, with the move and all."

His feet moved into her frame of view. Which meant he was really close again.

Gently, he placed his fingers under her chin and lifted her head. "Riley, you don't have to explain yourself to me—or anyone, for that matter. You've been through a lot in a short period of time. I think you're handling it better than most people would."

She shrugged. "At least I'm not day drinking." Yet.

He shook his head, and his thumb rubbed the side of her face. "No, I'm serious. You've had a lot thrown at you and here you are, every day, tackling life head on. I think you're very brave."

She stared into his eyes, the liquid pools of chocolate mesmerizing her and his words like a balm to her tired soul. Suddenly, her mouth went dry, like the cracked earth of a desert, and as she dragged her tongue across her arid lips, she watched his gaze drop to them. Her breathing quickened, like she couldn't draw enough air into her lungs, and she stood shock-still as, in slow motion, Ben lowered his mouth to hers.

The kiss was over as soon as it began, and she would have sworn she imagined it, if he hadn't dropped his hand like he'd been scalded and stumbled backwards like *he* was the drunk. He turned away from her, gripping the edge of the counter, his shoulders tense, his posture rigid. It'd been a while, but there was no way she was that bad of a kisser. If you could even call that a kiss. It was more like bumping into someone because you were looking at your phone instead of where you were walking. She chugged the rest of her wine and grabbed the bottle on her way out of the room.

Chapter Fourteen

That could not have gone worse. He hadn't planned on kissing her—not that he didn't want to. He wanted to. But it was complicated. She was his client. And Archie's niece. And not Sarah.

Suddenly the empty kitchen felt full of the ghosts of the past. Sarah, scrolling through dating apps, picking out the women she would approve of for him. Making him promise. Archie, reminding him Sarah wanted him to move on.

The memory of how broken he had been when she died.

He wasn't sure if he could do it again. He dug around in his pocket, seizing on the penny, pressing it between his fingers until they ached.

Could he open his heart to the kind of all-consuming love that burned a hole in his chest when it was taken from him?

He couldn't deny his attraction to Riley, and he certainly couldn't stand to be responsible for hurting her like her ex had.

Still not knowing how to explain what had happened, he went in search of her. She wasn't in the parlor, where the walls had been scraped within an inch of their life and furniture sat huddled under one of Sarah's drop cloths. She wasn't in the dining room, where art was piled high on the oversized table, a landscape of his late wife's balanced precariously on top. The front porch was empty, the swing swaying as if Archie sat upon it reading his daily paper. Turns out the kitchen wasn't the only place full of ghosts in this house.

A movement down by the water caught his eye.

Riley was sitting in the middle of the dock, her legs crossed, her hands bracing her as she leaned back. A passerby would simply think she was soaking up the last rays of sun before it set, but he doubted that was the case.

He didn't know her well enough to guess her reaction. Would she be disappointed and cry? Or pissed off and rage at him? Or would she act like nothing had happened at all? After watching her for a few minutes, he started across the lawn. He wanted to know. He wanted to know everything about her. Especially if she would give him another chance.

When his feet hit the dock, her shoulders tensed up, making him feel like an even bigger ass. He didn't want to be one of the things stressing her out. He approached her slowly, waiting to see if she'd snap like a gator or curl up in a ball like an armadillo putting on its armor.

"When we were little, we'd go to Lake Hartwell in the summer. My sister and I would spend all day jumping off the dock and swimming as far as we could before Mama made us turn back." She peeked one eye open and studied him. "There were no alligators in Lake Hartwell."

Option C it is.

"I swim in this river most every day. Haven't been eaten yet."

She leaned forward and scooted to the side to make room for him to sit. "Maybe you aren't meaty enough."

He laughed in spite of the serious conversation he wanted to have with her. "Riley—"

"It's not a big deal, Ben. Don't sweat it." She stared straight ahead, across the river, not at him.

"It's a big deal to me." He could tell by the set of her jaw and rapid blinking she was trying to put on a brave face. He didn't want that. He wanted to know her. All about her summers growing up, about her dreams, about every messy part of her life. He didn't want her to hide any part of herself from him. Which meant he couldn't hide from her either. "I haven't dated since Sarah died. Honestly, I haven't looked at another woman that way. I haven't dealt with my grief well. I think I mostly stuffed it down in a box and tried to ignore it."

A tear slid down her cheek, the late day sun glinting off it, but she didn't turn his way.

"And then I met you." He slowly moved his hand to cover hers, holding his breath to see if she would reject the gesture. When she didn't pull away, he continued. "I can't ignore how I feel about you. How you've made my heart wake up. I've wallowed in my grief longer than is healthy, I know that. I didn't have a reason to deal with it. Until now."

Her bottom lip quivered, and more tears joined the first.

"Riley." His voice sounded strangled, even to his own ears. But he'd plead if he had to. "Please, look at me."

She sucked in that lip, then turned to face him.

The sadness in her eyes was a punch to his gut. He didn't want to be responsible for causing her pain. He raised his other hand to cup her face, his thumb wiping the tears from under her eye. "It's not fair to you. But I'm going to ask, anyway. Can you be patient with me?"

At the slight shake of her head, his heart plummeted straight through the dock and into the depths of the river. He dropped his hand from her face, silently cursing himself. Knowing this was the risk he hadn't wanted.

He started to slide back, away from her, away from the rejection. *Of course, she would reject me. I couldn't even kiss her properly without being haunted by ghosts.*

Her perfect mouth formed an "O" and she reached for him. "Ben, wait."

He stilled, breathless, as her hands framed his face.

She leaned forward, their foreheads touching, her lips within inches of his. The world around them faded, and he focused on her breath, her quiet words. "I understand grief. Not letting go. It's not easy, it's not reasonable, it's not something you can turn on and off. I've spent the last year of my life hiding in the cave of my grief. I lost my marriage over it. I lost my spark. I lost myself." She was so close to him that she was blurry. Until he realized it was his own tears blurring her beautiful face. "I'm still not right, not altogether okay. Moving here was a kick start for me, but I'm nowhere near fixed. So, I'll be patient if you will too."

He had so many questions. But they could wait, because she was willing to. His breath escaped in a stutter, rushing out of him in relief. He wove his hand around her bare neck and up to underneath her ponytail, angling her head just right. He needed a do-over.

Their mouths met amid salty tears in a kiss more intimate than any he could remember. Her lips were lush and soft, and as her hands slid into his hair, his whole body heated. He used his other hand to pull her torso closer, in some strange hug/kiss/embrace. He wanted her as close as possible. He could feel her heart racing against his chest, only marginally slower than his own. In that moment, it felt like their souls collided and globbed onto one another like their tangled bodies on the dock.

Chapter Fifteen

There was no regret in that kiss. Ben might not be over the loss of his wife, but he committed a thousand percent to making it the kind of kiss they would never forget. Riley had been kissing the same man for her entire adult life, and honestly, she had no idea it could be that good. There was an entire conversation passing between them as they explored, sank in, and bared themselves for the other to see.

It was the first time she had admitted her grief to anyone. Those closest to her probably saw it, but she denied it fervently, insisting she was okay. That life went on despite the gaping hole in her heart. Eventually, they stopped asking, and she got really good at acting like she wasn't completely broken.

Larry cheated. But not until she had checked out of the marriage. Out of most everything. It was impossible to care about anything when the one thing she cared the most about was gone. Sharing that pain with Ben, knowing he would get it, connected them in a way Riley didn't think was possible. Sure, she got flustered around him, and he got her blood pumping, but she didn't actually think she would ever want to let someone into her heart again. She didn't think it was possible for her broken heart to beat.

That kiss. It was like a shot of adrenaline straight into the organ that betrayed her. As their hands groped for purchase, their bodies and mouths sliding together in exquisite harmony, as the sun beat down on them and a gentle breeze blew off the river, Riley felt hope for the first time since the day she lost her baby.

*****

The sun streaming through the window woke Riley from the most magnificent dream. She grumbled, reminded herself she needed blinds, or curtains, or something, and tried to recapture the feel of Ben's lips on hers. When her phone beeped with a text, she rubbed her eyes and slowly sat up.

Ben

Good morning! I left something on the porch for you. <Kissing emoji>

Ben sent me a kissing emoji?

Suddenly, the day before, the dock, the sun, Ben—THE KISS—all came rushing back. It wasn't a dream. She touched her lips, which were grinning so widely they might stretch right off her face. It wasn't a dream!

She bounded out of bed and raced down the stairs. Without a single thought about what her appearance might be, she threw open the front door, ready to tumble into Ben's arms. But there was no Ben. No one at all.

Pushing through the screen door, she glanced at the bench. There sat a fancy travel coffee cup with steam rising out of the little drinking slot. And a single flower. The gerbera daisy was a deep coral color, with large bold petals and a thick stem. Its leaves felt like velvet against her hand. She gripped it and her coffee and looked down the driveway where a dust cloud was settling.

Sad she had missed seeing him, but over the moon at his thoughtfulness, Riley floated over to the porch swing and sat, sipping her coffee. It was such a peaceful setting. She understood why her uncle chose to sit out here each morning. Maybe she should channel him and do some thinking.

Ten minutes later, she realized she wasn't much of a thinker, and as beautiful as the view was, her hands were itching to get back to work on the house.

She put her flower in a small vase she found in the pantry and set it in the middle of the island, then headed back upstairs with her coffee to get ready for the day. Her phone lay in the middle of the bed where she had dropped it in her haste to get downstairs. She shot off a quick text, thanking Ben for his thoughtfulness and wishing him a good day.

Humming to herself, she threw on some old clothes and brushed her teeth. Thankfully, Ben had been gone by the time she got downstairs, because her bedhead was at an extraordinary level this morning. It stuck up in several places, like the quills of a porcupine. *Only I could manage to get decades old wallpaper paste in my hair.* Finally, she wrangled it into some semblance of a ponytail and then headed for the stairs to finish the wallpaper removal once and for all.

In the hallway, she tripped, sloshing her coffee and nearly tumbling down the stairs headfirst. *I finally meet a hot, considerate, smart man and I plummet to my death after our only kiss.* (She was choosing not to count the first non-kiss kiss.) Turning, she assessed the culprit. The carpet had a gash in it, which the toe of her sneaker had managed to snag.

She glared down at the carpet, which was worn, dirty, and had been outdated the day after it was installed. Setting her beautiful new coffee cup on the banister, she hooked her hand in the rip and yanked. A fault line appeared down the middle of the hallway—a jagged chasm surrounded by fraying threads. Feeling empowered, Riley gripped one side of her conquest and heaved. A satisfying thwack sounded, and half the carpet ripped free from the baseboard.

She rolled it up, then took great pleasure sending it down the stairs, like an ugly, awkward Slinky. The cloud of dust it created when it crashed in the foyer made her congratulate herself on removing the health hazard. Within minutes, the other half of the carpet joined its mate at the bottom of the steps.

Now the hall stretched before her, dirty hardwoods gasping for life after being covered for so many years.

She rubbed the toe of her shoe in an arc and was pleased to see a gleaming oak floor under the decades of grime. A little spit and shine, and she was certain she could restore it to its former glory. Triumphant, she grabbed what was left of her coffee and headed downstairs to find cleaning supplies.

The dust was still settling in the foyer, which she would also have to clean thanks to the nasty rug, so she scooted the rolls out the door and across the porch. They tumbled down the next set of steps and landed with a plop on the gravel walkway. She'd have to take a load to the dump, or maybe even rent a dumpster, depending on how much demo she planned to do.

A plan. She needed a plan.

Riley had spent the majority of her life going along with everyone else's plans, making few of her own. She played all the same sports her sister did, kneepads and catching mitts passed down. She started dating Larry in tenth grade and he had big plans to open an auto body shop. Before she knew it, he was planning for her to run it. Instead of taking an extra semester of French, he signed her up for auto mechanics so she could learn the lingo.

So, she knew what a carburetor was, but she didn't know what she was going to do with her life.

She'd been in Eastport Beach all of three days and already she'd started on two different projects, in two different rooms, on two different floors. There was no rhyme or reason. She needed a list. A design. An idea. Something. Or she'd end up with a torn-up house with no direction.

For the first time in her life, she was completely in charge of her destiny. There was no one to follow or tell her what to do. She needed to figure out what she wanted to accomplish and how to go about it.

It was terrifying.

And pretty awesome.

She headed into the study and dug through the piles on the desk until she found a sketch pad and a pen, then took it out to the porch swing.

Number one. Rip out all carpet. She'd conquered the hallway, surely, she could manage the other rooms.

Number two. Rent dumpster. She took out her phone and tried to search for dumpster rentals, but her signal was crap.

Number three. Get Wi-Fi. She didn't know how she was going to pay for a luxury like the Internet, but if she was going to do this reno on her own, she needed the power of Google.

Number four. Finish removing wallpaper in parlor.

Number five. Paint over wallpaper in dining room. Because removing it was a pain in the ass.

Number six. Paint parlor.

Number seven. Sell art?

Riley was torn on that one. It almost felt like a betrayal to sell her uncle's art collection. She wanted to understand who he was and why he had been cut out of her family. Would she be selling off an important piece of the puzzle? Would he be rolling over in his grave?

Number seven. Sell art?

She wasn't ready to make such a final decision. Maybe she'd sell some plasma instead.

***

An hour later, Riley was moving furniture out of the bedroom next to hers so she could pull up the carpet when her phone beeped again. Her heart skipped a little beat when she saw Ben's name on the screen.

The man had a short memory. Or he liked her. She chose to believe the latter. Finally, she had a chance to get ready and look nice for Ben Ward.

She plopped into the chair she had been moving when Ben texted and dialed her sister. She hated it when Kelsey was right, but she was going on a real, actual date with her handsome attorney and there was no one she wanted to tell more than her big sis.

Chapter Sixteen

"**W**ow, Riley, you look beautiful."

A smile lit up her face, and she did a little spin. The yellow dress danced around her knees and his heart rate quickened. When he told her casual, he hadn't expected a dress. Most of the time she wore jeans or shorts and her fun assortment of eighties band t-shirts. She filled out a pair of jeans nicely (he had noticed), but this dress—wow. It was fitted to the waist with thin straps leaving her shoulders mostly bare and Ben felt an uncontrollable urge to place a kiss there.

"Thanks. I had to go to Bluffville to get cleaning supplies, because I tore up the carpet in the upstairs hallway. Ben, you should have seen me. I ripped that puppy up like Wonder Woman or something." She clenched her fists and made muscle arms. "Anyway, the floors were yuck, so I had to get some heavy duty cleaner because that dirt is older than old. And stubborn. So anyway, I saw this dress, and I thought, what the hell? I don't have anything nice to wear. So, I splurged. Not sure how I'm going to pay the power bill, but at least I'll look pretty in the dark."

As soon as she took a breath, he reached out, grabbed her by the waist, and pulled her in for a kiss. Partially to shut her up, but mostly because she was positively kissable. The dress was a complete knockout, but that smile—her pride beaming from her like a supernova—he couldn't resist her.

She melted into his embrace, a soft sigh escaping her, and he dove in deeper. This. He could do this forever.

His hand traced up her neck and into her hair, which she wore down, falling in gentle waves over her shoulders. Those delicious bare shoulders. He kissed his way along her chin, down her neck, and took his first taste of the delectable skin there. He could spend hours worshiping these shoulders.

But dinner. He had asked her to dinner. Not to be eaten alive on her porch.

So, he placed one last kiss where her shoulder met the curve of her neck and backed away, keeping a hand on her waist. Just because he stopped kissing her didn't mean he had to stop touching her.

Then what she had said penetrated his lust-filled brain. He'd kissed her twice and already he was shirking his duties as Archie's executor. "There's enough money in Archie's estate to keep the power on. You don't need to stress out about that. The bill gets paid automatically."

She was still catching her breath from that show-stopping kiss, but she cocked her head and narrowed her eyes. "There's an estate? I thought it was just the house. I've been freaking out about paying the utilities, but all that's covered? Seriously? Can I get Wi-Fi?"

He almost kissed her again to stop the barrage of questions. "Of course, you can get Wi-Fi. I sent all the account info to you in an email weeks ago. I assumed you knew most of those bills were automatically paid. I'm sorry you were stressed about it."

The spark in her eye dimmed, and she ducked her head. "I don't have a computer anymore, and my phone is ancient, so opening an attachment is almost impossible."

Anger churned in his gut. He'd bet anything that no-good ex of hers took the computer out of pure spite. "Riley." He hooked his finger under her chin and raised it so he could see her gorgeous hazel eyes. "I have an extra laptop. I'll bring it by tomorrow. It's yours. And until you get the Wi-Fi hooked up, you can use my hotspot when you need the Internet. I mean, it would mean you'd have to hang out with me, if that's ok."

Her eyes came back to life, and a smile eclipsed the worry on her face. "I guess I could manage to deal with it. If it meant I could get online and check for updates on the next *Bachelor*."

He pulled her in close, relieved to see her relax and joke with him. He didn't want her to stress about anything again. Kissing the top of her head, he steered them down the porch steps. "Let's go to dinner. Those gator bites are calling my name."

She pinched his side. "Are you ever going to run out of alligator jokes?"

"No plans to. Besides, The Landing really does have them on the menu. But I don't think they catch them fresh, if you're worried about depleting the local population." He opened the passenger door for her.

"It's a good thing I like you, Ben Ward." She chuckled as she ducked into the car, and he couldn't resist leaning down to plant a quick kiss on those delectable lips. The gator was tasty, but Riley tasted better.

***

"This restaurant is so cute. The crab traps on the walls, the anchors. I love the shabby seaside look. And this view. Whew." She gazed out over the water, which stretched all the way to Bald Head Island in the distance.

Ben's view across the table was far more enchanting, and there was little he liked more than a water view. It's why he lived on the river. But watching Riley take everything in, little spots of color on her cheeks, excitement evident in her reverent tone, he was as enamored with her as she was with his favorite hangout spot.

Justine Bridges waddled over to the table and handed them menus. No disrespect, she was eight months pregnant, and she'd nicknamed herself The Penguin. "Evening, Ben. Is this our newest Eastport Beach resident?"

"Justine, meet Riley Kirkwood." He mentally kicked himself. "Oh, wait, I'm sorry, it's Taylor, right?"

Riley flinched—he only caught it because he was staring at her—but she quickly painted a fake smile on as she looked up at their server. "No, it's Kirkwood." Her eyes flicked over to Ben. "Officially changed last week." Refocusing on Justine, she held out her hand. "It's really nice to meet you. This is such a cool restaurant."

He wished they were sitting closer together, because he was itching to give her some reassurance.

"My mama and daddy opened The Landing right before I was born. And pretty soon we'll have a third generation slaving away." She patted her basketball-sized bump. "Daddy's already talking about taking him out on the boat. He's over the moon to finally have a boy."

"Captain Dean goes out every morning to catch seafood for the day. I swear the man doesn't sleep, but I'm not complaining, because I practically live here." Eastport Beach didn't have a ton of options, but the places it had were top-notch.

"Yeah, he bought a bodysuit for the baby that says, 'First Mate.' After four daughters, I guess he deserves a grandson." She took a pad out of her apron. "Well, I'll stop rambling and let you two look at the menu. The special today is soft shell crab and scallops. What can I get you to drink?"

They placed their drink orders and Riley oohed and aahed over the menu and asked his opinion on what she should order. Coming from the mountains, she hadn't tried much seafood, and most likely what she'd had wasn't fresh, so she was in for a treat.

"Huh."

"What?" He took a swig of his beer.

"You weren't kidding. There really are gator bites on the menu."

Ben covered his mouth to keep everything in as a laugh broke through. "I told you. Are you saying you don't believe me now?" He mimicked Chesnee's mock indignation.

She gave him an over-the-top eye roll. "Not when it comes to the matter of alligators."

"Fair enough. We can order them if you like. Maybe if you know you're at the top of the food chain, they won't seem as scary. They taste like chicken."

She scrunched her nose up and shook her head. "I'm gonna stick with shrimp tonight. I'll keep my adventures to owning a fixer upper."

He scooted his chair closer. Because he wanted to. "So, Wonder Woman, huh? Puts quite the image in my mind." Like for any red-blooded American teenage boy, Lynda Carter had played a major role in his fantasy life.

"Well, I don't have a golden lasso or an invisible airplane. But I kicked that carpet's ass." She now seemed fully relaxed. Ben had been worried about the name thing putting a damper on their evening, but she appeared to have moved past it. And he had to admit he was relieved she had changed back to her maiden name. It showed she was ready to move on with her life. Now he just had to catch up with her.

"Did you finish the parlor already?"

"I may have gotten a tad distracted when the carpet tried to murder me."

"Murder you, huh? Pure evil."

"Not only that, but it's so gross. Like decades of dirt and dust. It's a health hazard. I ordered a dumpster today. All the carpet is getting torn out."

This woman was remarkable. She'd been here all of three days and she was ripping out carpets and shredding wallpaper. He doubted there was much she couldn't do once she set her mind to it. "Impressive. Need any help?" He wouldn't mind rolling up his sleeves and getting dirty with his new neighbor.

And help her renovate Heron House.

"That would be great. Archie liked really heavy furniture."

Riley was explaining, room by room, what she had accomplished upstairs, when he saw Chesnee enter the restaurant and the younger man's eyes zero in on Ben's date. Oh, *hell no.*

He slid his chair even closer to her.

"You must be Riley." Chesnee had her hand in his before Ben could even react. Damn, the kid was quick. "I've heard so much about you that I couldn't wait to meet you. I'm Chesnee."

Something burned in Ben's gut as Chesnee's lips met the back of Riley's hand. He hadn't taken the first bite of his meal, so he couldn't blame it on the food. "Don't you have a lesson with the Harrison girls tonight?" He gritted the question out as he shot his soon-to-be-former assistant a clear back-off glare.

Finally releasing Riley's hand, Chesnee grabbed a chair from a nearby table, turned it around and straddled it. He was far too close for Ben's comfort. "Nah, Emma got sick, and you know Eleanor won't do anything without her sister. So, I figured I'd find you here. But didn't know I'd find you here with Eastport's newest beauty."

Riley blushed and hunched those beautiful bare shoulders up. She was falling straight into the charming former frat boy's net. "Lessons?" She put her chin in her hands, fixated on the newest, uninvited member of their dinner party.

"I teach tennis at the country club over in Bluffville. Sometimes up in Wilmington, too. I played all through college. Even let this old guy beat me once in a while. You know, to keep me humble."

Ben rolled his eyes, but Riley was so fixated on the self-acclaimed tennis god she didn't notice. "Humble is not the first word I'd use to describe you."

Chesnee ignored his boss's comment and continued his blatant flirtation. "How are you liking Eastport Beach so far? Seen all the sights? Have you tried Ida Mae's fudge yet? It's almost as good as sex."

"She's been here three days, Chesnee." He couldn't believe the nerve of him bringing up sex in the first five minutes of meeting Riley. This wasn't some college girl here on spring break.

"I haven't really left the house much, although I did drive over to Bluffville today. Maybe after the reno, I can see more of the area." She smiled shyly. "I'll definitely have to look into that fudge."

It felt like steam was streaming out of Ben's ears. He was confident he could compete with Ida Mae's famous candy. As soon as he got rid of their third wheel. "Well, thanks for stopping by Chesnee. I'll see you at the office tomorrow."

Justine set plates of steaming food in front of Ben and Riley. "Can I get you a beer, Chesnee?"

"You know it, beautiful." He winked at the waitress and crossed his arms over the back of the chair. Like he was getting comfortable.

Riley picked up a fry and dipped it in ketchup. "Have you lived in Eastport Beach long?"

"I grew up in Wilmington, but moved here after school. You know, close enough to family I can see them when I want to, but far enough away they aren't up in my business."

Ben was getting ready to be up in Chesnee's business if he didn't take the hint and leave.

"Did you know my uncle?"

Chesnee snagged a hush puppy off Ben's plate. "Archie? Heck yeah, everyone knew Archie. He was an Eastport legend, like Captain Percy's weekly tribute and Ida Mae's fudge." He took the beer Justine offered, then directed his attention back on Riley. "Hey, you coming out tomorrow night?"

"What's happening tomorrow night?"

"Every Friday during the summer, we have live music on the boardwalk. There'll be food vendors and beer. It's a great time."

She glanced over at Ben, a questioning look in her eyes. "It sounds like fun."

The last thing Ben wanted to do was introduce Riley to a bunch of drunk Eastporters, but if he didn't step up quick, Chesnee was likely to make a date of it. "We could come down and check it out if you want."

She practically beamed, nodding her head vigorously. "I'd like that."

No longer the center of attention, Chesnee rose from the table, his beer in hand. "Come find me if the old man bores you to death, Riley. I'll show you how the younger generation cuts loose." He tipped his bottle and winked at her, then headed for the bar.

Ben started a mental list of all the excruciating tasks he would make his assistant do the next day at work.

"Old man, huh?" Riley's eyes sparkled with humor as she popped a shrimp into her mouth.

It took everything Ben had not to roll his eyes again. "Yeah, the kid can't handle the fact that an old geezer in his thirties can kick his ass on the tennis court."

She placed her hand on top of his and leaned close. "Well, lucky for me, I prefer my men well-seasoned."

"I'm not sure if I should be turned on or offended. I'm not that old."

Laughing, she moved in so close he could feel her breath across his lips. Definitely turned on. "Maybe I can make it up to you."

He closed the distance between them. She tasted like the fruity drink she'd ordered. He could have kissed her forever, but as it was, all of Eastport Beach would know by midnight that Ben had kissed the new girl in town. And he wasn't mad about it.

Chapter Seventeen

B en drove Riley home and gave her a socially acceptable goodnight kiss on the front porch before leaving. In her giddy state, she'd considered dragging him inside and taking advantage of him. But in the end, she knew he was still processing everything. She'd let him set the pace. As long as he kept showing up and curling her toes with his kisses, she was happy to go along for the ride.

Too keyed up to sleep, she changed into shorts and a tank top and headed into Archie's study. As in the other rooms of the house, art covered the walls. Behind his desk, shelves overflowed with books and papers. In one folder, she found letters from artists asking to come to Heron House for sabbatical or to study under Archie himself. Another contained thank-you notes from all over the globe. Her uncle had made an impact on so many people. What would it have been like to be included in his circle of influence? To have known him?

Frustration tamped down the excitement she'd felt from her date with Ben. She'd tried, unsuccessfully, to reach her father. All her emails had gone unanswered.

She plopped down in the desk chair and dialed her mom.

"Riley! How did your date go?"

Of course, Kelsey blabbed to their mother.

"It was great, Mom, but that's not why I'm calling. Have you talked to Dad?"

"How's the renovation going? Does the house need a lot of work?"

Her mother could avoid an uncomfortable conversation like a lion tamer avoiding the jaws of his beast. "Daddy's not answering my emails."

"I'm sure he's just busy. And he may not have Internet where he is."

Riley knew that was a possibility. But most of the time, when he did his reserve work, it involved flying out to a base somewhere in the US and doing training exercises. She couldn't remember a time she hadn't been able to reach him when she needed to. "It seems like he's been gone longer than usual. Is something going on?"

"It's nothing you need to worry about, honey."

"Mom, what aren't you telling me?" She could picture her mother at home, likely knitting, fingers working the needles faster as she tried to continue lying to her youngest daughter. "Mom..."

"He didn't want you girls to worry."

Now Riley *was* worried. "Tell me." Dread pooled in her gut where the frustration over not being able to drill her father about his relationship with his older brother had resided moments ago.

"This trip is a little different than usual."

Her father was career military. He had retired as a top-ranking naval officer. Technically, he was still a contractor for the Navy, but Riley had stopped worrying about him when he stopped deploying. Now that concern came rushing back like an unwelcome but familiar foe.

"All I know is he's overseas and he'll be unreachable until at least the end of the month. Maybe longer." It all came out in a whoosh, like she felt relieved to have finally set it free.

"Mom, you should have told me. I could have stayed there longer. Or you could have come here with me." Now she was worried about her mom being alone for that long.

She chuckled. "Riley, I'm a military wife. I can handle a couple months on my own. I've endured longer."

"Yeah, but back then you had me and Kelsey to distract you."

"Tell me about your date. That would be a pleasant distraction."

Riley stepped right on that land mine. She sighed, then leaned back in the chair. "Well, it turns out Eastport Beach is a really small town, and everyone knows who I am before I even introduce myself. So, it kind of felt like a date with the town."

***

Riley awoke to buzzing. It was like the time she left her vibrator turned on and loose in the bed with her, only this time there were no orgasms involved. She felt cramped, and when she tried to stretch her legs, she realized she couldn't.

The noise stopped suddenly and when she peeked her eyes open, she came face to face with Ansel. His look expressed how put out he was that she dared to move.

She'd fallen asleep in the desk chair, legs tucked under her head at such an angle that she'd likely have a crick in her neck all day.

At some point during the night, the cat had chosen her lap for a bed and was apparently comfortable enough with his new housemate to actually purr.

He was poised to jump down, obviously not caring to further their arrangement now that they were both awake.

Tentatively, Riley reached her hand behind him and stroked down his back. Large green eyes assessed her, and he tolerated the affection for about two point four seconds. Then he was gone.

Unfolding herself from her uncomfortable position, Riley looked at the mess she'd made after the phone call with her mother last night. If she wasn't going to be able to speak to her father for God-knew-how-long, then she'd have to figure this riddle out for herself.

Archie's filing system was about as organized as the parts room at Larry's shop, but instead of digging around for a 2011 Ford F-150 headlight, she was digging for clues as to why he had been eradicated from their family.

There was a series of journals she thought might lend some insight, but they were mostly from the nineties, and by her estimation, he would have made the split well before then. She paid special attention to the one covering the year she was born—in case her father had reached out with the news. But most entries were about artists visiting Heron House or projects Archie was working on.

Now, as morning light filtered through the windows, she felt overwhelmed by the sheer volume of paper on the desk. She'd have to put it in some semblance of order, in case she needed any of the information in the future. Some of the stories he'd written down were fascinating and there were a few names from the art world even she'd heard of. Maybe someday she could compile everything and release a book about her uncle's influence on the world of art.

The idea intrigued her, but seemed huge and unattainable. Maybe she could start by adding some of the information to the Heron House website. As soon as she got Wi-Fi. And a computer. And finished renovating the house. And the million other things needing to be done.

Maybe she'd start with coffee and see how the rest of the day went.

She padded into the kitchen and started a pot of coffee. While she waited, she attempted to stretch out her limbs, which were aching from sleeping in a chair. Normally, she could blame wine for not making it to bed, but she'd only had one drink with dinner. Apparently, she was drunk on something far more potent than alcohol.

She rolled her neck and thought back to her first first date since high school. It had definitely rated higher than cruising Patterson Ave in Larry's souped-up truck and eating at Taco Bell.

Ben's reaction when she appeared in that dress made it worth every penny she'd scraped together to buy it. She couldn't remember the last time she'd felt as beautiful. And she may have imagined it, but he'd seemed almost possessive of her, especially when his friend Chesnee joined them. There was a definite competitive-man-thing between them, and it was almost as if the younger man was purposefully pushing Ben's buttons.

Sure, Chesnee was good-looking in a suntanned, preppy, full-of-himself way, but Riley was far too enamored with his boss to pay the assistant any mind. It was hard not to be when he kissed like that.

The coffee finished, but suddenly she was burning up. She fluttered her tank, trying to create a breeze between her breasts. Just thinking about Ben's lips on her neck had her practically exploding. She grabbed a tall glass and filled it with ice, pausing in the cool stream emanating from the freezer. Then she added coffee and milk and took her iced latte to the porch. The sun hadn't fully risen yet, so maybe she could find a breeze outside.

She had settled on the swing when she heard a car approaching. Her pulse kicked up again, guessing who her likely visitor would be.

Sure enough, Ben's car appeared and bumped down the rutted driveway.

Riley fumbled to smooth her hair down and make sure none of her bits were hanging out. Hopefully, he wouldn't be able to tell the mere thought of him had evoked a full-on heat stroke.

She met him at the top of the steps, eager to get her hands on him, vanity taking a backseat to lust. The suit couldn't hide his broad shoulders and muscular arms. But it also highlighted that he was a mature, responsible man who had his shit together.

She just needed to catch up with him on that front.

He dropped the satchel he was carrying and wrapped those strong arms around her, lifting her off her feet. His hand dragged through her hair and down her neck, leaving a trail of goosebumps in its wake. "You should never cover up these shoulders." He dropped a kiss in Riley's new favorite spot and then turned his attention to her mouth. "Good morning." He didn't give her a chance to respond, instead tipping her head back and attacking her lips with vigor.

Lost in the kiss, she tried to remember the plan. The plan to let him set the pace. Because all she wanted to do was rip that suit off and lock him in her bedroom. She was going to ask him if he had to work all day, but all that came out was, "Hmmm, ugh mmm."

He answered with his own panting groan. "I need to go back down these steps if I'm going to make it to work today."

She raised her eyebrows, hopeful.

"And unfortunately, I have to go to work today." He released her and backed away, his eyes never leaving her face. "The laptop's in the bag. When I come over tomorrow to help tear stuff out, we can fire up the hotspot." He was back at his car door, straightening his tie, heat in his gaze. "I'll be back at six. We can go downtown. Or whatever."

Between the look and the sultry way he said, "whatever," Riley almost melted onto the porch. She was going to have to crawl into the freezer.

Chapter Eighteen

"I can't believe you didn't answer my texts." Chesnee pounced the moment Ben entered the building.

"Good morning, Chesnee." Ben stepped around his assistant and headed to his office. He had two cases to clear before he could get in his car and drive back to Riley. It had been torture to leave her standing on the porch in that skimpy outfit—especially after he kissed her senseless.

"You were on a date with the hot neighbor! A date!"

"Are we postponing the sleepover until tomorrow, or should we pass notes in court?"

Chesnee followed him down the hall and into his office. "I really wish you would stop comparing me to a teenage girl."

"If the training bra fits..." Ben clicked open his briefcase and pulled out the notes he'd made last night. They were mostly gibberish, because he'd been so keyed up after dropping Riley off. Which should have made him eligible for sainthood. Pretty soon, he wouldn't be able to stop after one kiss. Hell, they'd only been on one date, and it was already hard to leave her.

Kicking his feet up on his boss's desk, Chesnee continued the conversation as if Ben was participating. "I mean, I get it. She's gorg. Kinda sweet and innocent for me, but I can see how you'd be into that."

There was nothing innocent about the way Riley returned his kisses. She was feeling as connected as he was. At least he thought so. Unless he had, in fact, lost his game. "Do you have the Wilson file ready? I've got to be in court by ten."

Chesnee pointed to the stack in the middle of Ben's desk. If it'd been an alligator, it would have bitten him. According to Riley. "Damn, boss, you've got it bad. You're grinning like a hyena." He dropped his feet and stood up. "I'm stoked. You deserve to be happy. And besides, it proves once again I'm right."

Funny how the cocky little prick could turn Ben's amazing luck in meeting Riley into a success story for himself. "I'm going to review this file, then head over to The Coastal. I'm craving a bear claw."

Chesnee raised an eyebrow. "Did you get your run in this morning? Can't be letting yourself go now that you have a lady on the hook."

Tossing his head back, Ben pleaded with the tin ceiling for patience. "Thank you, Carb Watch. I'll take it into consideration." He was in a terrific mood. He would eat the damn pastry.

***

The afternoon hearing got postponed for two weeks, and Chesnee scored them a court at the club in Bluffville. If they were pounding it out on the clay, Chesnee couldn't snoop about Riley, and Ben could burn off the two bear claws he'd had that morning. He'd eaten the second one mostly out of spite.

They were taking a break between sets (the little prick was up two to one), when Marla Jefferies walked onto their court. The self-appointed queen of the country club always made Ben uneasy. She overtly hit on him, even in front of her husband at times. He always tried to be polite but firm in his rejections, however it was almost like the challenge turned her on more.

"Gentlemen, you're looking mighty fine out here, slamming that ball around like a shuttlecock."

The woman would use any excuse to say something suggestive.

"Looking good, Marla." Flirting with a woman was Chesnee's automatic response. Didn't matter she was old enough to be his mother.

She propped her hand on her hip and turned to Ben, obviously waiting for a compliment.

"Jeff feeling better after his surgery?" Only the uber wealthy had the gall to repeat their names. Jeff Jefferies, president of the Bluffville Country Club and all-around jerk. He was the one who decided there should be a dress code in effect everywhere on the property, which was why Ben was currently sweating his ass off in a stodgy polo shirt instead of a breezy tank.

Marla's look of disgust was brief, but he caught it. "Yes, much better. Thanks for asking. But he's unable to accompany me to dinner tomorrow night, so I was hoping you could escort me? It's the charity dinner for reading, or literacy, or some such thing."

Ben didn't point out they were basically the same thing, or that the dinner was benefiting the new library the county was building. He'd already made his donation, so he felt no need to attend the dinner. Now he had a reason not to. "It's a worthy cause, but I'll have to miss it, I'm afraid." His plans for tomorrow involved getting dirty with a certain new neighbor. Renovating, of course.

Marla jutted her collagen-filled lip out and possibly scrunched her nose. It was hard to tell with all the Botox. "I'll let you boys get back to your match.

Don't beat him too badly, Chesnee." She sashayed away, leaving a haze of flowery perfume in her wake.

"She may be nuts, but she knows I'm gonna slaughter your ass." He spun his racket in his hand and gestured at the court. "You ready for me to put you out of your misery?"

"Yeah, just need to send a quick text." Ben slid his phone out of his bag and fired a quick message off to Riley to remind her he'd be there at six.

"You could've gotten Marla to back off for good if you'd told her about Riley."

"Chesnee, I like Riley. I wouldn't sic Marla on my worst enemy."

"Ah-ha!" The younger man danced around like Steve Harvey had shown up with a giant check. "You admitted you liked her."

"No shit, Nancy Drew." Ben grabbed a ball and tossed it at Chesnee, but he was so indignant, it bounced right off his puffed-up chest.

***

Ben was early. The tennis match had been embarrassing, but he was too damn happy to care. He'd showered at the club and changed into khakis and a blue button down. He would probably get hot, but he wanted to look nice for Riley. Especially if she pulled another dress out of her bag of magic tricks.

He bumped along the rutted driveway to Archie's, straining his neck to catch the first glimpse of the woman he hadn't stopped thinking about all day.

The porch swing sat empty, the front door closed against the warm afternoon sun. She was probably still getting ready. It was barely five, after all. Some might even call him eager. At least Chesnee had.

He parked the car and jogged up the steps. Pieces of carpet and other debris littered the front porch. He glanced to the left side of the house, where a shiny new red dumpster sat. Rolls of carpet stuck out the top. Most women would have waited until they had help, but not Riley. She barreled ahead with what needed to be done.

Ben admired her resourcefulness. But he was ready and more than willing to help.

He knocked on the door, then turned to look out at the river. The late day sun glimmered across the surface, sending sparkles of light bouncing in all directions. A pair of egrets glided low over the water. It was like a scene from a painting. The peace he'd found when he met Archie.

Riley hadn't answered the door, so he tried the handle. It was locked up tight. He peeked through the transom window beside the door but didn't see any movement inside.

He checked his phone. Five-fifteen. Their last text exchange was nearly two hours earlier, and she said she'd be eagerly awaiting his arrival. No one could blame him for coming early.

Dialing her number, he walked to the windows that looked into the parlor. No sign of life. The phone rang and rang. He thought maybe he heard it inside, but he couldn't be certain. Her car was in the driveway. Muddy shoes sat beside the front door. Her purse was on a table in the foyer. A quick check of the dining room revealed the art still stacked high on the table.

Her voicemail recording came on, and he developed a knot of anxiety deep in his gut. "Hey Ri, I'm early. Call me back."

He practically flew down the steps and jogged around the side of the house. She wasn't at the dock or the gazebo. Wasn't on the shore of the river, or among the live oaks. At the back of the house, he tried the door leading into the kitchen, but it was locked as well, and a glance in the window showed a mug in the drainboard, but no sign of life. He considered sticking his head through the cat door, but if worse came to worst, he had a key.

He tried to convince himself everything was fine. She was in the shower. Or blaring music while she worked. Or hurt. Or abducted. He really needed to stop listening to those true crime podcasts.

He dialed her again. And again.

Panic was edging its way into his consciousness. He tried to slow his breathing as he put his hands up to look in the windows of the back bedroom Archie had spent the last year of his life in. The room hadn't been touched.

He completed his trek around the house and fired off a text.

Ben

I'm coming in. Hope you're decent.

He was too worried to make a joke about her not being decent.

Pushing the front door open, Ben darted to the stairs, taking them two at a time. "Riley? Are you okay?"

A muffled noise sounded far away, so he kept ascending the stairs, hoping beyond hope she wasn't tied up in a closet somewhere. The house was undisturbed and locked up tight, so the intruder theory didn't hold water, but he wasn't being logical right now.

"Riley?" He sprinted down the hall, glancing into rooms as he went.

"Ben! I'm up here." Panic tinged her voice, and his blood chilled to an icy level.

"I'm coming." He reached the end of the hall, where the door to the third floor was open. He hadn't been up there since, well, it had been nearly two years. His vision blurred at the edges, but all he cared about was getting to Riley and seeing her unharmed.

He scaled the narrow steps, his breath becoming shallow, his panic straining toward manic levels. Reaching the third floor, he bent at the waist, tried to slow his breathing. Tried to reason his way out of the anxiety threatening to paralyze him. The red door at the end of the hallway taunted him.

"Ben?"

Her voice penetrated his haze of grief. She needed him. He could focus on that. "Where are you?"

"I'm not sure, some sort of storage room or attic." Her voice still sounded muffled, like it was traveling through layers of drywall and insulation.

He was at the top of the house, there was no further to go. His purpose clear, he methodically searched each room, looking in closets and behind large pieces of furniture. "What do you see?"

"Uh, it's pretty dark. The room had boxes in it, and a couple easels." Her voice held an edge of irritation, but no fear. "I got stuck." She sighed. "I'm sorry."

The rooms on the third floor had been set up as studio space for the artists in residence and then later as storage. Except for the room at the end of the hall. But she couldn't be in there. The door had been locked tight for years.

When he reached the end of the hall, he averted his eyes from the bright red door, choosing instead to focus on the open doorway next to it. "Riley?" He ducked inside the room. Boxes were piled to the ceiling, and he briefly wondered how much junk Archie had collected over the years. Dust motes danced in the light streaming through the window, shining a beam, like a spotlight, on a denim-clad ass sticking out of the wall.

Laughter bubbled past the lump in his throat, and he felt his shoulders relax and his breath rush out in relief.

"I'm so glad you find this entertaining."

He had to admit, it was a delightful view. Her cutoff shorts barely contained her rear, and it was all he could do in the moment to resist grabbing two handfuls of the supple flesh. "I'm just relieved you're okay." He tried to shove down the remaining amusement over her precarious position.

"Who says I'm okay? I'm stuck in a strange portal to another universe, or some shit, and my date is currently staring at my big butt in the shortest shorts I own."

Ben was a big fan of the shorts. And the ass. "I promise I'm not staring. But if I was, it would be because you have a very nice rear end."

"I'm not a Honda. I don't need a new bumper. I need help getting out of this predicament. My phone is downstairs, and Lord knows how long I've been stuck between worlds."

He knelt beside her and assessed the situation. "Exactly what is in that wall? And how the heck did you manage this?"

The lower half of her body sagged. "I saw this little door, and I figured I'd see what was inside. But it was dark and stupid me left my stupid phone downstairs, so I didn't have a flashlight, but I figured I would fit." She wiggled her hips. "News flash. I don't."

"Let me see what I can do." He was enjoying the wiggling, so he took his time pondering a solution. He placed his hands on her hips, straddling her legs, and tried extra hard not to think about the position they were in.

He failed.

His pants were getting uncomfortable, and the heat in the room was unbearable. Stepping back from her lower half, he turned and shoved open the window, then rolled his sleeves up to his elbows.

Riley moaned.

Not helping.

"That breeze feels amazing. I'm hot enough to roast peanuts. I'm definitely gonna have to shower if I ever get out of here."

And now he was thinking about her showering.

Focus, Ward. "Okay, I'm going to try to pull you out. But I don't want to hurt you."

"I'm tough, just get me out of here."

He gripped her hips again, this time spreading his legs to brace himself. He pulled straight back. She slid out about six inches, then stopped.

"Oof."

"Sorry, I think your breasts are in the way."

"Since it feels like I just had my first mammogram, I'm going to agree with you."

And now all he could think about were her tits. This was going downhill fast.

"Okay, can you try to turn your body?" He slid his hands up the side of her torso and tried to angle her body so she could maneuver out of the hole. He was pressed up against her ass, practically laying on top of her. Pretty soon, she was going to realize just how entertained he was.

Under his hands, he could feel her breathing kick up.

"Uh, Ben? It's crazy hot in this little hell hole. Can you let go for a minute? I need some air."

Maybe he wasn't the only one getting hot and bothered.

Chapter Nineteen

Between the mortification of her position, the sweltering heat of the crawl space she was stuck in, and the feeling of Ben's "excitement" pressed against her ass, Riley feared she would spontaneously combust.

His hands slid up her sides, trying to grip her torso, creating trails of molten lava everywhere he touched. This was definitely not how her fantasy went. Sure, he'd be touching her, and maybe even from behind, but she never imagined his first time cupping her breasts would be to cram them through a too-small opening.

Sure enough, his fingertips danced across the underside of her most sensitive body part. Her nipples hardened and heat pooled between her legs. The only positive aspect of this situation was he couldn't see her face flaming red.

"Let me see if I can press things, um, in." At least if she vaporized, she wouldn't have to face him after this.

She squished her boobs and wiggled her hips, trying to slide out of the opening. Every time she moved, her ass bumped against Ben's impressive erection. If she wasn't so embarrassed, she would be supremely turned on. Who was she kidding? Her panties were a freaking slip and slide at this point.

He gripped her hips and moved her in a rhythmic motion. She could hear his breathing, which was labored, but not from exertion. Her pebbled nipples pressed against her palms, and soon she was panting along with him.

"That's it, Riley. Almost there." His voice sounded ragged, like he'd run a marathon. She was not the only one having a rescue fantasy.

Squeezing her hand through the opening, her right breast popped through to the other side, and then everything happened very fast.

She popped out of the hole, knocking Ben backwards, but because of the firm grip he had on her hips, she went with him, ending up like a she-crab stuck on top of a he-crab. At least that's how she saw it in her humiliated state. She wasn't an expert on crustacean sex practices. She wasn't an expert on any sex practices.

He grunted, whether from having the air knocked out of his lungs, or the rigor knocked out of his penis, she couldn't be sure. Scrambling off him, she yanked her too-short daisy dukes down and ran out of the room.

Before she reached the stairs, powerful arms grabbed her and pulled her in for an embrace. Warm hands stroked her dusty hair and soothing words calmed her down. "I've got you. Nothing to be embarrassed about."

She breathed in his scent and released a sigh. It felt so good to be in his arms that the anxiety of the last twenty minutes faded away. She could get used to this man rescuing her.

***

A shower helped wash the cobwebs from her hair and most of the embarrassed flush from her face. Digging through the suitcase she still hadn't unpacked, she once again cursed her lack of a decent wardrobe. Finally, she settled on a pair of dark jeans and a slinky tank top she bought off the clearance rack at a department store she had no business shopping in. She bit through the plastic piece attaching the tags to its label and tried to psych herself up to put it on. The skinny straps meant she needed a different bra, which had her digging through a box of unmentionables she hadn't unearthed for years.

She'd last worn the white strapless bra on her wedding day, but she tried not to think too much about that. Instead, she berated herself for not ever having a need for the lacy undergarment. She really hadn't put much effort into her marriage.

Some of the condemnation she felt for Larry melted away as she hooked the clasps between her breasts. He wasn't the only one at fault for how things ended.

Shaking off the unpleasant thoughts, she slid the tank over her head and turned to look in the mirror. Not too shabby for someone who hadn't made an effort in over a decade. She needed to get more new clothes and make a burn pit for her polo shirts and mom jeans. Maybe when Kelsey came to visit, they could drive up to Wilmington for the day. Her sister was the one who pressured her to buy the tank top she never thought she'd wear.

Blowing her hair mostly dry, she carefully applied her makeup, finishing up with a strawberry-flavored lip gloss. It would be a sweet surprise for Ben the next time he leaned in for a kiss.

She found him on the porch, leaning against the railing, looking down toward the river. Closing the screen door quietly, she studied him, appreciating the view—not of the Cape Fear River. The ass appreciation was certainly mutual. Stepping behind him, she wrapped her arms around his waist and leaned into his back. She felt him inhale deeply as his hands came up over hers, pulling her closer.

When she'd gotten back to her room, she'd heard the voicemails he'd left, each one increasing in intensity. To have someone be that concerned for her was almost as special as him constantly rescuing her from her disastrous predicaments. "I'm sorry I worried you."

He squeezed her hands. "Sorry I panicked."

"Thanks for caring enough to panic." When she was on the bathroom floor after her miscarriage, Larry had taken two hours to come home and take her to the hospital. He was more concerned she would get blood in his truck than about whether or not she would be okay. That was when she knew she was on her own.

Ben pulled her hands apart and turned in her embrace. He sucked in his breath upon seeing her. "Ri." His hands landed on her hips, squeezing her. "Damn." His gaze lit up and down her body, goosebumps appearing as he scanned her. He bent his head to place a kiss on her shoulder. Rockets of electricity shot out from where his lips trailed. It was why she chose the top. She planned to exploit his affinity for her bare shoulders as often as possible. It was going to be a hot summer, after all.

His hands slipped under the hem of her shirt, trailing up the bare skin of her back. His lips forged a path along her shoulder, up her neck and found her mouth—hot and waiting for him. Thankfully, she didn't have neighbors, because they would have been appalled at the heat level of the ensuing make-out session.

Eventually, his hands slid to her ass and lifted her. She wrapped her legs around his waist, pressing her pelvis against his. He groaned, then spun them, perching her on the porch railing and allowing his hands more freedom to roam.

And roam they did.

He pushed the slinky tank top up, and reverently stared at the lace covering her breasts, his breathing matching the frenzy of hers. Kissing along the top of her cleavage, his hands splayed across the skin below her breasts, setting her abdomen on fire. Everywhere he touched, looked, kissed, lit up like those old-timey Christmas lights that burn too hot and will set a real tree on fire.

Only she was the one on fire.

She was unbuttoning his shirt when his phone rang.

He paused long enough to pull it out of his pocket and glance at the screen, then he chucked it over the railing into the bushes lining the porch.

Riley broke into a fit of laughter. "Who was it?"

"Not important." He buried his face back in her cleavage.

She ran her fingers through his hair, never wanting his adoration of her body to end, but curiosity got the best of her. "Ben, who called?"

He pulled back from her, his eyes hazy with lust. "It was Chesnee, probably wondering where we are."

She had forgotten about the festival downtown. She was so completely lost in the "whatever" he had promised that morning. "Is he waiting for us?"

"He's a big boy. He'll be fine." Ben pulled her shirt back up and pulled the lace down on one of her cups, freeing her breast.

The light breeze off the river teased her bare skin and her nipple popped up, drawing Ben's immediate attention. He hummed as he drew it in his mouth.

Holy mackerel. Riley's legs straightened of their own accord, and she very nearly came right then.

The phone rang again from the bushes, insistent. She tried to ignore it and focus on Ben's lips, which were now on her other breast, which had also been freed from its lacy restraint.

She couldn't remember the last orgasm a man had given her, let alone one that didn't even involve her lady bits. But damn was that close to becoming a reality.

The phone rang again. "Argh!" The noise of frustration escaped without her permission.

Ben pulled away from her, and she immediately missed his heat. He mumbled something under his breath that sounded an awful lot like "freaking little cock-blocker" and stomped down the steps. He dug through the bushes, finding his phone as it pealed for a fourth time. "Where's the GD fire?" He stomped back up the stairs, listening with a scowl on his face. Finally, he blew out a sigh and raked his hand through his hair.

God, she loved it when he did that. And with his shirt open and his abs rippling with every breath, she couldn't stand not touching him again. She slid off the railing and ran her hands down his torso. He dropped his gaze to her, his eyes heated.

"Man, that sucks, really." He continued to listen to who she assumed was Chesnee, but his hand was tracing a path down her arm. "What?" He jerked his head up, his eyes widening. "No, don't come here. We'll be down there soon." His eyes flashed to hers, then he squeezed them tightly shut. "Yeah, man. I swear. We're leaving now." He disconnected the call and chucked the phone back into the bushes. Then his hands were back on Riley, his face buried in the spot where his neck met her shoulder. His spot.

"Uh, Ben? As much as I enjoy that, you promised someone we were leaving now."

"Now, an hour from now, whatever." He picked her back up, and she automatically wrapped her legs around him.

"What's wrong? Why was he calling so many times?" His lips felt so good on her skin, but she didn't want to be the reason Ben didn't keep his promise.

He threw his head back and sighed. "Mr. Confident is all worried because Gina is talking up some musician."

"Who's Gina?"

"She's a waitress down at the Spicy Mermaid that he's totally hung up on, but won't admit it. Says they're just friends."

"Aww, and he wants to be more than friends."

"Yeah, but he's too chickenshit to do anything about it, besides whine every time she dates someone else."

Chesnee had struck her as the type who flirted with anyone with two X chromosomes, so it was surprising to hear about his insecurities.

"He'll be fine." Ben started to pull her shirt up again, but she stopped him.

"It sounded like he was going to show up here if we didn't get down there."

He closed his eyes again and swore under his breath, before letting her slide down him and plant her feet on the floor. "Yeah, that's totally something he would do. And I don't want to have to rush with you." He gave her another mind-numbing kiss. "You ready?"

Yeah, sure. As soon as her legs re-solidified.

Chapter Twenty

The little prick owed him. Big time.

He'd finally been alone with Riley—no ghosts lingering near-by—and ready to take a giant leap, and suddenly insecure Chesnee decided to rear his immature, can't-face-reality head.

Ben parked behind his office, then took Riley's hand and led her toward the docks. It was a beautiful summer evening, with a breeze blowing off the ocean, but between the heat their make-out session generated and his fuming over the interruption, there was a significant risk he might combust.

He tried to keep his voice even as Riley asked about the businesses they passed on their way to the water. He didn't want to come across as some hothead that blew up at his friends—because he wasn't. Normally, he was easy-going and calm.

But his engine had been sitting idle for over two years and since Riley had turned it over, he was ready to drive somewhere.

She was excited about exploring Eastport Beach and bubbling with questions, but he could see the flush that still extended up her neck. Maybe once he got Chesnee through his crisis, he could take her back to his office and have a little more alone time. He wasn't looking forward to sharing her with the town.

It was one reason he had a vise grip on her hand. He wanted everyone to know he had staked his claim. It was a Neanderthal, alpha-male thing to do, but he couldn't help himself. The other reason was because he couldn't bear the thought of not touching her, and it would be inappropriate to latch on to her ass or tits in public.

The crowd thickened as they got closer to the stage, where a Nirvana cover band, decked out in full grunge, was playing "Come as You Are." He spotted Chesnee almost immediately, his arm draped across the shoulders of a woman with short, dark hair that Ben didn't recognize.

They were in line at Sharkey's booth, and he figured the least the kid could do was buy him a beer, so he steered Riley in that direction.

"Is that Gina?" Her eyes were wide at the sight of the barely dressed woman with an elaborate rose tattoo covering most of her back.

"No." He scanned the crowd again and found the waitress close to the stage, ogling the faux Kurt Cobain. He pointed. "Red hair, short purple skirt, leather top." It was easy to see why Chesnee had his panties in a bunch, although he appeared to have found a distraction.

"Wow, she's stunning." Riley fiddled with the hem of her shirt.

The shirt he'd almost had off her before Chesnee's barrage of phone calls. He turned to her and cupped her chin. "Ri, look at me." She slowly moved her gaze up to meet his eyes. "She's got nothing on you." He leaned down and kissed her delectable lips, pulling back quickly enough to maintain his composure since they had a couple hundred spectators.

Heat rushed to her face, making her even more beautiful, and he considered whisking her away right then, but Chesnee saw them and waved them over.

Begrudgingly, Ben took her hand and led her over to join his shit-eating-grin assistant and his flavor of the evening. Before Chesnee could open his big mouth and say something Ben would regret, he clapped him on the shoulder and turned to his tatted-up companion. "Hi, I'm Ben and this is Riley." He stuck his hand out in greeting.

She eagerly pumped his hand with the grip strength of a professional thumb wrestler. "I'm Rose, nice to meet you. Everyone here is so friendly. Not like where I come from." She shook Riley's hand next, and Ben saw the wince before she managed to cover it up.

"Where are you from?" Riley pulled her hand back, rubbing it.

Rose blew a large purple bubble, then sucked it back into her mouth before answering. "Philadelphia. Up there it's pretty much eat or be eaten, if you know what I mean."

Ben settled his hand on the small of Riley's back. Her eyes slid to the side, and she gave him a small smile before replying to the brash woman. "I've never lived outside of the South, but I imagine it has its own charms."

"Not even a little. City of brotherly love, my ass. Our homicide rate was through the roof last year. That's some messed up sibling rivalry, if you ask me." She continued to chaw on her gum.

He gave his friend a look full of what-the-hell-were-you-thinking. Chesnee shrugged, then looked back over at the stage, where Gina was full-on worshiping the lead singer.

While the men had their silent discussion, apparently the ladies had continued speaking and now they were looking at him, awaiting an answer to a question he hadn't heard. Luckily, the group in front of them departed with their drinks and Sharkey greeted them.

"Ben. Chesnee. The usual?" As was his style, the brewer spoke as few words as possible, nodding toward the women, questioning their drink orders as he filled two plastic cups with his 33rd Parallel IPA.

There was a small chalkboard with the night's selections scrawled across it. Ben turned to Riley. "Do you want beer or cider? The IPA is good, a little hoppy, but smooth. The cider is crisp, like a granny smith. If you like sour, you'll like it." He really had no idea her preferences, but she seemed more than willing to try any variety of wine. "Or we can order something at the Landing if you'd prefer wine."

She shook her head. "Nah, I'll try the cider. I love sour stuff."

"Make that two." Rose spit her gum into a nearby trash can. Chesnee was scraping the bottom of the barrel with this one.

Sharkey scratched his chin through his thick beard but filled two more cups from a different tap without a word.

When Chesnee conveniently struck up a conversation with a nearby vendor, Ben pulled out his wallet and handed the brewer a couple twenties. "I wanted you to meet Riley. She inherited Heron House. Is interested in selling some of the land." He handed her one of the cups. "Riley, this is Sharkey. He's our local brewer. He's been talking about moving his operation to a bigger place. Having a permanent spot."

Ben had been chewing on this idea since that day in the coffee shop (the whipped cream incident he would never forget). Sharkey wanted to stop vending festivals and have a casual place people could come and hang out. He didn't want a place right in the middle of town, so the location was ideal. He could be on the water without being overrun with rowdy spring breakers.

The other man stuck out his hand to Riley. "Pleasure. Let's talk later."

She shook it and then looked back at Ben.

"We'll set something up next week." He dumped the change into a large pickle jar that said, "Shark Bite Brewing Co, the beer with bite." He put his hand on Riley's back once again and steered her toward the pier.

She sipped the cider, then smiled at him. "Mmm. This is really good. Like cold apple cider spiked with Pucker Schnapps." Her tongue circled her lips, catching the bubbles from the carbonation. It took every ounce of Ben's willpower to keep following Chesnee and Rose to the pier and not take Riley somewhere they could be alone. But her eyes sparkled with excitement, and she was bouncing to the music as they walked. He had a feeling it had been a while since she'd gone out and had fun. He wouldn't take that from her. Even if his idea would be fun, too.

On their trek through the crowd, nearly everyone he recognized stopped them, most of them greeting Riley without having to be introduced. Word traveled fast in this small town.

Several of the men clapped Ben on the back and congratulated him. He wasn't quite sure how to take that, but it seemed like people meant well.

When people mentioned Archie, Riley would ply them for information. He hadn't realized how desperate she was to know everything about her uncle. He decided then and there he would tell her what he knew, but he feared the thing she wanted to know the most was the one thing he didn't fully understand.

Archie was full of stories—of his adventures, of artists that visited Heron House, of high-flying tales that sounded too fantastic to be true—but he refused to discuss his family and why he was estranged from them. Ben surmised it was simply too painful. But Archie wouldn't admit that either.

By the time they reached the pier, everyone had finished their drinks, so Chesnee volunteered to get back in line for refills.

Almost as if he was looking for an excuse to get away from his companion.

The women leaned against the railing, watching the pelicans dive into the water and come back up with their catch. Chesnee took a detour through the crowd and leaned down to whisper something in Gina's ear. The pale skin of her neck grew bright red, and she swatted a hand at Chesnee, playfully patting him on the chest.

Yeah, those two had it bad. Ben wondered when they would drop the pretense and the revolving door of dates. There was history there, but his normally gregarious friend clamped up tight when it came to Gina.

The band took a break, and Mayor Crenshaw stepped up to the microphone. "Happy Summer, Eastporters!" He waited out the resounding applause accompanied by the hoots and hollers of a couple hundred tipsy townsfolk and tourists. "It's so great to be back out here for our Friday Night at the Pier. For those visiting our glorious town, you'll want to check out our local businesses that stay open late for the occasion, as well as our vendors who set up to provide us with great food and delicious libations. For our locals, go easy on Sharkey's beer. And keep your pants on." The crowd roared with laughter and Riley looked at Ben, her eyes crinkled with a smile.

"Is taking your pants off an Eastport Beach tradition?" Her tongue peeked out from between her lips and suddenly he felt the overwhelming desire to take both their pants off.

"Woot! Take them off, Benny-boy!" Rose stood on a bench, her arms in the air like she'd just beat the Russian in Rocky IV.

Riley dissolved into laughter, which made the situation slightly more bearable. Where the hell was Chesnee? "Some locals have gotten a little rowdy in the past. Sharkey's beer has a high alcohol content, so it doesn't take much."

"Good thing I had the cider then, 'cuz I'm a lightweight."

Chesnee appeared at that moment with another round and Ben didn't have the heart to tell Riley her "apple cider" was almost as potent as the beer.

Next order of business, food to soak up the booze.

Chapter Twenty-One

BOOM!

Riley awoke, arms flailing, legs scrambling for purchase, kicking against something, but she couldn't place what it was.

"Umph."

Her eyes flew open, and the night before came screaming back. But not as loud as the sound that had woken her up. She was pressed between Ben and brown leather. And she had kicked him. Or punched him in the face. Either way, not the best early morning impression. She doubted her breath was any better.

BOOM!

"What the hell is that?" She tried to sit up, but his arm around her waist held her to the couch.

His eyes were squeezed tight, but a lazy smile grew on his face, and his hand started a delightful rhythm on her hip. "Captain Percy. Cannon." He nuzzled into her neck, his kisses sending tendrils of electricity down the length of her body, sparking somewhere in the middle and exiting the soles of her feet. When he came up for air, his eyes twinkled with humor, and possibly lust. "There'll be one more."

Did he say cannon?

BOOM!

"Holy hell. Is the man crazy?" Anyone who fired a cannon off at the butt-crack of dawn on a Saturday morning after everyone clearly drank too much the night before needed to be put in a padded cell.

Just how high was the alcohol content of that cider?

"Definitely." He winked at her and then lowered his delectable lips to kiss the tender skin above her bra.

Looking past his perfectly tousled morning hair, she took stock of her state of dress. Her shirt was gone, bra still on, legs still clad in tight jeans. She wiggled her bottom, and they shifted. Possibly unbuttoned.

Ben moaned and rocked his hips back into hers. She could feel another manly morning detail.

She tried to block out what his lips and hips were doing and concentrated on the events of last night. Had they slept together? Not that she was against it, but it seemed awfully fast, and she didn't want the entire town of to think she was a harlot. Even if she was possibly living in a brothel.

Her memory was fuzzy (damn Sharkey and his hard cider), but she remembered Nirvana, Chesnee and the Kat Von D chick, eating something on a stick, and dancing very close to Ben. So, the residents of Eastport Beach probably already thought she was a ho, fawning all over the handsome widower. "Did I eat alligator last night?"

His laugh rumbled against her stomach, where he was exploring her flesh with lazy kisses. "And you liked it."

She wondered what else she liked last night that she couldn't remember clearly. "Uh, Ben?"

He looked up at her, a half-smile on his lips, his eyes lidded with sleepiness or something else entirely. "Yeah?" His hand slid up her ribs and stopped just under her breast. He flicked his thumb along the underside of it and she momentarily forgot what she needed to ask him.

Soon it was impossible to forget. "Where's the bathroom?" She vaguely remembered a bathroom, with a porthole mirror and ships on the walls. Were they on the boat? It didn't feel like they were moving.

He sat back, lifting off her, and she got her first glimpse of full-on morning Ben. His shirt was also gone, and his khaki pants rode low on hips that looked good enough to bite into. Damn, if her bladder wasn't getting ready to burst, she'd explore every inch of his glorious chest and arms and back... "Down the hall, second door on the right." He stood then, adjusting his chinos, and shooting her a mildly embarrassed glance.

Absolutely nothing to be embarrassed about there. She dragged her gaze from his crotch and jumped up from the couch. Pain knocked around inside her skull like a pinball. That hard cider was a sneaky beast. Seemed so innocuous when she was drinking it, but now it felt like she'd drunk an entire carton of cheap wine. Pressing her palm against her forehead, she turned toward the direction he pointed.

A mission-style staircase climbed to the second floor and, despite her wobbling, she seriously doubted they were on the boat. She trailed her hand along wainscotting stained a rich cherry. She passed a small office and then found the bathroom. Porthole mirror and all.

Her pants were, in fact, unbuttoned, but her underwear (the nicest pair she could find amongst her paltry selection) were in place, so she hoped she hadn't forgotten her first time with Ben.

When she emerged from the bathroom, face washed and mouth rinsed with the handy mouthwash she found hiding under the sink, the smell of coffee lured her further down the hall.

She found Ben in a small vintage-style kitchen, working at a shiny coffee machine that looked like it belonged in a Starbucks. He cursed, sucked on his finger, and then waved his hand through the air. She had planned to just watch him, but before she knew what she was doing, she was at his back, her arms wrapped around that delectable body. "Did the mean old coffee maker bite you? Want me to kiss it and make it better?" Apparently, when she wandered around law offices in just a bra and jeans, she became some sort of vixen.

"I hate this machine. And yes, you may kiss it." He turned in her arms and held his finger up to her mouth.

His eyes heated as her lips puckered against his finger and when she sucked it into her mouth, he groaned.

"Morning!" The back door slammed against the counter and Chesnee entered the kitchen, loaded with a pastry box and a beverage holder with three cups.

Ben reacted before she could, grabbing her and shoving her behind him. "Christ, Chesnee! Ever heard of knocking?"

She clutched Ben's hips once more, but now in more of a cover-my-breasts-up sort of way than the take-me-now way of a few minutes before.

"Sorry, boss. Never had to worry about finding you indecent before." He nodded and winked at her. "Riley, it's lovely to see you this morning." He set the box and cups on the counter and left the room.

Mortified, she buried her face in her hands and leaned against Ben.

He turned again and wrapped his arms around her. "Sorry about that. I really need to discuss boundaries with him." He placed a kiss against her temple. "But he's right, I've been a monk the last two years."

"How is he so perky? He drank way more than either of us." Seriously, two ciders, and she couldn't remember if Ben had his hand down her pants.

"The secret is to not go to sleep at all." Chesnee reappeared in the doorway.

She kept her front pressed against Ben's chest and he angled their bodies so his assistant couldn't see much except his boss's back. And after spending the evening with Chesnee, Rose and a lot of PDA (she remembered something at least), she knew he didn't roll that way.

"Ah, to be young again. We appreciate the coffee, Chesnee, but could you beat it?"

"Well, I could, but the Sandersons are coming in to sign their paperwork in ten minutes, so unless you want to handle that, I should probably stick around." He plucked one cup out of the carrier and went back down the hall.

Ben cursed again and left her standing in the kitchen topless and wondering who the Sandersons were.

Before she could follow him, he returned, pulling his shirt on and holding hers out. "We should leave before they get here." He grabbed a donut from the box and waved it at her. "Denise Sanderson loves to talk about her rescue Corgis. We'll never escape."

She pulled her shirt over her head, grabbed a jelly donut and a coffee. "Any idea where my shoes are?"

He looked down at her bare feet and then at his own. A bell chimed at the front of the house. "There's no time." He yanked the last coffee out of the carrier and pushed her toward the back door.

"Ben, Chesnee? Are you fellas here? I've got to show you pictures of little Muggle!"

Chapter Twenty-Two

They ran barefoot and giggling over the gravel to his car. Their hands were full of donuts and coffee, so he set his cup on the roof of the car, balancing the cruller on top. He went to open her door but stopped when he noticed a bit of powdered sugar on her top lip. Leaning in, he licked the white dust off her lip and captured her mouth. She tasted like French vanilla and raspberries and had him ready to retire to France and become a pastry chef if she would kiss him like that every day.

When he finally pulled back, she pulled her tongue around those delectable lips and sighed. Her eyes moved to look over his shoulder and she swore softly. "We should probably go before you get disbarred for public indecency."

He glanced over his shoulder to find Denise Sanderson staring out the kitchen window in disbelief. He wasn't sure if the public display of affection appalled her, or the fact that he was finally moving on after two solid years of mourning.

His stomach dropped, and the situation suddenly seemed less comical. Was he letting his libido take over? And if he was, who would suffer more when he came to his senses, him or Riley?

He opened her door, and she slid into the seat, laughing softly.

The sound of her laughter wound through him, seizing his chest in a vise grip. She didn't only affect his body; she was definitely worming her way into his heart as well. He wasn't sure how he felt about that. Rounding the car, he reined in his emotions and put on what Chesnee called his court face. He didn't want her to be affected by his doubts.

"I hope you don't lose the Corgi clients over a little kissing in the parking lot." She laughed, but he could hear the underlying concern in her voice.

He buckled his seatbelt and started the car. "She'll get over it. But it will be the highlight of the Bible Study this week for sure."

She smirked. "I bet they'll pray for our souls." She took another bite of her donut, a glob of red jelly lingering on her bottom lip. His fascination with her lips was getting a little out of control. He shifted in his seat, pulling his pants away from his crotch. Maybe he needed some time away from her to get his head screwed on straight.

Unaware of the war inside his head, she licked the jelly off her lip and cocked her head. "You think people around here will think I'm, um"—she sucked her bottom lip in and stared in earnest at the gearshift between them—"loose?"

That got him out of his head faster than a bucket of cold water. "Riley, this town is hardly uptight. Did you not witness everyone drunk off their asses last night? Eastport gets pretty wild, especially in the summer."

She continued to look down, her mouth working back and forth.

He refused to let her feel bad about their relationship.

Which started with him not having any silly reservations. Sarah had practically demanded he move on after she was gone, so he had no excuses other than fear. And if it meant protecting this sweet woman's heart, then he would get past that fear right now. "Ri." He gripped her chin lightly and tipped her head back. "A couple kisses in public isn't going to get you a scarlet letter on your chest." He leaned down and kissed her softly. "As long as you aren't kissing a different guy every night."

"I'd like to keep kissing you every night."

"It's a date."

***

He dropped her off in front of Heron House and promised to be back as soon as he put on proper work clothes and some shoes.

When he pulled down his long driveway to the dock, the river sparkled invitingly, practically begging him to jump in. He tossed his shirt and pants on the deck of his boat and dove into the cool water. Swimming always allowed him to shut out the world and not think. He worked his muscles and cleared his mind, focusing on each stroke, each kick.

He swam upstream, enjoying the resistance and the way his body strained against the current. He passed Heron House, kicking harder to pound out the thoughts invading his mind. But try as he might, he couldn't get her out of his head.

Sarah sitting on the end of their dock, her feet dangling in the water while he treaded water below her, watching the sun set behind her. Her scrolling through one of the many dating apps she had downloaded when they found out it was terminal.

"I see you with a blonde. Bigger tits. Sweet natured. Not crazy like me."

He grabbed her foot, drawing her attention from the phone. "You aren't crazy. And your tits are perfect."

She bopped him on the nose. "I'm chaotic. You deserve some serenity in your life. Especially after a lifetime of never being good enough for your uptight family. She needs to have a solid family. Down to earth."

"Sarah, you are all those things. I can't just replace you." He was growing tired of this discussion, of talking about a future without her in it.

She set the phone down and slid off the dock and into his arms. "You can do better than me. Promise you'll try. I don't want to die knowing you'll be alone." She kissed him, wrapping her legs around his waist.

He supported her as they floated, soaking in every detail so he could remember. "I could never love anyone like I love you."

"Your heart won't stop beating when mine does, Ben. There's a woman out there who deserves to be loved by you. Because you're really damn good at it. Now promise."

"I promise."

They made love against the side of the boat and fell asleep under the stars. When he woke up the next morning, she was gone.

He stopped swimming, grabbing onto a branch jutting into the water to catch his breath. Water streamed into his eyes, mixing with his tears. Sarah's wishes and the reality of losing her were at such odds, he didn't know how to reconcile it.

He let go of the branch, allowing the river to take him back downstream, something he didn't have to decide. He bobbed along with the current, swirling with eddies and bumping against debris. A rather large log scraped his leg, and he realized he was at the spot where Riley and he had debated the presence of an alligator a few days earlier.

He looked up at the house as he floated by, his eyes going to the center window on the third floor, where an easel sat with a large canvas mounted on it. Sarah had spent her last bit of strength in that studio, pouring every ounce of her soul onto canvases. At least, that's what he assumed she was doing. After her death, he locked the door and never went inside.

Movement drew his attention to the porch, where Riley was dragging a large piece of carpet out of the house. *Dammit, Ward. You promised you would help her and instead you're wallowing in a river of grief.* He watched her heave the rug into the dumpster, then stare for a moment down the driveway, likely wondering where the hell he was.

Flipping over, he resumed his stroke and quickly returned to his dock. She was counting on him, and he wouldn't let her down. He'd keep pushing down his grief and doubt like he'd been doing for the last two years.

Chapter Twenty-Three

She took the stairs two at a time, anxious to keep her momentum. After a rough wake-up call, she was feeling energized and eager to work on the house. She'd done the best she could moving furniture and ripping up the decades old carpet underneath, but pretty soon she'd be stuck without help moving the bigger pieces.

Maybe Ben decided not to come help after all. But surely, he'd call if that were the case.

"Riley? You upstairs?" His voice rang out from downstairs, and relief flooded her system. He came. He wouldn't break a commitment. He was a dependable guy.

She leaned over the railing, taking in the sight of him in worn jeans, a tight T-shirt and wet hair. Of course, he'd taken a shower. That made sense. And suddenly she was picturing Ben in the shower.

"Hey, there you are." He smiled up at her from the foyer, popping her shower fantasy.

As he climbed the stairs, she breathed deeply, trying to slow her racing pulse. He was here to work. There was furniture to be moved and carpet to be ripped out. Which would get them all sweaty—and they would need a shower.

"Earth to Riley." He waved his hand in front of her face, and she snapped into reality. His wet hair was a dark brown, and she wanted to touch it so badly her fingertips physically quivered.

"Sorry, just thinking about my to-do list." Get Ben naked, get Ben in the shower, rediscover what an orgasm feels like.

He leaned down and kissed her on the cheek, which totally brought her to the here and now. In a public parking lot, he'd stick his tongue down her throat, but now that they were alone and she was horny, he kissed her on the cheek? Seriously?

"Which room do you want to start in?" He was already heading down the hall, leaving a confused and slightly miffed woman staring after him.

They'd only been kissing for a few days, and already she was completely addicted to him. Talk about zero to sixty. She didn't want anything to do with men after her divorce and now she was pissed off because a man only kissed her on the cheek. Obviously, she wasn't emotionally ready for a physical relationship. Her oxytocin levels must be skewed after over a year without sex.

"Riley?" He turned around and was staring at her like she had sprouted a second nose. "You okay?"

Shaking her head to clear the teenage hormones, she clapped her hands together, the noise startling them both. "Great! Terrific! Ready to Wonder Woman the hell out of this carpet!"

He looked a little scared at her enthusiasm, and honestly, she didn't blame him. She sounded manic to her own ears. Reining her crazy in, so as not to scare him away, she strode toward him, a smile on her face—not too big, like an orgasm—small, like a kiss on the cheek.

"Okay..." He looked ready to bolt for the stairs.

She pushed him toward the last bedroom, the furthest from escape. "Get those muscles ready, because we've got furniture to move!" Some of the mania was still leaking out. She had some caulk downstairs, maybe that could plug the crazy hole.

***

There were six bedrooms on the second floor. Which equaled six beds they had to move. Which wasn't awkward at all, since she was lusting after Ben, and he apparently no longer wanted her after sleeping half-naked with her the night before. She was beyond confused. These raging hormones and ninety-degree heat were not helping matters.

They were hauling the last piece of carpet down the stairs when she cracked. He was shirtless by this time, making the situation that much harder, because damn, his back. She was staring at said bare back when the dam broke.

"What the heck happened this morning, Ben?" She dropped her end of the carpet and it hit the stairs with a puff of dust.

He fumbled with his end, staggering down a few more steps before releasing the roll and turning to her, an exasperated expression on his face. "Huh?"

She plopped down on the steps. "I woke up in my bra with my pants un-buttoned and then we made out and had half-naked coffee and then made out some more against your car and everything seemed fine. Better than fine. Like spectacular. I mean, I don't really remember last night, other than some Nirvana and that weird girl Chesnee was using to make Gina jealous, and Sharkey's damn cider. But I kinda think we were dancing, and having a good time and then there was the half-naked sleeping..." She realized the rambling was full-bore, so she dialed it back a little. "Then you come back here and kiss me on the cheek. And we move six beds—six! And you don't throw me down on any of them and take advantage of me."

Her chest was heaving by this point and her brain felt like soup. She couldn't look at him, not after she vomited all her crazy right out there for him to see. This was why she was divorced, why she was going to die alone. At least now she had a cat. Although Ansel didn't seem to be her biggest fan, either.

He yanked the end of the carpet the rest of the way down the stairs and stomped up them without a word. When he reached her, he grabbed her by the waist and threw her over his shoulder. She flailed, trying to gain purchase, but his back was all sweaty, so her hands slid right to his ass. So, she grabbed that instead. Safety first.

He carried her into her bedroom and flung her down on the bed, then crawled into position over her. He looked stricken, like she'd told him his favorite show had been canceled after a huge cliffhanger. Or like someone died.

She couldn't possibly understand what he was going through. Guilt made tears well in her eyes. This couldn't be easy for him. She'd chosen to end her marriage, he hadn't. "I'm sor—"

Ben crushed his lips to hers, dragging his hands up through her hair, breathing her in deeply, holding her possessively. He kissed her like he was being shipped out tomorrow and would die before he made it back to her. He kissed her like she was a lifeline.

She was breathless when he finally drew back, only to bury his head in the space between her neck and her shoulder. His spot. "Ri, I'm so sorry. You deserve better than my constant back-and-forth. You deserve better than my doubts. I hate that I made you question how I feel about you." He finally pulled back and faced her. "Trust me, I want to throw you down on every single surface and take advantage of you. I just need to get my brain, my heart and my body all on the same page."

He was so earnest, his eyes pleading for understanding, or forgiveness, or something. The only thing Larry was ever earnest about was how important it was that he go to Charlotte for every single race. It was strange to meet a man who had emotions that weren't limited to tantrums when his favorite team lost.

She traced the side of his face, stroked her thumb over his cheek, then leaned up to meet his lips. "I'm not going anywhere."

He met her lips with fervor, kissing her deeply, saying so much without uttering a word. The way he touched her, held her, looked at her—she'd never felt so treasured, so adored. So much had changed in less than a week. It didn't seem real. Maybe Eastport Beach didn't exist at all. Maybe it was all an elaborate fantasy she had invented while she slept during her shift at the mini mart.

Chapter Twenty-Four

Admitting his doubts to Riley had lifted an incredible weight from his shoulders. Now Ben felt like he could enjoy their time together without over analyzing every thought, every action, every feeling. After their make-out session on the bed, they got back to work, getting the last of the carpet in the dumpster and discussing Riley's ambitious plans to refinish the hardwood floors.

"I'm pretty sure they rent those sanders by the hour. I've seen people do it on HGTV. How hard can it be?" She stood in the doorway of a back bedroom, watching him dismantle the bed. The plan was to move the furniture out of the room completely and use it as a "test." Unfortunately for his back, she got this brilliant idea after they had already played musical chairs with the massive antique furniture before they pulled the carpet out.

"Riley, I'm pretty sure the people on HGTV are professionals. Or at least the people behind the scenes who do the actual work are. Those sanders are heavy and powerful."

She squinted one eye at him. "Are you saying I'm not strong enough?"

He stuffed his laughter down, confident it would get her riled up. Not that he didn't like getting her riled up, because her spunk was a lot of what attracted him to her, but he'd already torn himself away from her body twice today and he didn't think he had the strength to resist a third time.

She hadn't even been in town a week. There had to be some etiquette around bedding a new neighbor too quickly. And if there wasn't, he was sure the ladies down at the Eastport Beach Christian Fellowship Church would develop their own. Denise Sanderson had likely already activated the prayer chain (ie. gossip line) about their early-morning debauchery.

"I'm sure you're plenty strong, but I don't want you to get hurt."

"Pretty sure you're patronizing me, but I'm going to let it slide since you're currently performing the manual labor."

"You know, if you sell that land, you could hire someone to refinish the floors for you." He spun the nut off the last bolt, holding the footboard to the rails. He gestured at her to grab the other side of the ornate piece of wood. They lowered it carefully to the floor, both of them panting. "Archie paid someone to deliver and assemble all this furniture. I think he had the right idea."

"I assumed all this stuff was as old as the house."

"Some of it is, but for years, the furniture was cheap and utilitarian. Over time, he replaced everything with antiques or fair replicas. Archie dragged me to auctions and estate sales all over the East Coast, trying to elevate the furnishings to a more sophisticated look. The man loved to haggle. Even if something was reasonably priced, it gave him great joy to get the price down, even if only by a few dollars."

"My dad is the same way. He refuses to pay full price for anything."

They each grabbed one of the rails and carried them into the room across the hall. "I'll get Chesnee to help me move the rest. I don't know about you, but I'm starving." He had worked off that donut hours ago.

"I didn't realize how late it was. You're here slaving away for me, the least I can do is feed you." She headed down the stairs, but looked back over her shoulder at him with a grin. "I make a mean PB&J."

"I'll be right down." Pulling out his phone, he shot off a text to Sharkey, asking if they could meet next week to discuss the land. Selling it would give Riley a cushion, so she wouldn't have to stress over how expensive a renovation could be.

His phone beeped with a response, and in typical Sharkey fashion, it was short and to the point.

He jogged down the stairs and into the kitchen to tell Riley the good news, but stopped short when he saw her standing inside the open door of the refrigerator, her head thrown back, trailing an ice cube down her neck. All the blood rushed straight to his crotch.

She startled and straightened, her cheeks heating in embarrassment. So damn pretty, with a healthy flush, full lips and the hairs at the base of her neck curling from the moisture.

Taking two giant steps, he joined her in the coolness from the fridge, but it wasn't enough to combat the heat between them. He bent down, licking the trail the ice cube had left on her skin, goosebumps popping up in the wake of his tongue. Her flush deepened, but this time he doubted it was embarrassment causing it.

Her body went limp, her arms loose at her sides, a sigh of contentment whooshing out of her. Worried her legs would buckle if she got any more relaxed, he lifted her up and set her on the closest counter. She leaned back, exposing her neck to him, and he got to work kissing every inch of it. He slid her oversized tee shirt off one shoulder and worshiped the juncture between her neck and shoulder. Never before had he been so enamored with this part of a woman's body, but with

Riley, he wanted to take up residence and mark it so everyone would know it was his.

She gasped when he drew her skin into his mouth. Backing off, he kissed the area lightly. He was in his thirties; he couldn't give a woman a hickey. Once again, his libido was taking over, and he was running out of reasons to stop it.

Her hands roamed his torso and the noises she was making would drive any man crazy. She had said she wanted him to take advantage of her, right?

He moved his hands down to her ass, getting ready to pick her up again and go back upstairs to one of the many beds, when he felt the vibrations. She moaned a little, and for a minute, he wondered if she had a vibrator in her pocket.

The rectangular shape of her back pocket combined with the shrill ringing noise made it clear it was a moronic idea. But a hot moronic idea.

In her pleasureful haze, it took her a full minute to realize what was happening. She slid the phone from her pocket, her expression showing her frustration at the interruption. But when she glanced at the screen, she straightened suddenly and pushed at his chest to move him back.

She answered the call, her breathing erratic, her free hand pulling her shirt back into place and smoothing back her hair. "Dad? Is that you?"

He knew she'd been trying to reach her father since Ben told her about the uncle she didn't know existed, so he did the honorable thing and left the room, trying to walk off his massive erection.

Chapter Twenty-Five

"Sugarbee, can you hear me? Hold on, let me move." The line crackled, then her dad's voice came through clearer. "Sorry, I borrowed a sat phone and reception here is hit or miss. But your mom said you needed to talk to me."

"Where are you? Why have you been gone so long?" Her head was jumbled with all the questions she wanted to ask, but those were the first to tumble out.

There was a blast so loud Riley could have sworn she felt the house shake. "The exercise is running a little long. Should be home in the next month or so."

"In time for my birthday?"

He sighed. "I hope so."

Staccato military speak echoed through the phone. Her gut clenched. "This isn't a training mission, is it?"

"No worries, Riley. Now tell me what's going on with you. Your mom said you moved."

"Yes, to Eastport Beach."

The connection wasn't great, but she heard his sharp intake of breath. "The coast? What brought that on?"

"Why didn't you tell me you had a brother?" Her leg twitched nervously, banging against the cabinet. She pressed down on her knee to still the tremor.

"Did Archie contact you?"

He didn't know. As angry as she was about his betrayal, she still felt the need to cushion the blow. If he even cared about the brother he had cut out of his life. "He's gone, Dad."

"Archie was never one to hang around long."

"No. He's dead. He left me his house."

The line went quiet, and if she couldn't hear gunfire in the background, she would have assumed the connection was lost. She waited, knowing this call was costing the US military a pretty penny.

Minutes ticked by, her chest tightening by the second.

"I"—he cleared his throat—"want to talk to you about this, but now's not good." Another loud boom sent a screech through the connection.

"Dad, promise me you'll be home soon." Suddenly, she was five, clutching her teddy bear, begging her daddy to come home. She'd spent most of her childhood worried he wouldn't return.

"Love you, Sugarbee." He never made a promise he couldn't guarantee.

The line cut out, and a sob broke free from her throat. Every ounce of anger she felt toward her dad morphed into fear that she wouldn't see him again.

Ben appeared in the doorway, and when he saw her face, he rushed to her. "Riley, what is it? Is your dad okay?" He cupped her face, his thumb wiping away a tear she didn't realize she'd cried.

Words couldn't break through the panic clogging her throat. She shook her head, letting the tears flow, unable to explain.

He wrapped his arms around her and pulled her in close, soothing her with his words and his hands. They stayed that way until she ran out of tears.

Crying on Ben's shoulder was becoming a thing. A thing that didn't sit well with her. This was not the independent woman she wanted to be.

"I swear I don't usually cry this much." She pulled back, already missing the feel of his embrace, but not wanting to get too dependent on this man she'd only known for a few weeks. She was supposed to be making it on her own. That was the plan. Not falling into the arms of the first guy to be nice to her.

"Do you want to talk about it?"

She shook her head, then swiped at her face. "I'll be fine. Now, I'm supposed to be making sandwiches." She slid off the counter, knocking him backward, a stunned look on his face. She opened the refrigerator door. "Grape or strawberry?"

"Riley, you don't have to..." His voice trailed off when she shook his hand off her shoulder.

"I'll make one of each, then we can split them." She grabbed the jelly and spun toward the counter, keeping her back to him so she didn't have to see the hurt look she'd glimpsed on his face. She dug the knife into the jar of peanut butter. Her hand was shaking and when she touched the knife to the bread, she tore a large hole in it. Swearing, she dropped the knife, unable to care when it fell to the floor, giant globs of peanut butter spraying the cabinet doors. Keeping her back to Ben, she fled the kitchen, throwing an apology over her shoulder. Her heart couldn't handle anymore messes today.

***

She awoke on her bed several hours later, her face streaked with tears, her body weary from the physical activity of the morning's demo. The sun was low in the sky but hadn't yet set and her stomach rumbled, clearly annoyed she'd only fed it a donut all day. She swung her feet off the side of the bed and glimpsed a plate on the nightstand. Neatly stacked on a bright orange plate were two triangles—one grape and one strawberry. Grateful, she bit into the top sandwich, which had the perfect proportion of peanut butter to jelly and not a single hole in the bread.

By the time she finished both halves, her hunger was abated, but her guilt was not. She'd been awful to Ben, and he'd still taken care of her.

She looked around for her phone and found it also lying on the bedside table, plugged into her charger. Definitely not a step she had taken in her meltdown.

She had a text waiting.

Ben

Give me a call when you're ready to talk. Take all the time you need. <heart emoji>

Grabbing the phone, she descended the stairs and pushed through the front door, heading for the thinking swing. She dialed, then waited, swaying gently back and forth, willing some of her uncle's big thoughts to soak in via osmosis.

"Auntie Wiwee! I went poopoo in the potty!" Noel screeched into the phone, causing Riley to pull it back from her ear and put it on speaker.

"Wow, that's awesome, No. Is your mama there?"

"Wiam didn't poopoo in the potty. Shoowee." The phone thumped against something, and for the next few minutes, Riley listened to the noises of a chaotic but loving home. Her sister cooing to her baby boy while she likely changed his diaper and her toddler niece singing Under the Sea at the top of her lungs.

She almost hung up, because she couldn't handle all the happiness.

"Sorry, Liam had a blowout. It wasn't pretty." Maybe her sister's life wasn't perfect, after all. "Noel, please go sing on the deck. Mommy needs to talk to Aunt Riley." The singing moved further away, and Kelsey turned her attention back to the phone. "What's up? You didn't call me last night. One might assume things went well, and you were indisposed. Were you indisposed?" She said the word like they were in a nineteenth-century work of literature. And Riley knew her sister only read books with naked men on the front cover.

Ugh, last night. So much had happened since then, and she didn't exactly remember what went down on that couch—just that they had woken up together half naked. She really needed to discuss that with Ben further. "I drank some cider at the festival, and I don't remember too much about what happened after."

Her sister gasped. "Did somebody roofie you? What kind of guy is this Ben, if he's not even looking out for you?"

"Hard cider, Kels. Really potent hard cider. No one took advantage of me." *At least I don't think so.* "I crashed on the couch in Ben's office." She left out the rest. Kelsey would want details she didn't have.

"Why were you at his office?"

"It's downtown in a converted house. So we parked there to walk down to the docks. They had music and food—I ate alligator, Kels—and alcohol, of course. It was actually really fun." She'd enjoyed meeting the townsfolk. Everyone had a story to tell about her uncle.

"As long as he watched out for you."

She thought about everything Ben had done for her since they met. "He always does. He's a really good guy. That's kind of the problem."

"Why is that a problem? You deserve a good guy after Larry the dud."

"What if I'm only reacting to how different he is from Larry? How do I know if my feelings are for him or just against Larry?"

"You're falling for him, and that scares you."

Of course she was. Maybe. Who the hell knew? "Dad called today."

"I'm going to let the sudden subject change slide for now, because where the heck is he and what did he say about this mystery brother?"

"I think he's somewhere pretty dangerous, Kels. And of course, he didn't tell me jack. But I'm worried. It didn't sound like his typical training missions. He called me on a sat phone."

"You think he's in the Middle East?"

"If I had to guess. But who the heck knows? I told him I'd moved to Eastport Beach, that Archie had died and left me his house. He said he wanted to talk to me but couldn't right now. Then he was gone." A heron landed on the fountain and stuck his head under his wing, preening. "He might not even be back by my birthday."

"He hasn't been gone that long since he retired. Maybe I should take the kids up and visit Mom. Hell, we could all drive out and see you and the house. I could meet Ben. I'd know in the first ten minutes if it's meant to be."

As much as she loved Kelsey, she wasn't ready for her to meet Ben. Riley needed to figure this out on her own. "The house is basically a construction zone, it's no place for little kids. Hopefully, I'll have it in shape by the end of summer."

Something glinted in the setting sun. She stood up and leaned over the railing, craning her neck to see what it was. A piece of gutter hung off the eaves of the porch, swaying in the light breeze off the water. *Summer of next year, maybe.* She sighed. "But going to see Mom is a good idea. And you can grill her for information on Archie. She knows more than she's letting on."

Noel's singing gained volume, and Liam started crying. "Sorry, Riley, things are breaking down here. Gotta go. Love you."

"Love you too, Kels. Give everyone kisses for me."

Archie's thinking swing had provided no major revelations, and while talking to her sister helped, she wasn't any closer to knowing what to do about Ben. Maybe the answer was not thinking at all. She still had wallpaper to remove upstairs, and that grunt work required very little brain power.

Chapter Twenty-Six

It'd been two days since Riley ran away from him in tears. He was ninety percent sure it had nothing to do with him.

Eighty percent.

He'd been a jerk sending mixed messages, but they'd talked it out and seemed to have moved past it, so he was seventy percent certain she was upset about the phone call with her father.

He'd told her to take her time, but their meeting with Sharkey to discuss the land purchase was tomorrow afternoon, so if he didn't hear from her before the day was over, he was going to have to reach out. And to be honest, he missed her. He'd awoken that morning missing her so badly he had to dive into the cool river to shock some sense into his body. All day at work, he'd jumped at every text and phone call, hoping it was her. Hoping she was ready to talk. If not about what had happened, then about anything at all.

He missed her voice. He missed her laugh. He missed the feeling of her body pressed against his.

"Do you want me to email that brief over to the court, or are you going to give it one more pass?" Chesnee was draped in the doorway like he'd been there for a while.

"If I sent it to you, it's ready to go." He tried to keep the irritation out of his voice. It wasn't his friend's fault Riley hadn't called yet.

"You sure?"

Ben huffed out a breath. "Yes, I'm sure."

"Even though you addressed it to Riley? I didn't realize she was an officer of the court now." He attempted to hide a snicker behind his hand, but failed miserably.

Slouching in his chair, Ben woke up his computer and clicked on the brief. Sure enough, Riley's name was front and center. "Let me give it another once over. And see if you can get us a court for later. I need to clear my head."

"Obviously," Chesnee mumbled as he turned away, still laughing at his lovesick boss.

Ben buried his head in his hands, counting to ten and then back down again. *Get it together, Ward.* He took a swig of nasty green juice and shook his fingers out, then read over the document again with care. After correcting four mistakes, he emailed it back to Chesnee and grabbed his briefcase.

He leaned into his assistant's office as he passed by. "What time?"

"Four-thirty. I'll meet you there."

The kid was efficient and could practically read his mind, which was a positive and a negative. "Thanks."

In the kitchen, he filled a jug of water from the filter on the tap and was headed out the door when his phone buzzed. *Please be Riley, please be Riley.*

God, he was pathetic.

The text was brief, but at least she reached out. Now maybe he could get his brain out of the fog that had settled around his head when she shut him out.

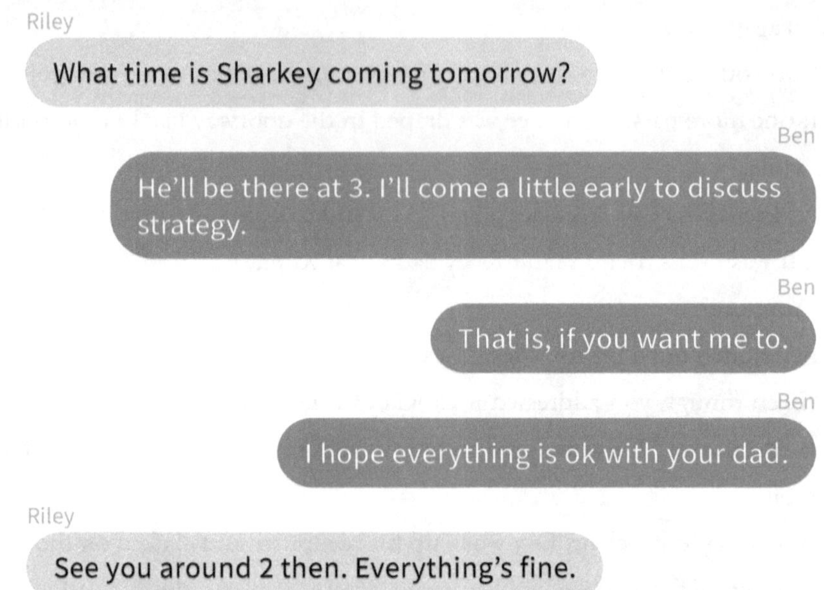

Were they back to being just business associates? What the hell happened on that phone call? He slammed the back door and stomped to his car, so wrapped up in his head he didn't notice the woman leaning against the car until he was almost in front of her.

"What's got your panties in a bunch?" The voice penetrated his subconscious before he even recognized her. She was dressed to the nines and her hair was done up in some fancy twist thing, a far cry from the braids and overalls she normally wore. But that was before.

"Aimee! What are you doing here?" He grabbed her and spun her around, his briefcase knocking against her side, causing her to squeal.

"Ward, put me down!" She flailed her arms, but was laughing by the time he lowered her feet back to the ground.

He stepped back to take her in, indicating with his finger she should turn around. "Why are you dressed like the CEO of some multinational company?"

She rolled her eyes, but flushed a little at the compliment. "I got a little promotion."

"A little promotion?" The last time he'd spoken to his sister-in-law, she was the assistant to the head of a conservation society in New England. How long had it been since they talked?

"My boss retired and put me up for the position. You're looking at the Chief Information Officer for the New England Oceanic Conservation Society."

He hadn't been far off. He grabbed her again for a congratulatory hug. "Aimee, that's amazing. I'm so proud of you." But it still didn't explain why she was in Eastport Beach. "Are you in town for long?"

"There's a conference at UNCW all week, but I couldn't be this close to you and not come visit."

He couldn't believe how happy he was to see her.

He couldn't believe they weren't both bawling like the few times they'd talked since the funeral. Maybe time really does heal some wounds.

"How about dinner? I can grab some fish from the market and grill out on the boat." He knew how much she loved fresh fish. When Sarah was alive, they would have a fish fry almost every night if Aimee was in town.

"I'd love that if you're free."

"Of course, I'm free. You know I don't have a life outside work." He left the "now" unspoken. "Give me one minute."

He jogged back inside and told Chesnee about the change in plans and asked for a rain check on their match.

"I should go say hi." The younger man started to rise from his desk, but Ben put out his hand. "Oh, hell no. The last time you got near Sarah's sister, you had her in tears." He'd spent a full week wooing the poor girl and then bailed on her last night in town with no phone call or anything.

"Hey, I've matured since then. I'm sure she'll forgive me."

"I'm sure I don't. I'll see you tomorrow."

***

The sun was sitting low in the sky by the time he fried up the fresh flounder from Murray's. Aimee chopped vegetables for a salad, the two working in companionable silence on the dock. She'd changed into shorts and a tank top and taken her hair down. This was more like the girl he knew. Only she wasn't a girl any longer. She'd grown into an accomplished, confident young woman. Sarah would have been so proud. He wanted to say the words out loud, but so far this had been a happy reunion, likely because they weren't acknowledging the elephant in the river.

A heron emerged from the reeds on the opposite shore of the river, shaking its wings open like it had just awoken from a nap. Aimee tossed a piece of romaine in that direction, and the bird lurched forward, investigating the lettuce. "I've missed this river." She glanced at him. "And you."

He bumped against her arm and grinned. "You're welcome anytime, you know that."

She looked pointedly behind them, where concrete poked out of the soil. "Still haven't finished the guest room, I see."

"Luckily, I have a neighbor with guest rooms to spare."

"How is Archie? We should invite him down to eat."

Belatedly, he realized she didn't know. So much for avoiding talk of death. "Archie passed away a few weeks ago."

Aimee turned and clenched his arm, her eyes welling with tears. "Oh Ben, how awful. I know how close the two of you were."

"Yeah, it's been tough. He was my best friend, and I leaned on him a lot."

She nodded, understanding the part he didn't say. "I would have come sooner, if I had known." She turned back to the cutting board set up on a folding table, tackling a cucumber with fervor. Likely trying to keep the evening from devolving into a crying fest.

"It's okay. I've got my work. And my camera." He flipped the fish over and closed the grill. He turned the heat down before stepping onto the boat. "I'll be right back." He slipped below deck and into the tiny bathroom to splash water on his face. If she could keep from losing it, so could he. Drying his face, he grabbed two plates, a bottle of wine and a couple glasses.

When he got back on the dock, Aimee was sitting in one of the camp chairs he had set up, staring across the water.

He poured them each a glass of wine and handed one to her.

She held it out to him. "To Archie."

"To Archie." They clinked their glasses together before taking a sip of the Sauvignon Blanc.

Her brow crinkled. "If Archie's gone, how could I stay at Heron House? Did someone buy it?"

"His niece is taking it over." He placed a piece of fish on each of their plates and heaped salad beside it.

"I didn't realize he had family. Honestly, I always assumed he'd leave it to you."

Aimee wasn't the first person to suggest that. But Ben had been adamant Archie leave his estate to family. If not his brother, then his niece. It was his legacy, and it belonged in his family. "His parents are both gone, and he isn't close to his brother, so I tracked down his niece. She was surprised, to say the least."

"Hmmm." She bit into her fish and rolled her eyes back. "No one can top your fish. Now tell me about the niece. Is she going to keep Heron House running?"

He finished his bite of salad and wiped his mouth with a napkin. "Yeah, she's fixing it up now. Archie was sick for a while, so it's a little rough around the edges. We tore out the upstairs carpeting yesterday."

"We?" She set her fork on her plate and faced him fully. "You're helping?"

Ben stalled with his wineglass halfway to his lips. It didn't occur to him how things might look to his deceased wife's sister. "I mean, yeah, Archie was like family to me, so I want to see Heron House brought back to life."

"What's her name?"

"Uh, Riley." He searched Aimee's face for anger, or sadness, or any hint of what she was thinking.

"Nice. Single?" She took another bite of her fish, but kept her eyes trained on him.

Seriously, where was she going with the interrogation? "Divorced." He held her stare, not wanting to upset her, but also not wanting to back down.

"When can I meet her?"

"Why would you meet her?" He took another sip of wine, trying to calm his nerves over the direction this conversation was heading.

"I'm not Sarah, but I'd say my stamp of approval is the next best thing."

Wine spewed from his mouth before he could stop it. "Aimee! She's been here a week. What are you thinking?" He wiped his face with his napkin and looked down at his plate of food, now dripping with moderately expensive droplets of wine.

She leaned back in her chair, a Cheshire grin on her face. "Sarah told me it took you four days to fall for her."

He plopped his ruined dinner on the dock beside his chair and sighed. She wasn't wrong. "It was different then."

"Because you didn't know what it was like to lose someone you love, and now you do." She turned her chair and put her hands on his knees. "I would be surprised if you weren't gun shy, Ben. Losing Sarah"—she sucked in a breath—"was brutal. But she wanted us to have a life when she couldn't. She made me promise and I know she made you too."

He stared down at her hands, so much like her sister's. "I don't think I can handle losing anyone else."

"We can't stop loving because it's too hard to lose someone. People die. It's inevitable. But is it really much of a life without love?"

"When did you get so wise?"

She laughed. "I've fallen head over heels in love like three times since I last saw you. It'll toughen anyone up." Scooting her chair back a little, she dug back into her food. "Seriously, I want to meet this girl."

Chapter Twenty-Seven

She'd tried the tough girl, figure it out on her own, Miss Independent thing and she didn't feel any better. All she'd accomplished in the last two days was tearing the house apart. Demolition was cathartic, but it also gave her too much time in her head, and she was more jumbled than when she started.

She showered, wound her hair into a wet braid, and added a little mascara to her lashes. She was ready to talk about the phone call with her father. And apologize to Ben for being a brat.

In the kitchen, she squeezed a couple lemons, then added the sugar-water mixture she'd made up that morning. Testing the lemonade, she smacked her lips. Hopefully, it'd be sweet enough for him to forgive her.

Pouring two glasses over ice, she headed out the front door and set across the lawn. She wasn't quite sure how to get to Ben's dock, but she could see the mast of his boat bobbing over the trees, so she assumed she could figure it out.

She shouldn't have taken so long to get ready, because the sun was setting, and pretty soon she wouldn't be able to see the gators hiding in the tall grass lining the shore of the river. Maybe she should have sent a text. And not like the stodgy one she'd sent earlier.

Up ahead, she saw concrete pilings poking through overgrowth and realized this was probably the house they had started to build before his wife passed away. It sat on a small hill overlooking the river, and when she turned to take in the full view, she saw the sailboat moored against a long dock.

And she saw Ben.

He was talking animatedly to a woman about Riley's age with straight brown hair. The woman laughed and leaned over, her hand touching his knee.

Riley froze. They were far enough away she couldn't hear what they were saying, but if either of them turned in her direction, they would easily see her.

Her hands felt stiff and cold, so she set the glasses on one of the pilings. Her breath was coming in sharp gasps, and she feared it was so loud it would draw their attention. It would look like she was spying. Which she absolutely wasn't. She was simply bringing her neighbor forgiveness lemonade. Nothing wrong with that.

Except for the woman on the dock.

Two days ago, she was under the impression Ben didn't have any other women in his life. That he hadn't since his wife died. Because that's what he said, if she remembered correctly. Had she made it all up in her head? Had she manufactured their chemistry?

Had her inability to face her demons chased him into the arms of the first brunette he came across?

Slowly, she picked her way through the overgrowth, trying to determine where she had come from, be quiet as a field mouse, and not break down in tears. She was really tired of crying. The last year and half, she'd become like a Victorian woman with the vapors. Crying over her miscarriage: legitimate. Crying over her failed marriage: jury was still out. Crying over her boob in whipped cream: how was that even a thing? Crying over her dad possibly dying in a foreign country on a secret mission for the government: classified.

She definitely wasn't going to cry about Ben swooning over another woman. Especially not after he claimed to want to take advantage of her.

It was fine. She was fine.

She definitely wasn't lost, and the sun hadn't just set beyond the trees.

Okay, maybe she was in denial about a few things.

Loblolly pines surrounded her, stretching tall up to the sky. The first few stars were visible through the branches, and something rustled in the pine straw on the ground. She wasn't going to think about what could be hiding in the pine straw. She absolutely would not wonder about that.

Taking her phone out, she tapped on the maps app, but it spun and spun. So, her cell signal wasn't any stronger when she was lost in the woods. Great.

Taking deep breaths, she started counting. When she reached one hundred, she cursed her therapist and started over. She kept walking as straight as the trees allowed, figuring eventually she'd find the road, or a clearing, or the river, or something. This patch of woods couldn't be that big.

The ground started to soften and soon she was sloughing through marshy soil, convinced they'd never find a trace of her after the alligators ate her.

As she almost gave in, as the first tear leaked out, she broke through the tree line and stepped onto the tarmac of River Road. The road she knew would lead to Heron House. To home.

Relief surged through her, and a bit of pride.

She stuck it out, she didn't give up, she didn't become a gator snack.

Soon she could see the house outlined against the night sky, a light on in an upstairs window she didn't remember turning on.

She hadn't been to the third floor since Friday. Memories of getting stuck and Ben's eventual rescue flooded her with heat, which, on top of her exertion and the sticky summer evening, made it feel like she might melt into the tar of the road.

But he was either a player, or he had moved on from her variety of crazy.

She trudged up the porch steps, collapsing on the swing. What a freaking night.

Chapter Twenty-Eight

After spending most of the afternoon together, Riley had said maybe ten words total to Ben.

When a person made Sharkey look chatty, something was off.

She obviously wasn't over whatever had happened during that phone call on Saturday.

They stood side by side on the porch, watching Sharkey's van bump down the driveway, silence stretching out between them. Once it was out of sight, she turned to go into the house.

"Riley, please talk to me." After practically getting Aimee's seal of approval last night, Ben was ready to get past this awkward part and get to the good stuff. He'd had a little taste of it and Riley's stuff was really good.

She kept her back to him but stopped with her hand on the screen door. "Thanks for setting up the meeting."

Sighing, he started down the steps. Sharkey had agreed to their purchase price. They should be celebrating right now. Once he reached the bottom, he turned around, determined not to give up so easily. "Is this about me not taking advantage of you? 'Cause I'll throw you down on this porch right now if that's what it'll take."

She turned, as if in slow motion. Her brow was scrunched up and her eyes narrowed. "I don't like cheaters, Ben."

"Excuse me?" He stomped up the steps and lined up with her. "Who's cheating in this scenario? Because from my point of view, all that's happening here is you giving me the cold shoulder over some phone call I wasn't even involved in." He started to leave and then realized he had much more to say. "And didn't you get mad at me for a kiss on the cheek? Am I misremembering that?" He paced the porch, huffing out his frustration instead of screaming like he wanted to.

"This isn't about Saturday."

"Well, you weren't talking to me on Sunday, and you barely texted me on Monday, so what is this about? You won't even look me in the eye today. What is it, Riley?"

"I went down to the boat last night." She practically whispered the words, staring at her shoes intently.

The boat? "Aw, Ri." He stopped in front of her, pulling her to his chest. She was stiff, her arms plastered at her sides, like a nutcracker whose body was stuck in that position. Suddenly, the two glasses he'd seen this morning laying in the grass around his foundation made sense. "You saw me with Aimee. My sister-in-law. She's Sarah's sister, Ri. That's all."

Her body relaxed slightly, but she didn't give in to the hug.

He pulled back, tucking her hair behind her ear, stroking his thumb down the side of her face. "I spent the entire evening telling her about you."

Her eyes rose to meet his, searching—he guessed for the truth. "I brought lemonade. To apologize."

"And you saw me with Aimee and thought, what? That we were on a date?"

Her head tipped forward in a nod, and her gaze slid back to her shoes.

"She's basically my little sister. And she's insistent about meeting you. The woman who has woken up my heart."

Her eyes met his, wide as saucers. "Really?"

He leaned his forehead against hers and grabbed her hands. "Yes, really. Not talking to you for two days was pure torture. Please don't make me miss you like that again."

She angled her head and pressed her lips against his and suddenly, all was right with the world again—at least his world. He released her hands and drew her closer, deepening the kiss, holding her tight so she wouldn't change her mind.

When they came up for air, she clung to him, buried her head in his shoulder. "I got lost in the woods. I was basically seconds away from becoming alligator food."

"When, last night?" The thought of her being lost and scared gutted him. She nodded her head, clutching him tighter. "You should have called me."

"There was no signal and besides, I thought..." When she burrowed in further, he stroked her hair and murmured reassurances.

"No more adventures in the woods at night without me, okay?" But the thought of him and Riley alone in a tent after dark didn't sound so bad.

She leaned back and looked up at him. "There should be lights. A path. Between us." She still looked unsure, and Ben wanted to erase any doubts she had.

"We'll light it up like the Fourth of July." He kissed her again, relishing the way she sighed into his mouth, the way her hands roved his body. It was getting hot out here. He pulled back. "Did you say something about lemonade?"

***

He leaned against the counter, watching as Riley squeezed several lemons. The little grunts she was making were driving him crazy, but that's why he was on the other side of the kitchen. There was some talking that needed to happen before naked time.

She filled two glasses with ice and poured the juice in, then added a watery mixture from the fridge. Like a master bartender, she shook the concoction, garnished it with a slice of lemon, and handed it to him.

It was the perfect blend of tart and sweet, a lot like the woman who made it.

"Man, that's good."

"My grandmother taught me how to make it. Be careful, it has enough sugar in it to put a rhino into a diabetic coma." She sipped from her own glass, her tongue peeking out to swipe a drop off her lips.

Talk, smalk. They could talk later.

He pushed off the counter.

"My dad's mom. Archie's mom, I guess." She leaned back against the opposite counter, like she was settling in for a Sunday visit.

He mimicked her position and took another sip of the refreshing drink. If she was ready to open up, he could maul her later. "Were you close to your grandparents?"

Nodding her head, she smiled. "Yeah, when Dad was deployed and Mom was working, we'd go over there after school and sometimes on the weekends. My mom's family didn't live close by, so they were our built-in babysitters."

"Your dad was gone a lot?"

"Oh yeah, career military. Just like my Gramps and his father." She swirled her glass, watching as the lemonade made a tiny eddy. "I think he wanted me to enlist, but he never pressured me to do it."

"Did you ever consider it?" He tried to picture Riley buttoned up in a uniform, standing at attention. It was a stretch.

"Ugh, not really. I mean, I love the idea of fighting for our country and all that, but the working out, and the getting up early..." She crinkled her nose and shook her head. "I'm not exactly what you'd call tough. And I'm a complete klutz. I'd probably blow myself up by tripping over my own feet."

As usual, she wasn't giving herself enough credit. She might not be physically tough, but she had been through a lot in the last year, and she was doing pretty darn well from his viewpoint. He thought back to that night on the dock when she'd spoken about grief and wondered what she had been referring to. "I'd have to agree you should probably stay away from munitions. But you're smart and brave, so if you wanted to do it, you could."

She shrugged. "That ship has sailed. Besides, I don't think my mom could take it. She barely let me go to sleep-away camp, so I seriously doubt she would have wanted me to enlist. I'll let my dad save the world."

"I thought he was retired." He saw a shadow pass over her face as she set her empty glass on the counter.

"He's supposed to be. But every summer he goes back for a couple weeks and usually does trainings or something." Her brow creased.

"But something's different this time?"

She met his gaze, her eyes swimming with moisture, and gave a small nod.

He crossed the kitchen in three strides and pulled her to his chest. "Is that what upset you? Is your dad in danger?"

"I don't know for sure. But he's definitely not in the States and he's been gone well over a month. This feels different." Her arms tightened around his waist.

"Did you tell him about Archie?"

"Yeah, he was shocked, but said he couldn't get into it until he got back."

"And you don't know when that will be?"

She shook her head, her ponytail swooshing over his hand.

His heart broke for her. She wouldn't get answers about Archie until her dad came back, and in the meantime, she had to worry *if* he would come back. "I'm so sorry you're having to deal with this. I can't even imagine."

She stepped back, swiping at her cheeks. "I'll be fine. I'm an old pro at worrying about him."

"Ri." He pulled her back to him, gripped her chin lightly. "You don't have to do it alone this time."

The right side of her mouth ticked up. "Thanks."

He kissed her lips softly. "How about some dinner?"

"I could eat."

Chuckling, he tucked her into his side. "I say we grab a pizza to celebrate your sale and watch the sunset from the deck of my boat."

"Ok, but I'll bring the wine. And you can show off some more of your magic."

Chapter Twenty-Nine

The house was coming along, and she and Ben had settled into a comfortable routine. Thanks to the money from the sale of the land, she'd hired a crew to refinish the floors and focused her Wonder Woman prowess on the walls. Every hideous strip of wallpaper had been removed, and when Ben showed up tonight with dinner, they'd start priming the walls.

On the third floor, Riley rifled through closets, looking for more drop cloths. She hadn't accomplished much up there, choosing to focus on the bedrooms and main level. And ever since getting stuck in the wall, she hadn't been too eager to get back to exploring.

Ben had explained the top floor had been used as studio space for guests of Heron House. She wasn't sure if she would continue to use the space the same way. As much as she wanted to carry on her uncle's legacy, she also felt strongly about opening up the property to anyone who needed a retreat, not just artists.

She pictured yoga out by the river, bridal shoots in the gazebo, families gathered around the large dining room table. The possibilities were endless. She'd even toyed with the idea of a bed-and-breakfast. But mornings weren't her forte, so she ruled that out rather quickly.

After searching the three rooms on the left, she'd only found one extra drop cloth. Stepping back into the hallway, she stared at the bright red door at the front of the house. All the other doors were white. What made this room special? Was it her uncle's studio?

She tried the knob and found it locked.

Running downstairs, she grabbed the set of keys Ben had given her the first day she arrived in Eastport Beach, and jogged, panting, back up the two flights of stairs. With all the manual labor she'd been doing lately, she'd noticed her arms had a little less jiggle and a little more definition. Crazy how scraping wallpaper was more effective than years of gym membership. Although going regularly might have helped.

With a three-story house, she had a built-in stair master. And once she had guests staying, she'd be scaling the steps constantly to keep up with the cleaning.

Maybe she could work some of the jiggle out of her butt as well.

Returning to the red door, she tried every key on the ring, but none of them fit. She stood for a few minutes, scratching her head (although that was more about the dust from sanding the walls, causing her scalp to itch, and less from thinking too hard) and trying to figure out the significance of this room.

Ben would be arriving soon, so she put the puzzle on hold and searched the remaining rooms on the floor, finding two more drop cloths and one ugly pair of drapes paint could only improve.

She stopped on the second floor and did a quick mirror check. No wonder her head was itchy. She looked like she was auditioning for the role of Casper, The Friendly Ghost. She was covered head to toe in a fine white powder. Glancing at the time, she stripped off her clothes, leaving them in a heap on the floor, rather than infecting all the clothes in her hamper. She cranked the shower to hot and stepped under the spray. She didn't have the luxury of waiting for it to warm up.

According to Ben, Archie had upgraded the plumbing a few years back, but she was guessing the hot water heater was a bit older. It was fickle about when and for how long it would dispense hot water. Scrubbing herself under the cool water, Riley thought about what needed to happen after the painting and floors were done. She ticked through her list of must haves and then nice to haves. The money from the sale of the land helped a lot, but she didn't want to blow it on unnecessary things. Yes, a fridge with an ice maker would be nice, but was it necessary?

As she was rinsing her hair, the water suddenly went from a lukewarm baby bath temperature to boil a lobster. She jerked the knob to the right, and it switched to ice cold mountain waterfall.

She was bumping a new hot water heater up to the top of the list.

Once her hair was soap free, she turned off the water and reached for a towel. Her phone rang, but she'd left it in the bedroom, and she wasn't about to trail wet footprints over the freshly sanded floors. The guys were coming back next week to stain them, so she had a deadline to get the painting done before then, or risk messing up her newly finished floors.

She finished drying off, then wrapped the towel around her chest. Padding to the nightstand, she checked her missed calls.

Larry again.

He'd taken to calling every day and then texting when she didn't answer. Sure enough, her phone dinged with an incoming text.

He'd spent her last birthday with Brandi, so she wasn't sure what his idea of tradition was. She'd spent the day curled up in a ball, wishing she had died along with her baby. She wasn't even sure she would celebrate this year. No one here knew, so it'd be like any other day if she had her way.

She hadn't responded to the other twenty-odd texts he'd sent, so she wasn't about to start now.

Grabbing a pair of the new underwear she bought last week, she pulled them on under her towel and then grabbed the matching bra. If tonight went like most, Ben would get a peek at her pretty underthings, even if they didn't take it much further. They'd agreed there was no hurry and were enjoying each other's company.

She pulled a pair of cutoff shorts over the lacy purple panties and was digging around for a shirt she didn't mind getting paint on when she heard Ben call her name.

Figuring she'd give him a little preview, she stepped into the hall and leaned over the banister. "Hey hand..." The word died on her lips as she jumped back, covering her breasts with her arms.

"Good to see you, Riley." Chesnee's voice held more than a hint of mirth.

Not only had Ben's assistant seen her pretty new purple bra, but so had a tall, slender man with dark brown hair she didn't know. She wasn't sure which was worse, giving a peep show to a stranger, or to a man she saw regularly.

By the time she ducked back into her bedroom, Ben had scaled the stairs and met her in the doorway. "I'm so sorry, Ri. I brought the guys as a surprise, figured we could get twice the painting done."

She grabbed the nearest shirt and pulled it over her head. "It's fine, I'll stay up here until they've had time to forget about my pretty new bra."

He laughed and pulled her in for a hug. "I promise, it was so fast no one saw anything. In fact, I think I need to see it again."

Relaxing into his arms, she giggled. "No more strip teases until the painting is finished."

"That's a powerful motivation." He kissed her on the head and released her. "Do you want me to take these drop cloths down with me, or leave them up here?" He gestured to the pile of linens on the floor of the hall.

"Downstairs, please. Hey, that reminds me. I was upstairs today, and that red door is locked. None of my keys fit. Do you know what's in there?"

He straightened, his arms full of paint-splattered dropcloths. "Hmm, weird, should be a key somewhere." He was down the stairs before she realized he hadn't answered her question. She trailed after him but couldn't pursue the conversation because Chesnee and the mystery man came out of the kitchen, both sipping beers.

"Riley, hope you don't mind"—he held up his bottle—"but Ben promised us booze in exchange for manual labor."

"Of course, as long as it doesn't impair your ability to paint a straight line."

"Maybe we'll save the rest for after."

She grinned at him. "Probably a good idea." She approached the new guy and held out her hand. "Hi, I'm Riley."

Chesnee slapped his palm to his forehead. "Duh, sorry. Riley, this is Trip. Trip, Riley. She's super cool, even if she was lame enough to fall for the old man."

Trip pointed down the hall. "Dude, he's right there."

Ben appeared in the doorway. "Don't worry, he's called me worse." He wrapped his hand around Riley's waist and pulled her to his side. "Besides, I did get the girl."

She had become accustomed to the guys' teasing over the last few weeks. She loved how close they were. "Yeah, Chesnee is great and all, but he's easily distracted by anything with breasts."

"I can't even deny it." Chesnee drained his beer with a flourish. "And yours looked lovely in that purple lace."

She buried her head in Ben's chest and groaned.

"Maybe we should start the painting." Ben, ever the mediator, patted her back.

"So, what are we painting?" Chesnee asked.

"Everything," Ben groaned.

Riley pulled away from Ben to amend his answer. "All the walls, that is. I want to leave the trim stained. Tonight is all about priming. Let me grab a couple extra rollers." She stopped before she went into the dining room. "And thanks for offering to help."

"Beer and pizza. The universal payment accepted by men worldwide." The two younger men slapped their palms together in the air.

She'd get them started and then head out to find more payment.

***

An hour later, they'd finished off two pizzas, and the guys were starting on their second six-pack. Riley and Ben had primed the dining room and study, and Chesnee and Trip had focused on the parlor and kitchen. After they ate, she sent everyone else upstairs to tackle the bedrooms while she finished up the hallway that split the ground floor in half.

She had just stepped off the stool to reload her roller when she felt hands encircle her waist.

"I'm kind of jealous Chesnee got a better look at that bra than I did." Ben nuzzled her neck, and she felt her pulse tick up.

"I'm not taking my shirt off again with those two in the house. And we aren't done painting, so I don't want to kick them out."

He kissed the sensitive spot under her ear.

"Well, maybe a brief break is in order." She dumped her roller in the tray and looked around, but all the walls were covered in wet primer. Then she spotted the coat closet under the stairs. Spinning around, she grabbed his hand and pulled him inside the closet.

She'd pulled all the coats out last week and took them to the church for their ministry, so all that was in the closet was a bare bulb fixture and a couple boxes on a shelf.

Ben pinned her against the wall and kissed her like she had the oxygen he needed to breathe. His hands slid under her shirt to cup her breasts, and she sucked in a breath as her nipples hardened against his palms.

She splayed her arms out against the wall to help support her from his onslaught of passion and suddenly, it felt like the world was tipping sideways. Then the wall was no longer behind her. Flailing her arms into the empty space, she tried to call out his name, but he was too deep in the kiss to notice.

Stumbling backwards, she fell, taking Ben with her. They landed with a *thunk*, his weight knocking the breath from her lungs.

"What the hell?" Ben jumped off her, then reached for her, feeling his way down her arms. "Are you okay? Where did the wall go?"

Rubbing her chest, she sat up with his assistance, looking around the dark space. "Apparently that kiss was so powerful, the Earth moved. Right from behind us."

He pulled his phone out and turned on the flashlight, illuminating a narrow passage with slatted walls. "Whoa, it's a secret passageway."

"A creepy passageway, if you ask me." Cobwebs stretched along the tops of the walls and through the space between the slats, she caught sight of something scurrying by. She jumped up, not wanting to be a sitting duck when whatever critter lived in the walls decided to attack.

"Let's see where it goes." Ben took her hand like he intended to go down the dark, spider-infested passage.

She pulled against him, trying to get back into the closet that felt like a suite at The Plaza compared to the dingy space they were standing in. "I'm good. Not the least bit curious."

"You were curious when you got stuck upstairs."

"There wasn't anything living in the wall upstairs."

"That you know of."

She glared at him.

"Come on, I'll protect you."

She doubted he could keep her safe from black widows or rabid rats. "If we go back in the closet, I'll show you my bra."

He barked out a laugh, then placed his hands on either side of her face. "Riley, I promise there are no alligators living in the walls of your house." He kissed her on the end of her nose.

"Don't patronize me. I know there aren't alligators in here. I'm more worried about my leg falling off after being bitten by a brown recluse spider."

He shined his light on the closest spiderweb. "Just your ordinary, run-of-the-mill cellar spiders."

"We aren't in the cellar."

"Well, maybe he's lost."

"Maybe we're lost."

"We're two steps inside a secret passageway. You could take one step backwards and be back in the closet."

"Let's do that."

Ben chuckled and pulled her into his arms. "Okay, I won't make you go with me. I'm sure Chesnee will do it." He walked her backwards until they were safely inside the closet.

She fumbled to push the door open, then took gasping breaths once she was back in the open hall.

He laughed at her, then went to the foot of the stairs. "Hey guys, come down here. Check out what we found."

"I had a traumatic childhood spider incident."

"A little PTSD? Post-traumatic-spider-disorder?"

She shoved against his chest, but he barely moved, and his eyes twinkled with laughter. "It's not funny."

"What's up?" Chesnee and Trip jogged down the stairs and joined them in the hall.

"We found a secret passageway in the closet." Ben pointed at the door.

Chesnee smirked. "What were you doing in the closet?" He elbowed Trip in the ribs and they both laughed.

Ben sighed. "Who's going to be man enough to explore it with me? Riley has a spider thing."

Trip backed away from the door. "I'm man enough to admit I hate spiders. I'll keep Riley company."

"A few spiders won't bother me. Let's go." Chesnee was inside the closet with his phone out before Ben could join him. "Cool, there's a sliding panel in the wall. Seriously, how did you find it?"

"Just go down the dark, creepy passageway, Chesnee. And don't let any rabid rats bite Ben!" Riley leaned into the closet and watched as their backs disappeared into the dark.

She turned to look at Trip, who was as far away from the closet as he could get without leaving the hallway. Glad she wasn't the only scaredy cat. She sat on the steps facing him. "So, Trip, what brings you to Eastport Beach?"

He leaned awkwardly against the front door, because of all the wet paint on the walls. "Chesnee and I went to undergrad together at UNC. I just finished law school and needed a breather, so he said I could crash on his couch for a while."

"Wow, law school. What are your plans?"

A dark cloud passed over his face, but he quickly tacked on a smile. "Not completely sure yet. My family has one idea, and I have a few others."

At least he had options. She'd skipped school altogether to run Larry's auto body shop, and now she had nothing to show for it. "It's hard when you feel like you have to live up to other people's expectations."

He nodded. "Yeah, that's for sure." Suddenly, he jumped forward as the front door opened against his back.

Ben and Chesnee, covered in a layer of grime, appeared.

"How? What?" She looked back at the closet they had disappeared into. She couldn't put words together to form her thoughts.

The two were proudly strutting around the foyer, like peacocks preening for a mate. Ben was the first to speak. "The passage was short but led to a set of stairs."

Chesnee pointed his thumb at his boss. "This one didn't want to go down, but I cleared it for him first."

Ben rolled his eyes. "If by clearing it you mean jumping down the stairs and shouting 'Aya!' while striking a karate pose."

"Where did the stairs go?" Riley stayed in her spot on the steps, not convinced the two hadn't brought spiders inside with them.

"It was a room in the cellar I've never seen before."

Chesnee dusted dirt off his shirt. "It was full of boxes, but old stick in the mud here said we shouldn't go through them."

"Technically, those are your boxes, so it didn't seem right to go through them without you there."

"It wasn't a secret sex dungeon, then?" She recalled their texts from a few weeks ago.

"Not a whip or chain in sight." Ben shook his head solemnly.

The look on Chesnee's face was priceless. "Are you telling me old Archie was into some kinky shit?"

She and Ben laughed, and Chesnee scowled.

"But we should see what's down there." Ben sat on the step beside her.

She scooted away from the potential arachnids currently calling him home. "I'm going to need a few more bottles of wine to make it down a spider-filled hallway to a dark, creepy cellar. Maybe some other time." She stood up and clapped her hands together. "How about we finish the painting? There's an extra six-pack in it for you." She smiled and pointed at Chesnee and Trip.

The two grumbled a bit, but headed back up the stairs.

Ben rose and came toward her, his arms outstretched. "Now, back to our closet activities..."

"Oh, no, Spiderman. You can go take a shower and burn those clothes before you touch me again."

Chapter Thirty

Chesnee stuck his head in the doorway. "Hey, Boss. Mr. Martine canceled his four o'clock. If it's cool with you, I'm going to knock off early. Trip is down at the marina waiting for me."

"Sure, go ahead. And thank him again for helping out last night." Ben closed his laptop. He'd head out too and stop by the hardware store to grab bug spray. He wanted to bomb the secret passageway so he could talk Riley into exploring it with him.

"It was fun. And not just catching Riley in the buff."

He glared at the younger man. "What did I say about forgetting that ever happened?"

"Sorry, but the image is burned on my retinas."

"Well, keep it to yourself." He honestly couldn't blame Chesnee; she looked amazing in that purple lace. He'd like to take a better look himself.

Laughing, his assistant started to leave, but then turned back. "I gotta say, I'm impressed you managed to snag her. Maybe you do have moves."

He wasn't about to discuss his sex life with Chesnee. Especially not the fact he and Riley hadn't slept together yet. "I'm so glad you approve." He started piling up the folders he needed to take home.

"Don't take too long to close the deal, or she might lose interest and check out some younger, more virile options."

Ben snapped his head up, his jaw going slack. *How did the little prick know?*

"It's your posture—so tense. Once you're getting some regularly, I bet you'll hit better, too."

"I beat you last week."

"Yeah, but it took three sets. Think how quick you'll take me down after a round with Riley." He winked, and wisely departed before his boss could wring his neck.

Ben buried his head in his hands and sighed. It'd been almost a month since that first hot kiss on the dock. (He still wasn't counting the first non-kiss in the kitchen.) They'd gotten pretty close a few times, but something always stopped them.

She'd been getting a lot of phone calls and texts. And while she didn't answer most of them, it usually put a damper on the mood. He wanted to ask her about them, but they hadn't defined what was between them, so he didn't feel like it was his place to stick his nose in her business. He just knew the look that crossed over her face every time the phone buzzed, and she swiped the screen like she was poking someone's eyes out. He'd bet his boat it was the ex.

Eventually, they'd have to broach the subject, but he also knew that meant him revealing what lay behind that red door on the third floor, and he wasn't ready quite yet.

One night, they'd been making out on his boat, and he could have sworn he saw Sarah standing on the dock, staring out at the river. It spooked him so badly he feigned a reaction to the fish they'd cooked for dinner. As she'd walked away from him, he felt like such a fool. To not be able to pull the trigger with a woman he was intensely attracted to and felt something for, and then to lie to her on top of it. He had to get a handle on his psyche. It was definitely mental.

His body was ready and willing to take the next step with Riley. It'd gotten to the point that the sound of her voice made him hard, which was fairly inconvenient when she called him at work.

As he locked up the office, he vowed that he would bring it up tonight. Her ex and the red door. It was time.

***

An hour later, he pulled down the rutted drive to Heron House, his backseat full of groceries for dinner, a half a dozen bug bombs, and a broom to knock down the spiderwebs after he'd killed all the little buggers.

Riley's car wasn't in its usual spot, so he used his key to let himself inside. He called her on his way to the kitchen to put away the perishables.

"Are you leaving work? I'm out, but I'll be back in less than an hour." Her cheery voice had its usual effect on him, and he had to adjust his pants.

"No, my last appointment canceled, so I'm at the house now."

"Oh, I'm sorry, I'll hurry back."

Murrays had a sale on steak, so he'd stocked up. He slid two in the freezer and left the other two on the counter to marinate. "No, no. Don't rush. It's probably better that you aren't here. I'm going to bomb the secret passageway. Get rid of all those scary spiders."

"I'm not going to say no to that. I'll run to Murrays and grab something for dinner."

"Already been there, too. Got us two fat steaks." He popped a can of beer and poured it into a baking dish, then settled the steaks in the bubbling liquid.

"You are too good to me."

He sprinkled seasoning on top of the steaks, then covered the dish with foil. "Maybe you can find a way to thank me later."

"Hmm. Maybe. I'll have to google what the appropriate thank you is for steak and spider removal."

"Pretty sure it involves you in that purple lace bra."

"Pretty sure that can be arranged." Her car door slammed. "Hey, I'm at the pharmacy, I'll see you in a bit, okay?"

"Okay. Take your time." He ended the call and headed outside to grab the bug bombs. He'd change clothes, set up the foggers, and then fire up the grill. All the manly stuff. Now if he could just be man enough to talk to Riley about their relationship.

***

He was putting the potatoes on the grill when he heard Riley's car pull down the drive.

He rounded the side of the house, hoping to catch her before she made it inside. Not seeing her right away, he soon realized she was still sitting in her car. He approached, ready to open the door and greet her, but he stopped short when he saw her head leaning against the steering wheel and her shoulders heaving.

She'd been fine when he talked to her less than an hour ago. Cheerful, even.

Concern clinched his gut, and he wrenched the driver's side door open, kneeling in the opening. "Riley, what is it?"

She turned to face him, her cheeks streaked with tears and her breath coming out in mournful gasps. She opened her mouth, but only a sob escaped.

He unbuckled her seatbelt, then pulled her from the car, cradling her in his arms. She burrowed into him, hanging on desperately to his neck, her body shaking. His brain whirled through the possibilities, but he couldn't fathom what had happened since they spoke to have her in such a state.

He carried her up the porch steps and settled on the swing, keeping her in his arms, whispering what he hoped were soothing words while he stroked her hair and her back.

Finally, the sobbing subsided, and she took a shuddering breath.

"Tell me what I can do, Ri." He would do anything in his power to take this grief from her.

She sat back a little, so he could see her beautiful tear-streaked face, and it gutted him once more.

"Anything."

Shaking her head, she wiped her eyes. "There's nothing anyone can do. My father is missing." She dissolved in another fit of tears and buried her face against his chest.

No trip to the hardware store could fix this.

Chapter Thirty-One

Ben held her all night. She slept in fits and spurts, but usually awoke to some horrific dream. His presence was calming, but she needed to actively keep her mind from wandering down terrifying paths.

So, after he left for court, she got up, changed into painting clothes and set to work. If she concentrated on cutting in and rolling smoothly, she could focus on Caribbean Sea and Celadon Breeze. She painted through lunch, then curled up on a drop cloth for a quick nap, then sprung up when the nightmares crowded back into her mind. She ate a granola bar and drank half a bottle of wine, then painted the dining room.

By the time Ben reappeared with dinner and a concerned look on his face, she had finished the main floor.

"Riley, I can't believe you've gotten all this done. I was worried when you didn't answer my texts, but I thought maybe you were sleeping." He held her, pressed tightly to his side, while he went from room to room, celebrating her hard work. He kissed her temple, lingering there like he was trying to peer inside her mind. "Are you sure you're okay? You're awfully quiet."

She'd spent the day in silence. No music, no phone calls from Kelsey or her mom. Her lips hadn't parted except for the wine. She hadn't cried since last night, her tear ducts little dried up raisins, exhausted from overuse. The only person she wanted to speak to was her dad.

"Ri, you're scaring me." He turned her into his arms and pulled her in tightly. She felt safe in his embrace, but he couldn't protect her from this. No one could. She'd spent her whole life worrying about this. Preparing for this tragedy. It hurt almost as much as her miscarriage. Because she still had the tiniest morsel of hope. Her mother's stream of texts, declaring there was nothing to worry about, that it was temporary, and he would be home in no time. It's what mothers did—they lied to their children to keep them from hurting.

She squeezed Ben back, the only comfort she could manage for him right now. Besides, she still had the second floor to finish.

"Okay, well, at least eat something." Not letting go of her, he led them to the kitchen, where he had set a bag of tacos.

Normally, she'd dive in and suggest margaritas, but how could she when her dad was probably being held hostage by some hostile regime? How could she enjoy anything until she knew he was safe?

Ben picked up the bottle of wine and tipped the remainder into her glass. She reached for it, swearing silently she wouldn't enjoy it, she just needed to numb the pain.

Sliding the goblet as far away as possible, he held out a taco. "Eat the taco and I'll let you have the wine."

She glared at him but took the taco from him and bit into it, letting bits of lettuce and broken shell drop to the floor. She'd clean it up later, not like she was planning to sleep.

Ben ate his taco, neatly catching the inevitable crumbs with a paper towel. He watched her the whole time, like he expected her to hide the remainder of her meal behind the toaster if he turned his back. Not that she considered it or anything. She needed the fuel to keep painting.

When she finished, he slid the glass toward her. She sipped it slowly, because no matter how bad things got, she wasn't going to open a second bottle. She wouldn't be an orphan *and* a lush. Okay, even she had to admit she was in a dark place. Her mother was still alive and in denial. As if to reinforce the thought, her phone beeped again.

Mom

Your father has endured far worse than this, Sugarbee. Keep your head high.

Oh, hell no. No one called her that except her daddy.

The wine must have gone straight to her tear ducts, because they plumped into little grapes again and started releasing moisture.

"Oh, Ri." Ben set his taco down and pulled her back into his arms. "I wish I could fix this for you."

***

Mortars sounded all around, lighting up the night sky and the desert sand below. She huddled behind a stone wall, wearing a combat helmet and holding a bayonet so tightly her hands ached. In a ditch a few feet in front of her, she could see her father stretched out, his rifle sighted on some distant target, but he didn't fire the weapon. The enemy approached, unconcerned about the bullets whizzing past him. Just as she could make out his features, her father pulled the trigger, sending a bullet straight into Archie's chest. She cried out and jumped from behind the wall, running forward, but not getting anywhere.

"Ri. Riley, I'm here." Strong hands shook her, but she fought back, shaking her head from side to side.

"No, no!" She shook her head, not wanting to believe what she'd seen. How could her father kill him? Why?

"Riley." A hand smoothed her hair back from her forehead and she peeked one eye open to find Ben over her, his eyes filled with concern. "It's okay, you're okay." He pressed a kiss against her forehead, then slid a hand down to clasp hers.

She came fully awake, taking in as much of her surroundings as the dim light would allow. She was in the parlor, stretched out on one of the sofas. Ben was sitting on a coffee table pulled close to her side, his hair sticking out like the first night he had run up to Heron House. She sighed, relieved she was here, that this was real, not what had been in her mind.

He laid his head down on her stomach, looking up at her. "What can I do?"

She dragged her hand through his hair, wishing she had an answer, a simple solution to this torturous problem. The weight of him across her abdomen comforted her, held the knots in place for the time being, so she stroked his hair, soothing them both, until he fell asleep.

A vibration captured her attention, and she grabbed her phone off the table. It was a text from an unknown number. At forty-thirty in the morning.

She pressed her phone to her chest, silent tears of relief coating her cheeks. Her dad was alive. Her world had been righted.

Chapter Thirty-Two

Ben awoke to the sun streaming through the leaded glass windows, creating fractal patterns across his face. He was in an awkward position, with his lower half on a coffee table and his upper half leaning on the sofa. Slowly, he untwisted his torso and searched the room for Riley. He'd spent the first half of the night watching her, praying she could sleep without the nightmares that had plagued her the night before. She didn't share the content of the dreams with him, but he could imagine the horrific images that haunted her sleep.

After she had woken up, flailing, screaming and terrified, he'd felt so helpless. All he wanted was to comfort her, and instead, she had soothed him to sleep by stroking his hair.

Checking his watch, he swore, then quickly shot off a text to Chesnee that he wouldn't be by the office before his two o'clock hearing. He circled the ground floor, looking for Riley, and grabbed a cup of coffee when he passed through the kitchen. He heard music coming from upstairs, which was a positive sign after the deadly silence that echoed through the house yesterday. She hadn't spoken a single word to him, unless he counted her calling out in her sleep. It was unnerving.

Jogging up the stairs, he followed the strains of early eighties Madonna to a back bedroom. There, he found Riley atop a step stool, cutting in the corners of the room with a pale peach color. She was singing along with "Material Girl" and shaking her hips to the rhythm. The sound of her voice soothed his soul, and he wanted to grab her off that ladder and kiss her, he was so damn happy to see her back to normal.

"You could have woken me up to help."

She turned her head and smiled at him over her shoulder. "You needed the sleep after babysitting me for two nights."

"It's not a hardship to spend the night with you." He wanted to know what had changed, but he was scared to burst this bubble of normalcy. "Did you sleep?"

"A little." She dipped the paintbrush in the red plastic cup she was holding. "My dad reached out last night. He's okay."

"Oh, Riley. That's amazing." He stepped closer to her, grabbing her waist and lowering her to the floor. "You definitely should have woken me up to tell me the good news!" He hugged her while she laughed, holding her paintbrush high so it wouldn't touch either of them.

She pulled away from him and set the cup and the brush on her stool. "Sorry I was so"—she paused, considering the right word—"unreachable, yesterday."

He slipped his hands back around her waist. "You don't ever have to apologize to me for your feelings. It was completely valid."

"Well, my feelings right now are that I want to kiss you." She hooked her arms around his neck.

"And you definitely never have to apologize for that." He leaned down and met her lips, savoring the smile he felt there, so relieved to have her back. Sliding his hands up under her shirt, he savored the feel of her soft skin, the warmth that radiated from it. He tightened their embrace so she could feel the effect she had on him.

She moaned against his mouth and pulled at the hem of his shirt, yanking it up, but not breaking the kiss.

He pulled back long enough to jerk the shirt off, then found her mouth again—hot, with a hint of cinnamon. She backed him up against the wall, luckily one she hadn't painted yet, and kissed his chest, her mouth following the path her hands made over his torso. Everywhere she touched, his skin lit up, like the sun beating down, followed by a light breeze. Her mouth and hands working in tandem to set him on fire.

Suddenly she stopped, stepped back, and pulled her own shirt over her head.

Purple lace covered her perfect breasts, the pale skin begging to be kissed. He grabbed her hips and pulled her closer, lowering his head to explore this new territory. They'd fooled around a few times, but this seemed different. More intense, more real. He vaguely remembered wanting to address what was keeping them from taking the next step, but here they were, teetering right on the edge of the stairway to heaven as far as he was concerned.

Her skin tasted salty, like an ocean breeze, and her chest swelled as she gasped with the contact. She threaded her fingers through his hair, holding him in place as he kissed along the line of her cleavage. The bra did little to cover her glorious breasts, which momentarily pissed him off, knowing Chesnee and Trip had gotten a glimpse of her in the lingerie.

He circled her nipple with his tongue and felt her suck in a breath. He moved to the other side, trying to keep things equitable. She moaned and pulled his head closer.

His pants were getting tighter by the minute, so he hooked his hands under her ass and yanked her up, not breaking contact with her breasts. Her legs encircled his waist, and his erection throbbed at the contact with her center. There was no longer a need for conversation. He only needed to be inside her. Ex-husbands and red doors be damned.

He stopped worshiping her breasts long enough to carry her down the hall to her bedroom. Right before he dropped her on the bed, he flicked the clasp on her bra and watched in awe as the purple lace fell away to reveal smooth skin and pert nipples.

Riley laughed at the expert move and her face lit with joy.

"You are so beautiful." He tucked a loose strand of hair behind her ear and kissed her softly. As he started to pull away, she leaned up and kissed him fiercely. Her hands slid down his abs to his pants, where she undid the button and had the zipper down before he even knew what was happening. He wasn't the only one ready to take the next step.

They helped each other out of their pants, then it was like time suspended while they each took in the scene, raking gazes over heaving, sweaty, gloriously naked bodies. She had curves in all the right places, hips he could grab a hold of when the time came, the soft lines of a woman. And he was hard as a rock.

He lowered himself over her, hovering, drawing out the moment before they would be skin to skin. Sparks of electricity flickered between them, his skin pricking with goosebumps, her body quivering in anticipation.

When they finally did touch, it was like his world slid into place. Every doubt he'd had over the last few weeks dissipated, and if someone had asked him what he'd been so worried about, he would have been unable to answer. It felt right. Like forces outside his control had orchestrated it.

Their gazes locked as they explored the sensations of their bodies meeting, sliding against each other, savoring the contact. He trailed his fingers up her arm, twining their hands together, wanting to be linked to this woman in every possible way. Her eyes were glazed and her mouth slack, her face the perfect picture of pleasure and serenity. He knew in that moment he was attached. It would hurt if he had to let her go. And that thought gave him pause.

Was he really ready to feel that kind of pain again? Then she ran the fingers of her free hand up his ribcage, pulling him closer, meeting his lips with a fervor that sent a chill through his body. She might as well have reached inside his chest and squeezed his heart. He was in deep—no matter the risks.

She mumbled his name between kisses, her moans sending even more blood to his erection and urgency to their embrace.

One minute they were kissing, and the next, he was inside her, barely conscious of it happening, but becoming fully aware once the sensation reached his brain. Being inside Riley made him feel whole again, and he hadn't even realized he was missing anything.

Chapter Thirty-Three

Sex with Larry had never felt like that. It wasn't bad, per se, but it never even bordered on the universe of spectacular. Earth-shattering, epic, ruined for other men. Sex with Ben was all the things she'd read about in romance novels. Except more somehow.

Between finding out her dad was okay, and the two orgasms Ben gave her before he left for work, Riley was riding a shiny, rainbow-colored wave of happiness. It was as if every mundane, pathetic moment of her existence had been justified. This was her reward for surviving the last twenty-nine years of ordinary life.

She had no idea sex could hold that power. Something told her it wasn't just the sex, but she wasn't ready to face that quite yet. Maybe after the glow of her multiple orgasms wore off.

As soon as her legs could support her again, she bounded out of bed and went back to painting. By lunch, she had finished the back two bedrooms and most of the hallway. She made a peanut butter and jelly sandwich and took it out on the porch to eat. It was a beautiful day, with the sun high in the sky, very few clouds, and the temperature holding steady in the low 80s. Everything felt better, looked better, tasted better. It was like she had donned orgasm-colored glasses.

She finished her sandwich and headed back upstairs. Four more rooms and she'd be done. Well, with the first two floors at least. The third floor needed a little touch up, but the wallpaper extravaganza hadn't extended up there, so it wasn't nearly as hideous. Besides, she still needed to figure out how she was going to utilize the space—and she needed to get that darn red door open. No telling what treasures Uncle Archie had tucked away up there.

Ben sent her a brief text that he was going into court and would be unavailable for the afternoon. He followed it up with several hearts and kissing emojis. She grinned and sent him back a series of eggplant and fireworks emojis.

Several laughing emojis later, she turned her music back on, choosing a nineties station this time, and continued her work.

***

She shook the paint can, then popped her flathead screwdriver into the groove to open it. *This should do it. Last room, last can.*

Turning the lid over, she stared in disbelief at the bright blue paint. It was definitely not Sunny Veranda. She flipped the lid back over. Sure enough, the label said Blue Bonnet. The hardware store had given her someone else's paint.

She'd chosen to paint each of the bedrooms a different pastel shade, a tribute to the colorful row houses in Charleston. They had lived there briefly when she was little, and she'd loved the multi-colored homes.

Muttering under her breath, she put the lid back in place and rapped it with the hammer until it was sealed. The floor guys were coming in two days, and she needed to finish this room. The inconvenience poked a tiny hole in the sunny cloud of bliss following her around.

Slipping on her nearest pair of flip-flops, she clomped down the stairs and out the front door.

She set the can of paint on the rear floorboard of her car and tossed her phone in the passenger seat as she slid in. Punching the gas in irritation, she sped down the rutted path, hoping to get back quickly so she could finish the bedroom before Ben got back.

THUNK!

No, no, no.

Her car shuddered to a stop and echoed her groan. Leaning her forehead against the steering wheel, she tried counting, and when that didn't work, she tried cussing. Her cloud of bliss was shrinking quickly.

Her phone pealed. She grabbed it and swiped the screen without even looking. "Hello?"

"Whoa, darlin' don't go bitin' my head off right off the bat."

At the sound of her ex's voice, a few more choice epitaphs slipped free.

"Let's save the dirty talk for the reunion, baby."

"It's not a good time, Larry."

"Seems like it's not been a good time for a while since you've been dodging my calls."

She pushed the door open and got out to see how bad it was. Cloud of bliss, nowhere to be seen. "I'm busy, Larry. And we're divorced, so we really don't have a reason to talk."

"Well, that seems a bit hasty."

This from the man who shacked up with another woman within a week of Riley's miscarriage. "Not a good time, Larry." She didn't have the energy or desire to fight the man and deal with her car, which was currently stuck in an especially deep rut with a fist-sized dent in the rear wheel well. "Lisa's gotten herself into a bit of trouble."

"You still driving that old Honda?"

Did the man live in some parallel universe where two months after their divorce he thinks she could afford a new car? She had to get a surprise inheritance to afford new underwear. "There's nothing wrong with my car. Save the dented wheel well and hopefully not a broken axle."

"I can take care of that for you, baby. No problem."

There were too many issues with that statement to count. "I can handle it on my own. Talk to you later, Larry." Or not.

Riley ended the call and rubbed at her temples. She wouldn't be able to reach Ben for a couple hours and she wanted to get the painting done today. So she opened a ride share app, but it spun and spun, kind of like her tires. She was too far outside a small town. Did they even have Uber drivers in Eastport Beach? Why hadn't she made an effort to meet more people in town?

Unsure whether Chesnee would be in court with Ben, she shot him a quick text to see if he was free. He replied almost immediately, saying he was happy to help.

She grabbed the paint and her purse out of the backseat and plodded down the remainder of the driveway. While she waited, she called a gravel company and ordered a load. It wouldn't be delivered until next week, so she had time to get a tow truck to haul her car somewhere to get it fixed.

Chesnee pulled up in a sporty two-seater, the top down, his golden blond hair blowing in the wind like he was in an ad for California.

"Thank you so much!" She climbed in the car and positioned the paint can between her feet. "You are my hero."

He grinned and put the car in gear. "You're almost in as good a mood as the boss. If I didn't know better..." He glanced at her, eyebrows raised.

She knew the two were close, but had no idea if Ben talked to his assistant about his sex life. However, it was nice to know she had put a smile on his face.

"I was in a terrific mood until my car met with an untimely demise. I'm almost finished with the painting. But they gave me the wrong paint." She tapped the can wedged between her feet.

"Painting, huh?" He winked, but didn't press any further.

This was the first time she'd spent time alone with the younger man. He was an affable guy, fit, Ken-doll good looks. And he was confident to the point of being cocky. She had a feeling that if Ben wasn't interested in her, Chesnee would have already asked her out. "You seeing anyone?"

"Why? Second-guessing your decision to date the old man?"

"Nope, really happy with that decision. Just making small talk." She tightened her ponytail, as the wind was threatening to rip it out of the tie. "What about the woman I met downtown? Rose?"

"Who?"

She snickered, but the wind covered it up. "The one with the giant back tattoo?"

"Oh, yeah." He grinned sheepishly. "We just hung out that night. Nothing serious."

"Anything serious with anyone else? Gina, maybe?"

He rolled his eyes. "Don't let Ben give you the wrong idea. I've known Gina forever. She's like my sister."

Your sister you want to kiss, maybe. "She seems great. I met her at the diner last week when I stopped in for lunch."

"She's the best. But we're just friends." He turned into the parking lot of the home improvement store. "I've got to run to the post office for Ben, can I come back and get you in a few minutes?"

"Sure, I'll only be as long as they take to change out this paint."

"Okay, but don't tell Ben I left you unattended in a store crawling with horny men."

She laughed. "I think I can manage fine, horny men and all."

"I'm just telling you what he would say. He's an old fogey."

"Do people even use that word anymore?"

He shrugged. "Who knows? But my grandma says it all the time."

"Aww, it's sweet that you're close to your grandma." Maybe he wasn't as shallow as she pegged him to be.

"My grandma is the best. I'll invite you next time she makes Sunday dinner. You'll think you've died and gone to heaven. But don't tell her you and Ben are 'knocking knees' or she'll kick you out on your duff."

Riley choked. She wasn't sure which was more shocking, that he knew she and Ben had slept together, or that he talked like an eighty-year-old woman.

She stumbled out of the car, unsure how to respond to Chesnee outing her. She feared he'd be able to read the orgasms all over her face.

The parking lot was completely full, with cars and trucks lined up outside, loading wood and cases of bottled water. She fought her way through the crowd and found the customer service desk. Several people fielded phone calls, while others were ringing up customers, and one man appeared to be guarding a stack of generators.

When an older woman finally acknowledged her presence, she plunked her paint up on the counter. "They gave me the wrong color. I ordered yellow. This is blue." She dug in her purse for the receipt.

"Take it up with the paint department, if there's anyone working. I think they pulled Kenny to help load plywood." She waved to the next customer to step forward.

Carrying the Blue Bonnet to the paint counter, Riley kept her eyes peeled for a name tag that read "Kenny." If she remembered correctly, he was the one who mixed her original order, so hopefully she could get this resolved quickly.

Customers rushed by, their carts loaded with bags of sand and large plastic totes. One guy had piled every box of plastic sheeting on the shelf into his cart. If she didn't know better, she'd think a snowstorm was coming. But no one was fighting over shovels or bobsleds.

Finally, a balding man in a gray vest came behind the paint counter and plopped down on a five-gallon bucket. It wasn't Kenny, but she wasn't going to be picky at this point.

"I—"

He held up his hand. "Give me a minute to catch my breath. You'd think it was the apocalypse the way people are acting." He wiped his brow with a torn bandana. "Sure, we don't get too many hurricanes, but these folks have just lost their minds."

Hurricanes?

"Now, what can I do for you?" He rose from his temporary seat and put his hands in his pockets.

She pushed the can forward, still processing. "Blue Bonnet. I need Sunny Veranda."

"Ma'am? I'm not following."

Riley shook her head to clear it. "Did you say hurricane?"

"Sure did. Connie's heading this way, looking to be quite a storm. Aren't you here for supplies?"

She was guessing a snow shovel and ice melt weren't going to help this situation. She glanced at the time. Ben would be getting out of court soon; he would know what to do. "I'm all good with hurricane supplies." It wasn't nice to lie to a stranger, but somehow it felt more wrong to start wailing and freak out. "They gave me the wrong paint. Can you please swap this out for a gallon of sunny veranda?" She pushed the paint can and receipt toward him.

He screwed up his face like he'd seen straight through her lies, but took the can and set it under the counter, then started mixing up a new batch. She watched carefully as the paint turned yellow, not blue, and tried to ignore the panic rising in her chest.

Correct color in hand, she headed back outside to see Chesnee casually leaning against his convertible, chatting up a couple young women who didn't look old enough to drink. Seeing her, he said goodbye to the girls and opened the passenger door for her. She gave him the side eye, certain he was showing off for his newest fans.

"Did you know there's a hurricane coming?" She set the new can of paint between her feet and reached for her seatbelt as he rounded the car.

He hopped over the door and slid behind the wheel like some action star in a movie. "Yeah, think I heard something about that. Is that why this place is swarming with people at four o'clock on a weekday?"

"I guess. I've never been through a hurricane. Do I need to be worried? Should I leave?"

"Nah." He waved his hand through the air like he was swatting a gnat. "It's just a little wind and rain. People always overreact." He slid his sunglasses on as he pulled out of the parking lot.

Somehow, she didn't feel reassured. "What time will Ben be out of court?"

He glanced at his watch. "Anytime now. Want me to take you back to the office or home?"

Murray's Market was a few doors down from Ben's office, and it sounded like she might need to get some groceries. "The office will be fine. Ben can take me home later."

"Sure thing."

A few minutes later, they were cruising down Main Street.

Businesses along the road were boarding up windows and bringing in outdoor decorations and furniture. An older woman was pulling a wagon that appeared to be full of liquor bottles.

"Are you sure there's nothing to be worried about?" Riley tensed as Chesnee slammed on the brakes to keep from hitting a pack of old men crossing the street, each of them carrying a twenty-four-pack of beer.

"Nah, they're getting ready for the hurricane party."

"There's a party?"

"Add a little booze and there's always a party."

Well, at least she had a pantry full of wine.

They pulled into the parking lot behind the old house that had been convert-ed into Ben's office.

"Thanks for the ride, Chesnee. I'm going to run down to Murrays for a couple things. Will you let Ben know I'll be back soon?"

"Sure, I'll leave him a note. I need to head up to Wilmington to close up my grandma's house. She can't manage the hurricane shutters on her own. I'll probably stick with her. It's no fun to have a hurricane party by yourself."

Riley followed him inside and left the can of paint on the kitchen counter.

He told her he'd leave the back door unlocked for her as she headed down the street.

Murrays looked like it had been ransacked by vandals. The shelves were practically bare, displays of vegetables and fruit had been picked over, and the beer cooler was completely empty. She managed to find a loaf of nine-grain bread, but she wasn't that desperate. As she strolled down the paper goods aisle, she found an abandoned pack of hot dog buns. She grabbed it, then headed for the deli. There were no hot dogs left, but she did find a single pack of yellow cheese and a pound of bacon. Gram's favorite quick meal was open-faced bacon and cheese sandwiches. She'd cook the bacon up tonight in case the power went out. They could broil the sandwiches on the grill if necessary.

She grabbed a bag of off-brand chips, because beggars can't be choosers—and she was also happy to find a box of chocolate snack cakes wedged between the feminine hygiene products and the enemas.

The youngest Murray was manning the register. He looked like he'd been through battle. Well, they'd have nothing left to ring up soon, so maybe he could go home.

She took her single bag of groceries and headed back to Ben's office. Hope-fully, the storm would pass quickly, because they would run out of food faster than Chesnee got to second base.

Ben's car was in the parking area when she got back. She ran up the short flight of steps to the back porch, but before she reached the door, it flew open, and he met her on the deck. He pulled her into a tight embrace, kissing the top of her head.

"Man, it was hard to leave you this morning."

She smiled against his chest, loving the smell of him, like leather and saltwater. "Well, you certainly left me happy."

He pushed back, a grin on his face, and crushed his mouth to hers. She was having flashbacks to the multiple orgasms, but the bag in her hand grounded her to the present emergency. She pulled away, her breath coming in quick gasps.

"Apparently, there's a hurricane coming?"

"Oh yeah, I forgot to mention it. I wondered if you knew." He wrapped his arm around her shoulder and led her inside to the small kitchen.

"No, I didn't know. Do I need to sign up for some hurricane newsletter or something, so I'm not left in the dark?"

He laughed. "Maybe check the Weather Channel now and then."

"Archie didn't have a TV, so I don't have a TV." No way Larry was letting his big screen get away.

"There's a TV in his bedroom, but you could also download the app."

She waved her crappy phone at him. "Oldest smartphone on the planet. Haven't been able to download an app in two years." She replayed what he had said in her head. "Archie's bedroom? I didn't see a TV in any of the bedrooms."

Ben opened the fridge and pulled out a sports drink. He downed half the bottle in one swig. "His bedroom at the back of the house."

She mentally walked the first floor of the house. Parlor, kitchen, study, dining room, half bath, coat closet with creepy, spider-filled secret passage. No bedroom. "There's no bedroom on the ground floor."

"It's behind the butler's pantry." There was a hint of a smile on his face, which he failed to hide behind the bottle.

"Are you messing with me again? Is this like the alligator thing?"

He set the bottle on the counter and grabbed her by the hips, holding her close. "I'm not messing with you, although I intend to later." He bent down to kiss her, but she held up a hand to block him.

"Seriously, I've been in that pantry a hundred times. And not always to get wine." She narrowed her eyes at him, daring him to say something he'd regret.

"Come on, I'll show you." He grabbed her hand and the paint off the counter in one swoop. The man was damn charming.

Chapter Thirty-Four

Riley peppered him with questions the entire ride to Heron House. Some were about the hurricane, others about the house, most were about how demented her late uncle was. Ben just smiled and kept his eyes on the road.

All day he'd been floating on a cloud, and nothing, not even a Cat 3 storm, would rain on his happy parade. In court, the judge had actually asked him if he was ill. Apparently smiling too much was a sign of sickness.

They pulled down the driveway to the house and as soon as they turned the first curve, found Riley's car sitting, well, more accurately, hunched, in a rut. "What happened to your car? And did you walk to my office?"

She filled him in on her paint and subsequent car fiasco, and Chesnee's helpfulness. He made a mental note to thank him with a six-pack later.

"Well, we probably won't be able to get anyone out here before the storm. You'll have to be at my mercy until we get it fixed." For the first time he could remember, he was looking forward to being stuck indoors during a week-long weather event. "By the way, I was hoping I could stay with you. A boat isn't the safest place to be during a hurricane." Normally, he'd just hunker down at the office, but spending the time with Riley held infinitely more appeal than reading court briefs.

She let out a whoosh of air. "Thank God, because I was starting to freak out about being alone in that big house with no electricity."

"Perfect then. I'm sure we'll find some way to occupy the time." He slid his hand across her thigh and squeezed.

He rounded the fountain and parked the car at the foot of the steps. He wanted to take her inside and have an encore of this morning, but first, he'd promised to let her in on Archie's little secret.

She grabbed the paint and raced up the steps before he could come around and open her door.

"Slow down, speed demon."

Unlocking the door, she smirked at him over her shoulder. "Think you can catch me?"

Apparently, she wasn't too intent on solving the mystery of Archie's bedroom, because she raced up the stairs, the can of paint banging against her leg. He wasn't happy about the bruise it would likely leave on her smooth skin. But he was more than happy to chase her.

***

Riley was as eager as he was to continue their earlier mattress aerobics. He found her in her room, naked on her bed, not trying in the least to get away from him.

After an hour rolling around in the sheets, he was convinced this morning hadn't been a fluke. They really were that damn good together. Yup, this was going to be the best hurricane ever.

She sighed and rolled to rest her head on his bare chest. Her foot slid up and down his leg and if he wasn't so out of practice, he'd probably have gotten back on top of her and gone for a third time. But it'd been years since he'd participated in this form of activity, and he felt like his muscles had turned to mush.

"I don't have a lot of experiences to draw from, but I think we do that really, really well. Like spectacularly. Like we could enter the sex Olympics and medal the first time out."

Damn, he loved her rambling.

And the way her hair curled around her face when she got sweaty.

And making her get sweaty.

"Gold for sure."

A lazy smile graced her face, and he wanted to take a picture of the moment. Sheer contentment.

"As soon as my legs re-solidify, you're going to show me where the secret bedroom is."

So, she hadn't forgotten, she just had similar priorities. Orgasms, then secret doors. "Happy to finish the tour that got interrupted a few weeks ago."

"Can I ask you something?"

"Anything."

"And you'll answer me seriously?" She pushed up on one elbow, attempting to screw a "serious" look on her face. He grinned. "To the best of my ability."

"Do you slowly seduce all of your client's nieces to get them into bed?"

"You're the first. But next time, I don't think I'll drag it out so long."

Her face remained neutral, but there was a sparkle in her eyes. "You could have taken me on the dock."

His exhausted member sprung to life. Pulling her on top of him, he pressed her hot body against his erection. "Maybe I still will."

***

There was only so much sex a thirty-five-year-old man could take in one day, so they got dressed and found something for dinner. One look in the cupboards made Ben realize how unprepared they were for the storm.

"First thing tomorrow, we need to get supplies. Food, a fresh propane tank for the grill, maybe some plywood for the windows. The house is on a hill, so I don't expect any flooding, but the wind could be an issue."

Riley leaned against the counter, sipping a glass of wine, wearing only his button-up shirt. "Murrays was trashed. I managed to get enough for possibly two meals, but I left the bag at your office."

"We may have to go further inland, where people aren't acting irrational yet." He set her wineglass on the counter and took her hands. "You ready?"

She sighed. "I want to be, but really, Ben, five orgasms in one day is my limit."

God, she made him laugh. "I meant to see Archie's bedroom."

A blush crept up her neck and graced her cheeks. "Oh, yeah."

He led her into the pantry and showed her the lever hidden under the small appliance shelf. The entire wall swung open, and she gasped. "I had no idea!"

"That's the point. Archie wanted to have privacy from his guests, so he made it appear to only have an outside entrance. But it's way more convenient to get a midnight snack using this door." He winked at her and led the way into what he thought of as Archie's inner sanctum.

The room was large—a true master suite that had been added on to the house in the eighties. It had a walk-in closet, a full bathroom, and a small studio space with a view of the water. Both nightstands were piled high with books, a garish red and purple striped jacket hung on a full-length mirror, and a half-finished painting of an alligator sat on the easel in the alcove. He unsuccessfully suppressed a laugh. He'd forgotten about the visitor last year that inspired the piece. Maybe he'd save that story for another time.

Riley took in the room, her face in awe, her fingers trailing along bookcases and idly rubbing the head of the four-foot-high heron statue beside the TV armoire.

It made sense for her to eventually move into the space, but right now it was so full of Archibald Kirkwood it was hard to imagine anyone else living here.

She stepped into the bathroom, and he could hear her gasp from where he stood. She ran out, her eyes wild. "That tub!"

Well, maybe if he strained, he could imagine her in that tub. He might even be able to picture himself in it with her. "Archie spared no expense on this addition. It's probably a little outdated now, but it was top-of-the-line when he built it."

"It's so retro, it might even be back in style, but I don't care. I could live in that tub!" She turned back toward the bathroom, but that's when she spotted the walk-in closet. "Whoa, somebody liked clothes."

He laughed. "Oh yeah, Archie was a clotheshorse. Always flying up to New York and buying hideous pieces from fashion icons." The man had his own style, that was for sure. Ben was more of an off-the-rack suit guy, and only when he had to appear in court. He was happiest in khakis and a light sweater. A solid-colored sweater, preferably.

She leaned out of the closet, her eyes sparkling. "If I move into this room, I'm going to need to buy more clothes."

"As far as I'm concerned, you should only wear my shirts." He wagged his eyebrows at her. "Or nothing at all."

The pink returned to her cheeks, and she shyly ducked back into the closet. "What am I going to do with all these clothes? I'm not even sure the homeless would want them."

"Some of them are probably worth a pretty penny. You should check out one of those resale apps."

"I'll add that to my to-do list, right after 'get new phone.'"

He kept forgetting she was living on a tight budget since the divorce. Well, he could do something about her phone, at least. As soon as the storm passed, he was buying her a new one.

They spent the evening sorting through Archie's clothes, Riley occasionally modeling something utterly ridiculous and Ben feeling like he'd won the lottery—getting to spend time with this vivacious woman.

Chapter Thirty-Five

Ben's car was loaded with supplies and the hardware store would be delivering the plywood later that day. He eased the car down the driveway, and Riley cursed herself for not ordering the gravel sooner.

They turned the corner, and the fountain came into view, along with her car and a big ass white truck. Oh, *hell no.*

She was out of the car before Ben put it in park, stomping across the driveway to where her ex-husband was wiping his hands on a towel next to Lisa, who sported a new tire and a less obvious dent. "What the hell are you doing here?"

"Good to see you too, baby." Larry stepped forward, his hands outstretched.

Riley sidestepped him and put her hands up. "Don't 'baby' me." She sensed Ben behind her, quiet and strong, and it gave her confidence. "How did you even know where I was?"

Larry grinned, his chipped tooth in the front taking center stage. She felt zero nostalgia for the goofy smile. "Nate down at the post office, gave me your forwarding address."

She was pretty sure that was a federal offense. She'd have to ask her legal counsel later, after they got rid of the vermin and sealed the house up for the storm. "You need to leave, Larry."

"But your birthday is tomorrow. I can't leave yet." He tried to slide his hands around her waist, but she jumped out of his reach, catching the shocked look on Ben's face as she stepped back.

"Tomorrow's your birthday?"

Probably the kind of thing most people would tell the person they just got naked on the stairs with.

She blew out a sigh. "Yeah. I wasn't going to make a big deal out of it."

"Not make a big deal? My girl's turning thirty! Of course, we're making a big deal."

"Larry, I haven't been your girl since you gave Brittani my engagement ring."

"You weren't using it, on account of your fingers swelling."

She caught a questioning look from Ben, but she would deal with him later. She tried another tactic. "In case you haven't heard, there's a hurricane coming. You need to go back to Ashford."

"Can you believe she won't give the ring back? I mean, it's been in my family forever." The weather situation failed to penetrate his thick skull. "That's when I knew I'd made a stupid, momentary lapse in judgment, baby."

Momentary? He'd been living with Brittani for over a year. "Stop calling me that. I'm not your baby." Her scream was lost as a gust of wind blew across the lawn.

Ben started unloading the car. "We're running out of time. We need to start prepping." Thankfully, he left out the reason they were behind in their storm preparations (the stair sex).

"Who's the suit?" Larry jerked his thumb at Ben, who was wearing chino shorts and a polo shirt.

They hadn't had the "talk," or used labels for the relationship yet, but part of Riley wanted to tell her ex this was the man who proved to her she could have the big "O" during sex. Five in one day, no less.

Ben set down the bags he was carrying and held out his hand. The juxtaposition between the two men was striking. Riley's ex stood at 6'4" and most of the muscle of his youth had morphed into flab. His hairline started receding in high school, and he was dressed in ten-year-old basketball shorts and a Big Larry's t-shirt.

Kelsey had been so right about her settling. She'd have to tell her next time they talked.

She watched as the two men shook hands, ready to jump between them if Larry got out of line.

"I'm Ben Ward. Riley's boyfriend." He didn't hesitate or equivocate; he just stated the fact loud and proud.

He had to be loud, because the wind was really picking up.

"If you'll excuse us, we have to get the house ready for the storm." He picked the bags back up and headed for the porch.

Larry turned to her, his eyes wide. "You're living with this guy? After we just broke up?"

She rolled her eyes. "We broke up a year and a half ago after you got a girlfriend. And we aren't living together, he's just staying here during the storm." She grabbed the rest of the bags from the car. "Bye, Larry."

He turned to stare at the house and the surrounding land. "I can't believe you didn't tell me you had a rich uncle."

Riley was seconds away from launching herself at him and pummeling his sagging chest. Then she heard tires crunching slowly down the deathtrap that was her driveway. She looked at her car, good as a twenty-year-old car could be. "Thanks for fixing the car. We've got windows to board up, and that's our plywood delivery."

Only it wasn't a truck from the hardware store that came around the bend. It was an SUV that looked a lot like Kelsey's.

The car crunched to a stop and her sister jumped out, their mother exiting the passenger door just as quickly. "What the hell is he doing here?" Kelsey pointed her finger at Larry, vitriol spewing from her mouth.

"Larry, you promised me you weren't coming." Margaret Kirkwood approached the group, limping slightly, likely from too many hours in the car.

"You've been talking to him?" Riley dropped her bags and spun on her mother.

She twisted the Marine Corps pendant she always wore. "He was missing you. But I told him he needed to work his way up to it."

Riley threw her hands up in the air. "Mom! I can't believe you. He cheated on me. We're divorced. I'm dating Ben." She gestured at the porch where her new boyfriend stood shell-shocked. Hopefully, he'd still be her boyfriend after the dust cleared.

"It's very nice to meet you, Ben." Her mother smiled up at him, then turned back to her ex-son-in-law. "Now, Larry. I explained that you needed to woo her."

"I fixed her car."

"And that's very nice, but you can't show up un— "

"Argghh!" Riley turned Larry's lumbering bulk toward his truck. "Larry, go away." Then she turned to her family. "You guys should head back. There's a hurricane coming, and the house is still a construction zone."

Kelsey's face crumbled. "But it's your birthday." She threw her arms out and made jazz hands. "Surprise."

Suddenly, a distinct newborn wail rose over the wind. Her sister hustled toward the car and fussed with the baby. She got him out of his car seat and headed back to the group. "I've got to change and feed him. Riley, will you get Noel out of the car?"

"No one is listening to me! You can't stay here. It's not safe for a three-year-old." And she wanted to have hurricane sex with her new boyfriend.

Kelsey stopped at the foot of the steps and turned around. "Don't worry, sis. It looks like a big house. You won't even know we're here." She climbed the steps and pulled Ben into a hug. "It's very nice to meet you, Ben. I've heard really O-mazing things about you."

Riley buried her face in her hands just as the truck from the hardware store pulled down the drive, and the first big plops of rain bounced off the back of her neck.

Chapter Thirty-Six

He wanted to hate the guy; he really did. But the truth was, without Larry's help, Ben would still be outside in the rain, hanging plywood over the windows.

They talked about cars and football, and while Ben was no expert on either subject, he held his own. It sounded like Riley's ex was something of a football star in high school. At least in his mind. The man was enormous, so tall he didn't need the ladder until they got to the second-floor windows.

He'd driven across the state to fix Riley's car and now, here, he was wielding a hammer in driving rain.

So, while Ben couldn't hate Larry, if he found out he had ever raised a hand to Riley, he didn't care how big he was or what his tackle stats were.

Ben stepped out of Riley's shower, reaching for the towel, his eyes closed against the water dripping from his hair. His hand hit something soft, but not terry cloth.

"I'm so sorry about everyone showing up. I swear I had no idea." Riley thrust the towel into his hands and he wiped the water from his face.

"You don't have to apologize to me. It's your family." He dried himself off quickly, then wrapped the towel around his waist, distinctly aware of the fact he was naked while she was fully clothed. And he wasn't about to get her naked again until they were alone.

"He's not my family anymore." She tilted her head back, as if she was studying the ceiling, which he noticed she had painted in her burst of energy. "I cannot believe he came all the way out here to fix my car."

Ben suspected that wasn't Larry's only motivation for the trip, but he kept his mouth shut for the time being. "He was a big help getting the house boarded up."

She sighed. "Think he still has time to get out of here before it gets bad?"

"He seemed pretty intent on being here for your birthday."

She cringed. "Sorry about that."

He knelt in front of the toilet where she sat. "Why didn't you tell me?"

"I was trying to ignore it." She balanced her hands on his bare shoulders, sending a signal to his crotch that he couldn't act on.

Trying to keep things rated G, considering their unexpected guests, he gripped the sides of the toilet seat instead of her hips, like he wanted to. "You don't like birthdays?"

Her eyes slid to the right, and she studied the shower curtain, like she was trying to decipher hieroglyphics.

"Hey." He raised his hand to smooth the hair back from her face, and angle it so she would meet his eyes. "Talk to me."

"I didn't think I'd be starting over at thirty. Having accomplished exactly nothing."

He'd been wondering how old she was ever since Chesnee asked.

"Nothing? Look at this place." He gestured at the freshly painted walls. "You've transformed this house in a matter of weeks. That's not nothing."

"It's just some paint."

"Riley, you've taken a rundown old house and made it beautiful again. And you've accomplished something else."

Her gaze raised to him, questioning.

"You've made me fall in love with you. I hope that's a new beginning you can be excited about."

Eyes widening, she raised a hand to cover a gasp.

She looked almost as shocked as he felt over the revelation. This was not how he pictured telling her he loved her. "Don't feel any pressure to reciprocate. This is not the ideal time. There's a literal hurricane beating down the door, but I thought you should know."

Grabbing his neck, she yanked him closer, meeting his lips with fervor. Next thing he knew, he was on the bathroom floor, a half-naked Riley on top of him and his towel thrown over the shower rod. He was trying to remember why he couldn't get her all the way naked when someone pounded on the door.

"Riley? You in there?" Larry's booming voice filled the small room.

Riley froze, her mouth open against Ben's chest.

His penis suddenly remembered why he couldn't get her naked.

"Your mom needs to know where the mixer is. She's baking your cake tonight in case the power goes out."

"I'll be down in a minute, Larry." She groaned, but not the oh-my-God-I'm-getting-ready-to-come kind.

"Is Bart in there with you?"

The two men had spent nearly two hours working as a team to get ready for the storm and he thought his name was Bart? Ben managed to muster up a little hate for the man.

"Goodbye, Larry."

Heavy footsteps descended the stairs. Riley reached for her shirt. Ben prayed for the storm to pass quickly.

***

Downstairs, Riley's mom and sister had cleared off the dining room table and pulled the drop cloths off the furniture in the parlor. Her niece was happily flipping the pages of a book under an antique floor lamp and the baby was sleeping peacefully in a portable bassinet. He found the three women in the kitchen, cabinet doors open, and pans pulled onto the floor.

Luckily, Larry was nowhere to be seen.

Outside, the storm raged, but the boarded-up windows effectively muffled the sounds.

"I hear we're baking a cake."

"Not if we can't find baking soda." Margaret Kirkwood looked like June Cleaver in her dress and frilly apron. Had she packed that? He didn't remember Archie owning a pink checked apron. "You think you can run out and get some?"

He grinned. "Sorry, ma'am, but the stores are closed until the storm passes. Did you check the refrigerator?"

Riley's sister stuck her head inside the fridge and cheered in victory. "Found it!" A low wail started from the parlor. "Riley, do you mind getting Liam? He's probably just wet." Kelsey plopped the box of baking soda on the counter in front of her mother and started digging through drawers. "Where's the measuring spoons?"

Riley glanced at the butler's pantry, sighed, and then headed down the hall, calling back over her shoulder. "Drawer beside the sink."

Ben grabbed the bottle opener and ducked inside the pantry. Selecting a bottle of Bordeaux, he popped it open, then poured four glasses. Back in the kitchen, he slid one in front of each of the women, then took the other two to the parlor.

Riley was re-buttoning the bodysuit Liam was wearing. Colorful dinosaurs somersaulted and cartwheeled across the outfit. The baby stared up at his aunt, his pudgy lips blowing tiny bubbles. She leaned down and kissed his belly, making the little guy squirm.

"You look good with a baby."

She startled, then looked up with a cautious smile. *Way to freak her out, Ward.*

He held out the glass to her.

"Thanks." She downed half the glass in one sip, then set it aside.

Noel looked up from her book. "Wiwee, can I have a waweepop?"

"Sweetie, if I had a lollipop, I'd give it to you in a heartbeat, but I'm fresh out." She picked up the baby and sat down beside her niece on the couch. "How about we have some cake after dinner?"

"Okay." The little girl flipped the page of her book, then stopped and looked up again. "What's for dinner?"

Riley's gaze flew up to meet his, panic evident in her eyes. "Ha ha, great question, sweetie."

"Your mom has the oven occupied and it's raining too hard to grill, so how about omelets?" He had no idea if three-year-olds ate omelets, but when they bought groceries that morning, they'd been lucky to find a pack of eighteen eggs with only four broken ones. He'd cleared out his galley on the boat, so they had veggies and cheese.

Noel screwed her little face up. "What's an omewet?"

"It's eggs and cheese, yum. I'll make you some toast with jelly, too." Riley smoothed the little girl's hair and smiled at her.

"Swawberry?"

"Of course."

The sight of Riley with the two little kids was almost more than he could take. He sat beside her on the couch and kissed her cheek.

Noel's eyes grew to the size of quarters. "Mommies and daddies kiss. Are you Wiwee's daddy?"

A beautiful blush hit Riley's cheeks. "Not exactly, honey. Ben is my special friend."

"Do you wove him?"

Yeah, Wiwee, do you wove him? Ben sat back, enjoying the way the question made her squirm.

"I need to check on the cake." Riley jumped up from the couch, plopped the baby in Ben's arms, and hightailed it into the kitchen.

Noel shifted her gaze to him.

"Yes, Noel. I love Riley."

The side of her mouth quirked up, and she tucked a strand of brown hair behind her ear before returning to her book. "Good."

Chapter Thirty-Seven

Riley slid into the kitchen and grabbed the wineglass out of her sister's hand.

"Hey! Get your own."

"Mine is back in the living room." *With Ben and that nosy little girl.*

Kelsey narrowed her eyes, but simply commandeered her mother's glass. "Who's watching my kids? It better not be Larry."

"Ben's got them. They're fine." She assumed. "Where is Larry, anyway?"

"Hopefully washed out to sea."

Their mom pointed a rubber scraper at her oldest daughter. "Be nice. I think he went upstairs to check the third floor."

"Check it for what?" She swung towards Riley. "Ooh, are there ghosts?"

"There aren't any ghosts." She wasn't telling her about the secret passageways either, or Kelsey would drag her down there with the spiders, no doubt. "He won't find much up there, just a decade's worth of dust."

"Riley, if you'll leave out some cleaning supplies, I can clean up there tomorrow." Margaret slid two round cake pans full of batter into the oven.

"Mom, you don't have to clean while you're here. I'll get to the third floor eventually."

Kelsey drained the rest of their mom's wine and wiggled her empty glass. "What's up there, anyway? More bedrooms?"

Riley tilted the wine bottle up, but there were only drops left. "I think they were studios. I haven't decided what to do with the space yet. And there's this one room that's locked." She ducked into the pantry and grabbed another bottle with a label to match the first.

"Ooh, a mystery! Maybe we can jimmy the lock!"

"You are getting way too excited about everything. Maybe we shouldn't open another bottle of wine." Not that Riley could if she tried. She had yet to master the fancy bottle opener.

Luckily, Ben breezed into the kitchen at that exact moment, Liam cradled in his arms and Noel clinging to his leg. "Did someone say wine?" He plucked the bottle and opener out of her hands, and like the legit magician he was, opened the bottle while still holding a baby and a toddler.

Kelsey's jaw was hanging open and Riley imagined hers was a carbon copy. "Damn, Riley, who is this guy? He tamed the beasts and opened the wine. You have to marry him."

Closing her eyes, Riley prayed for the storm to suck her out of this reality. Okay, so it wasn't a tornado, and this wasn't Oz, but a girl could dream.

"She's already married." Larry chose that moment to come out of hiding.

Riley prayed harder.

"You're divorced, stupid." Kelsey stuck her tongue out at her ex-brother-in-law.

"Kelsey." Their mother's tone left no doubt she wouldn't tolerate the childish behavior.

Ben ducked his head in the refrigerator, taking an unnecessarily long time to pull out a carton of eggs and some cheese. She wished she could hide in there with him.

Kelsey filled both their glasses and grabbed Riley by the arm, yanking her out of the kitchen. Conspiratorially, she whispered, "Let's go mess with that lock while they're distracted."

"We can't leave Ben in there with Larry! And your kids, for that matter."

"Pshaw! Mom will handle them." She vaulted up the stairs, then turned back, gesturing at Riley, wine sloshing from her glass. "Hurry, before they notice we're gone."

Riley rolled her eyes. Even someone as dense as her ex-husband would have noticed they were gone by now. But she was a little excited to get her sister alone to talk about what Ben had told her in the bathroom. When she caught up with her on the third floor, Kelsey was standing in front of the red door, head tilted to the side, sizing up the situation.

"It's locked."

"Duh. That's why we're going to have to get creative. Got a crowbar?"

"Ben told me he loved me."

Kelsey whirled around and grabbed Riley by the shoulders. "He what? When?"

"Maybe you could keep it down, so the entire house won't hear you."

She waved her hand through the air. "We're two stories away. He actually said he loved you?"

Riley replayed the scene in her mind. "Well, he said he had fallen in love with me. Is that the same thing?"

"Did you say it back?"

"I wasn't sure what to say, so I attacked him."

Kelsey bobbed her head, as if that made perfect sense. "He seems pretty great, Riley. And he's good with my kids."

She sighed. "Yeah, I'm a little worried that could be an issue."

"How is that an issue?"

"I don't think I want to have children."

Pigs must have been picked up by Connie's winds and were flying through the air, because Kelsey was speechless.

Riley turned and slid down the red door to the floor, burying her head in her hands. It was the first time she'd said it out loud.

She felt her sister sit beside her, her presence comforting as they sat in silence for a long time.

Finally, Kelsey found her words. "Riley, you've always wanted to have a baby. Is this because you're turning thirty? I'm thirty-five and I just had Liam. You've got plenty of time."

"I can't lose another baby, Kels. It nearly killed me the first time."

"Oh." She slid her arm around Riley's shoulders. "There's no reason to think that will happen again, honey. Plenty of women who have miscarriages go on to have normal, healthy pregnancies."

"I'm not willing to take that risk."

"What if Ben wants kids?" "Then it's not meant to be."

The two of them sat in silence until they heard heavy footsteps on the stairs, and then Larry barreled through the doorway. "I don't trust that guy as far as I can throw him. And that's about forty yards. He's too goody-two-shoes, down there, sweet talking your mama and coddling those rugrats. He's up to no good."

The sisters looked at one another, rolled their eyes, and helped each other to their feet.

"I'll go get the rugrats." Kelsey passed Larry with a glare and headed down the stairs.

"Larry, I'm not really interested in your opinion on who I choose to date."

"Riley, baby." He took two giant steps and stood in front of her. "You can't *date* him. What about us?"

How many times did they have to go over this before he would get it through his thick skull? "Larry, maybe that fifth concussion left you with a little memory loss, but there is no us. Remember going to court a few weeks back?"

He grinned that goofy, chipped-tooth smile. "Baby, we can't let a little thing like a divorce come between us. We're supposed to be together." He slid his hands onto her hips. "We can try for another baby, baby."

Suddenly, it felt like the storm was raging between her ears and not merely outside. "No, Larry." She pushed his hands off her. "We cannot try again. I don't want you, and I don't want a baby." She turned to stomp away, and that's when the lights went out.

Chapter Thirty-Eight

Ben was sliding the last omelet onto a plate when the power went out. Margaret and Noel shrieked in unison, and he heard an "oomph" come from the hallway.

"Noel? Are you okay?" Kelsey's voice was nearing panic level as well, so Ben grabbed his phone and turned on the flashlight. He watched as she limped into the kitchen. "My kids?"

"Liam's sleeping and your mom has Noel. They're in the parlor. I'll take you."

He led her down the hall with his light. "Where's Riley?" He wanted to add, "and Larry," but he refrained.

"She's on the third floor with Larry."

Noel was huddled in her grandmother's arms, but jumped off the couch when she saw her mother. Liam was still sleeping peacefully in his bassinet despite all the screaming.

"I've got lanterns, hold on." He'd prepared a staging area of sorts in the study, so he grabbed two lanterns and a hand-held flashlight. If he'd known they were hosting guests, he would have bought more. Turning on the lights, he brought them back into the parlor. "Go ahead and eat before the food gets any colder. Sorry, Noel, but we can't toast the bread." He patted her on the head. "I'm going to take Riley and Larry a light."

Using the flashlight, he raced up both flights of stairs. Once on the third floor, he swept his light across the hall, passing it quickly over the bright-red door. The hallway was empty. "Riley?"

"In here." Her voice sounded muffled and wavered too much for his liking.

He reached the room where she had been stuck in the wall in time to see Riley wiping her eyes and Larry patting her on the back. Rage roared through his chest at the thought that this man might have hurt her. "Are you okay?" He rushed to her, and Larry wisely stepped back.

"I'm fine, we were just talking.""Yeah, we've got a lot of history, you know?" Her ex puffed out his chest and placed his hand on her shoulder.

She shook it off and glared at him. "I'm okay, Ben, really. I'm not hurt."

He flashed the light over her, trying to confirm there was no blood or bruises. Because if there was, he could think of a pretty effective way to dispose of a body with a hurricane raging outside. "Come on, I'll help you downstairs."

"What about me?" The big dope stood with his hands out, like he couldn't possibly figure out how to get down the stairs on his own. *What did she ever see in this guy?*

"Use the flashlight on your phone, Larry." Riley leaned into Ben's embrace as he led them down the dark hall to the stairs. "Sorry to worry you."

"Better get used to it, because I'll probably worry about you for the rest of our lives."

She froze, and he worried he'd crossed another line, but then she started moving again.

When they made it to the kitchen, Margaret and Kelsey had moved the lanterns in there and were washing their cold omelets down with a third bottle of wine. Apparently, someone else had figured out how to use the wine opener.

Kelsey raised her glass. "We may not have power, but we have enough booze to last the rest of our lives!"

"We should probably cut her off. She's breastfeeding." Riley snatched the glass out of her sister's hand.

"Hey!" She swayed a little in her effort to get her glass back. "I can have a glass of doctor, the wine said it's fine."

"A glass, Kelsey, not a crate." Riley drained her sister's wine before she could take it back.

Margaret picked up Noel from where she was sitting on the counter, running her fork through an omelet that had been hacked into a thousand pieces. "Come on, Noel, let's get ready for bed." She put her other arm around her older daughter and led her out of the room. "Liam will probably sleep through the night with all you've had to drink."

"Amen to that!" Kelsey leaned her head on her mother's shoulder, and they made their way to the parlor with one of the lanterns.

"The eggs are cold, but we probably better eat something." There was no telling how long the power would be out, and how long they'd be stuck in this house.

Larry grabbed a plate and took a huge bite of the omelet. He spoke before he finished chewing. "I used to eat raw eggs when I was in training, so this is some gourmet crap compared to that." He threw open the door of the fridge, apparently not understanding it was best to leave the door closed while the power was out. "Please tell me there's something to drink in this place besides wine."

Riley closed the door and stood in front of it. "Larry, we need to keep the fridge closed so the food will stay cold longer. Like when we have a snowstorm?"

He nodded. "Oh, yeah. Does that mean you have a couple six-packs out in a snowbank?"

She closed her eyes and Ben imagined she might be counting.

"Afraid we're all out of snowbanks, and beer, big guy." As soon as the words left Ben's mouth, he regretted them. He waited for Larry to pound him into the floor.

But apparently, all Larry could focus on was the lack of beer. "This sucks. Where's the closest mini mart?"

"Hurricane, Larry. Nothing's open, even if you could leave." Riley looked like she was about to snap.

There was a rattle and clank outside. If he had to guess, he'd say the awning over the back door was gone. He hoped he'd tied the grill secure enough not to blow away. "Riley, eat something. Then we'll go to bed. Maybe the storm will pass by morning." He held a plate out to her, but she shook her head.

"I can't eat." She grabbed the closest glass of wine and headed for the stairs.

Larry tossed his empty plate in the sink and leaned against the counter. "Where'd you stash the beer, dude?"

He was going to be pretty upset when he realized no one had hidden the beer from him.

***

Ben got Larry settled in the bedroom farthest away from Riley's and then checked to make sure everyone else had what they needed for the night.

Kelsey was snoring loudly, and Noel was singing to herself beside her mother, something from *The Little Mermaid,* perhaps. They had carried the bassinet up the stairs, and Liam was asleep in it, swaddled like a little caterpillar in a cocoon. Margaret was in the room next door and assured him she would be backup if Kelsey remained comatose.

Then he crept quietly into Riley's room. It was dark, but he saw her form in the bed when he passed his light over the room. He turned off his phone, hoping to save the battery, and quickly undressed and slid into the bed behind her.

She settled into his embrace, but didn't say anything for a long time. It was hard enough getting through your first hurricane, but Riley had had the kitchen sink thrown at her when Larry and her family showed up. He placed a kiss on her shoulder and wrapped his arm tightly around her waist. They could talk about everything once things were back to normal.

"Ben?" Her voice quivered, and he tightened his hold on her.

"Yeah?"

"Do you want to have kids?"

The question shouldn't have surprised him, after all the hints Kelsey and Noel had hurled at them. But the answer was easy. "Of course. I love kids."

She sighed and pressed her body closer to him.

Hopefully, with that reassurance, she could get some rest.

Chapter Thirty-Nine

Riley woke up to a dark room with no idea what time it was. She'd wanted curtains or something to keep the sun from waking her up, but the plywood was a little extreme. She fumbled for her phone and saw it was a little after seven.

Ben was still asleep, so she slid out of the bed trying not to wake him. For a minute, she stared at him, wishing she could stay with him. Not just in bed, but forever.

Slipping out of the room, she was met with banging. Had the storm blown a drum line up here from New Orleans?

Hurrying downstairs, she found the source of the clamor. Noel was sitting in the middle of the kitchen floor, a dozen pans surrounding her, beating out the rhythm of "Kiss the Girl" with wooden spoons. It was pretty spot on. There were no adults in attendance for her show, so Riley backtracked to the parlor, where she found Kelsey asleep on the couch and their mom holding Liam by the fireplace.

"Your sister went back to sleep after she found out there would be no coffee."

Ugh, she couldn't believe she had to face Larry and the man she had to break up with on the same day with no coffee to aid her. "Is it still storming?"

Margaret shrugged. "I haven't checked. Liam and I were talking about how he'll serve in the Marines."

Riley rolled her eyes. No way would she encourage her nephew to do something so dangerous. Even if it was brave. Not after the panic her father put her through. She went to the front door and stared out the peephole. All she could make out was Larry's big-ass truck.

She unlocked the door and wrenched it open. It was raining, but it wasn't blowing sideways, and it didn't feel like the wind could carry her away. She pushed through the screen and stepped out onto the porch. There were branches and leaves everywhere she looked, the fountain was overflowing with muddy water and the copper heron that usually perched on top was laying at an awkward angle on the ground beside it. The rowboat had come untied from the dock and was now resting on the bank of the river, and it looked like the gazebo had lost about half of its roof. Basically, everything looked soggy and tattered.

She heard the screen door open behind her and before she could turn around, arms slinked around her waist, pulling her against a hard body. Definitely not Larry. She sighed, hating she wouldn't get to enjoy this man for much longer.

"The storm is on its way inland. Should just be rain from here on out. I'm going to go down and check on my boat if you're okay." Ben rested his chin on her head, his hand idly stroking her hip and sending surges of pleasure up her spine. Life really wasn't fair.

"How long 'til they get the power restored?" She had a houseful of people to feed and keep entertained and electricity would make that so much easier.

"Hard to say out here, but in town it will likely be later today or tomorrow, so we can get food and more supplies soon. I'll call and find out when the restaurants will reopen. It'll depend on how they fared during the storm."

The door banged open again, and heavy boots stomped across the porch as Larry flashed by them. "If I'm staying here, I need beer."

It was seven o'clock in the morning, and no one had asked him to stay.

"I doubt anything's open yet, and I could use your help taking down the plywood." Ben's grip on her tightened protectively.

Larry stopped cold as he rounded his truck, his hands going up in a defensive position. He started to back up, shaking his head.

Riley opened her mouth to ask what was wrong just as he cleared the back of his truck and his reason for retreat became obvious.

Stalking slowly towards him, mouth open and about a billion pointy teeth on display, was an honest-to-goodness, real-life, no-doubt-in-anyone's-mind alligator. His front right food was missing, that wasn't slowing him down.

Riley leapt out of Ben's arms and flew inside, breath coming fast as she clung to the screen door, watching in morbid fascination as the beast stalked her ex across the driveway.

"Ben, that is *not* a log."

He took a step, so his back was pressed against the house. "Nope, not a log."

Larry reached the porch steps and fell twice, trying to scale them backwards. He didn't take his eyes off the at least nine-foot-long reptile.

"Can crocs climb stairs?" She'd never heard panic in her ex-husband's voice before, but right now he sounded like a man who had fallen out of a plane without a parachute.

"Don't know, but alligators can!" Ben grabbed the screen door and jumped inside, Larry close on his heels.

"What's all the commotion about?" Margaret joined them in the foyer, Liam draped over her shoulder. She looked between Riley and Ben in time to see said alligator mounting the stairs. "Holy shit!" She gripped the baby tightly and ran back to the parlor.

Riley wasn't sure if she'd ever heard her mother cuss, so it was right on par with a three-legged alligator climbing her porch steps as far as shock factor.

"I'm betting they can also tear straight through this screen." Ben pushed everyone back and slammed the front door just as the gator cleared the last step.

"You're on your own with the plywood, Barney," Larry threw over his shoulder as he headed to the kitchen. "Too bad my gun's in the truck."

Kelsey came in from the parlor, rubbing her eyes. "Can you guys keep it down? Some of us aren't used to expensive wine."

"Sorry, guess the ten-foot alligator on my front porch didn't realize you were hungover."

Her sister blinked a few times, attempting to process the information. "Call me when the porch is reptile free. I'm going back to bed." She dragged herself up the staircase, Noel following close behind with her mermaid book. When Kelsey reached the top, she turned back around. "Happy Birthday, Riley." She covered her yawn with her hand and shuffled toward her room.

"Good thing you didn't want much fanfare for your birthday. It's so chill we don't even have lights." Ben kissed her cheek. "As soon as everything is back to normal, we'll celebrate properly." He leaned in close. "And by that, I mean, alone and naked."

A familiar shiver rocketed up her spine at his breath on her neck. It took so little for her body to react to his. Maybe she could keep him a bit longer. It was her birthday, after all. "How'd you know what I wanted?"

He grinned, and her heart melted. *Not fair, not fair, not fair.*

A crash on the porch popped their little bubble. "I think we'll wait until it stops raining to take the wood down."

She laughed at his attempted nonchalance. "What? I thought you wrestled gators all the time. It's not even Sunday."

He grabbed her and pulled her close, burying his face in the crook of her neck and kissing his favorite spot. "Har har. We should get you a spot down at the comedy club."

She linked her arms around him tightly, wishing she didn't have to let him go.

Chapter Forty

The gator had gotten bored on the porch with nothing (or no one) to eat and had wandered back to the river. Larry had retrieved his gun from the truck, where it was now strapped to his waist for when the beast returned. They had pulled all the plywood off the windows and were storing it in the shed behind the house.

"What are your intentions towards Riley?"

Ben dropped his end of the wood. Grappling with the plywood, and the right thing to say to Riley's ex-husband, who two days ago had basically announced his intentions for them to reconcile, Ben stammered under his breath. He finally decided to be brutally honest and hope the gator was the only thing in danger of being shot. "I love her, so I imagine I'll marry her at some point."

"You ever been married before?"

Was he going to get a lecture from Riley's cheating ex-husband on the secret to a good marriage? "Yes, I have. My wife passed away two years ago."

Larry appraised him over the pile of wood. "Sorry to hear that."

Ben nodded once.

"Whelp, I guess all I got to offer is that she's a pretty great girl, and I was a dumbass." Larry pointed a meaty finger at him. "Don't be a dumbass."

Unsure how to respond, Ben continued to nod.

"When she lost the baby, I didn't know how to fix it. How to fix her." He wiped a hand across his wide forehead. "I gave up too easy."

Suddenly, the pieces began to fall into place. Her grief, the sadness in her eyes when she held her nephew, her question last night. Losing a baby—he couldn't possibly imagine. Despite all his loss, he couldn't fathom losing a child. The hole she must have in her heart. "I won't give up on her."

Larry nodded once, a silent agreement between the two men.

***

When they finished outside, Ben thought about going to find Riley but realized he wasn't ready to face her with this new information. They'd only been together for a few weeks, but he wondered why she hadn't told him.

He had shared his struggles about moving on after his wife died and told her he was in love with her, and she hadn't shared any of this. Maybe she didn't care about him as deeply as he did about her. Maybe this was more of a rebound for her—a way to move on.

Instead, he picked his way through the mounds of debris the storm had kicked up to check on his boat. A trip that normally took about fifteen minutes—less if he was running—took closer to forty. Branches littered the well-worn path between the two properties and at one point, two trees had been completely uprooted, their gangly roots pointing toward the sky. He'd have to rent a chainsaw and clear the path, but it wasn't an emergency.

He took the long way around, slogging through the muddy foundation of the home he and Sarah had begun to build.

He leaned against a cement piling, picturing the plans she had drawn up. He'd be standing in the kitchen right now.

He wondered how the house would have fared in the storm. He wondered if he would ever finish it. If Riley would want to live here someday. If she even wanted to stay with him long term.

The buzzing of his phone interrupted his rambling thoughts.

"Hey, man," he greeted Chesnee, "how are things up in Wilmington?"

"The house came through better than Grandma."

"What happened?" Ben picked through the mud toward his dock.

"She broke her hip when she fell off the table."

"Why was she on a table?"

Chesnee snickered. "Performing her version of Proud Mary after one too many cocktails."

He tried to picture the elderly woman gyrating like Tina Turner, but it was too disturbing to contemplate. "I hope she has a quick recovery."

"She'll be fine. She's got a thing for her orthopedic surgeon. Poor guy gets all flustered around her, but I guess I would too if a purple-haired lady kept grabbing my ass. What about you? Did you and Riley get busy in every room in the house?"

Ben shook his head, almost tempted to tell him about their escapades on the stairs, but thought better of it. "Her ex-husband, mother, sister and two little kids showed up."

"Dude. That's an epic cock-block."

"You're telling me."

"Are they all still there? Is the sister hot?"

He stopped in his tracks, finally taking in the sight of his boat, which was listing to the port side. "Chesnee, I've got to go, the boat doesn't look good."

As he lowered the phone to his side, he could hear the younger man yelling, "What about the sister?"

He ended the call and left the phone on the shore—in the only dry spot he could find. No telling what kind of mess there'd be on the boat. His home.

He tested the dock as he stepped onto it, but it seemed sturdy. Two of the ropes securing the boat had come undone, so he had to reel it closer and retie the leads. As he stepped on board, water sloshed over his shoes. A little water on the deck was to be expected, but his primary concern was the leaning.

He rounded the wheelhouse and immediately saw the problem. The door that led below deck was open, likely unable to bear the brunt of the wind, and there was about a foot of water on that side of the boat. He found a bucket and started bailing it out, attempting to salvage his belongings as they floated past.

The water was concentrated in the main living area, and his bedroom was dry. The cushions that comprised his "couch" would dry out on the next sunny day, the small TV that got precisely one channel was toast, and his to-be-read pile of law journals would have to be replaced. His primary concern was his photography equipment, which was safe inside the waterproof case under his bed.

A couple hours later, his boat was sitting level again, and he'd filled a garbage bag with trash to haul away. He sat in the built-in banquet in the galley and popped a beer from the fridge. He supposed he could have told Larry he had cold beer on the boat, but he wasn't feeling quite that generous toward his girlfriend's ex.

The sun was sinking toward the horizon, so he knew he should get back to the house, but instead, he propped his feet up and opened another can. His mind drifted to thoughts of Riley naked underneath him. No chance of that happening anytime soon with her family hanging around.

Then he remembered why they showed up in the first place. It was Riley's birthday, and his dumb ass was hanging out alone on his boat.

He'd promised Larry he wouldn't be a dumbass.

Chapter Forty-One

After a dinner that looked a lot like lunch (the power was still out and they only had so many options), Margaret announced she was doing a deep clean of the kitchen cabinets and everyone needed to split. Ben hadn't returned from the boat yet and Larry took off up the stairs to do God-knows-what, so Riley grabbed her sister and dragged her into the butler's pantry.

"I'm all for choosing another bottle of wine, but don't let me drink as much tonight. I wasn't coherent until mid-afternoon."

"Mid-afternoon is a bit of a stretch. Try happy hour."

"I must have missed the cocktails." Kelsey propped Liam up on her shoulder and patted his bottom.

Riley laughed. "The cabana boy must have floated away in the storm. But I do have a little trick up my sleeve."

Noel, always tagging along, perked up. "You do magic, Wiwee?"

She put on her best magician pose and flicked the hidden lever. The wall swung open, revealing Archie's inner sanctum.

"Shut up." Kelsey slapped her sister's shoulder. "A freaking secret passageway?"

Feeling pretty smug, Riley nodded. "Turns out old Archie was full of surprises."

"I mean, I already love him just for the wine."

The sun was making its descent, so the room was shrouded in shadows. Riley stepped back into the kitchen and grabbed one of the lanterns. "You gotta see his wardrobe, Kels. The man had style." *Tacky is a style, right?*

Kelsey situated the baby in the middle of the enormous bed, creating a pillow fort around him. Riley set the lantern on a shelf so it would illuminate part of the bedroom and shine some light into the closet. Noel settled on the floor with her mermaid book. Thank goodness she was as obsessed with it as with the movie.

For the next hour, the sisters dug through Archie's clothes, a veritable time capsule of the last five decades. They tried on shirts and jackets, sorted through boxes of memorabilia, and added to the "donate" pile Riley had already started.

Noel fell asleep, her head resting on a picture of a crab, and Liam started to fuss.

Kelsey scooped him up, pulled out her breast, and plopped down in the chair behind Archie's desk. "You think you'll move in here? It's way bigger than your room upstairs."

Riley leaned in the doorway, watching her sister breastfeed her nephew, feeling her heart break in a million pieces. She swallowed the lump in her throat. "It makes sense. Once I start having guests, it will give me way more privacy, and another room upstairs to rent out."

"You'll need more clothes if you're gonna come close to filling that closet. I volunteer to take you to the outlet mall in Myrtle Beach."

"Such a sacrifice." Her sister could have made a career out of finding bargains and knew every outlet mall in a five-state area.

Kelsey shrugged. "Anything for my sis..." Her mouth dropped open, and she reached for a frame on the desk. "Have you seen this?"

Riley crossed to her side of the room, bringing the lantern closer. "I haven't looked through his desk in here yet, just the one in the study."

Her sister turned the frame around, and Riley's heart seized. No way.

The picture had been taken on Riley's first birthday. Six-year-old Kelsey sat in one of those giant beach chairs they have in tourist towns for pictures, holding her sister on her lap. Obviously, she didn't remember the events of the day, but that picture had hung in her parents' living room her whole life.

"Guess old Archie knew we existed, even if we didn't know he did." Kelsey switched Liam to the other side, never taking her eyes off Riley. "You okay?"

Slowly nodding her head, she tried to process what this meant. Archie and her dad had apparently been in contact as recently as twenty-nine years ago. The fact that it was framed, and on the desk in his bedroom, where he would see it every day...

"Riley, say something. You're freaking me out."

"Sorry. I just have so many questions." She wondered how long until her dad was back in the states, so she could finally get some answers.

Kelsey started yanking open drawers and pawing through Archie's belongings. Riley sank down on the bed, staring at the picture.

"Look." She dangled a key ring from her finger. "Maybe one of them goes to the mysterious red door." She plunked the keys on the desk and kept digging. "Check this one out." She read from the tag dangling from a single key. "Sarah's Studio. Who's Sarah?"

Riley's eyes slid over the frame in her hand and landed on the key Kelsey held, the one with the red tag hanging from it. "Sarah was Ben's wife."

"Shut up!" Kelsey jumped, startling Liam, who cried in protest. She propped him on her shoulder and tucked her breast away. "We've got to go see if it fits!"

It couldn't be the key to that door. It couldn't be Sarah's studio. Because that would mean Ben lied to her. That would mean every time she mentioned the locked room was another instance, he kept that secret from her. And she was guessing he had a key he had withheld from her as well. "We don't know that it's *the* key."

"Girls!" Margaret's voice drifted through the open door. "Come see what I've accomplished."

Kelsey tucked the key in her pocket. "We are so going up there as soon as Mom shows off her organizing skills." She checked that Noel was still asleep and preceded Riley through the secret door in the pantry.

Riley followed behind her and when she stepped into the kitchen, her mom was holding a cake that was on fire and illuminated the people in the room who had started to sing "Happy Birthday"—including her father.

She raced to her dad, wrapping her arms around his neck, so relieved to see him again and so overwhelmed he had made it for her birthday.

"Happy Birthday, Sugarbee." He hugged her tight and then kissed her cheek.

"Blow out the candles before you burn the house down." Larry towered over the group, a party hat perched at an angle on his head.

She scanned the room, happy to see Ben was back and surprised to find Trip there as well.

"Chesnee is sorry he couldn't make it, but his grandma is in the hospital." Trip also wore a hat, which she realized said Happy Retirement.

She may have been dreading thirty, but she wasn't that old.

"I hope she's okay." Her gaze landed on Ben, who wasn't wearing a party hat, but he was wearing a hell of a smile.

"I'll tell you about it later, the cake is melting." He gestured at Margaret, who had lost her cheerful grin after holding a burning cake while Riley was catching up with everyone.

Briefly, she closed her eyes, thought of a wish, discarded it, thought of a better one, and then huffed until all the candles went out.

"Cheers." Larry saluted her with his beer bottle (thank goodness he finally got his beer) and left the room. He had been acting weird the whole time he was there. And where did he keep disappearing to?

Margaret dumped the cake on the table and Ben turned up the lantern since the blaze had been put out and they no longer had the ambient light from a million candles.

"Happy Birthday Ri." Ben wrapped his arms around her waist and pulled her in for a hug that lit up her whole body. Then he kissed her—like he wasn't the least bit concerned her father (a colonel, no less) was in the room.

When he released her, she looked heavenward and double wished for her wish to come true.

Her mom was handing out slices of cake and everyone was talking about the storm, her birthday and why they hadn't opened any wine yet (that was Kelsey). Ben grabbed a bottle from the pantry and poured a few glasses. The men drank the beer that had arrived (thanks to Trip). The women ate cake and washed it down with a fruity red.

Larry came back long enough to grab a slice of cake, but didn't linger. He wasn't exactly on her dad's good side. After he cheated, there had been "a discussion" according to her father, and "a threat" according to Larry. Riley was guessing this was the first time they'd seen each other since, but they only glared at one another briefly.

She wanted to get her dad alone and grill him about Archie, but she was the guest of honor at this pathetic little party. After two glasses of wine, Kelsey proposed a game of charades but was shot down by everyone in attendance. She huffed and went to put her kids to bed. Trip left shortly after that, and Margaret started cleaning up the mess in the kitchen. Riley seized the opportunity and grabbed her dad by the arm. She would deal with Ben later.

Pulling him through the doorway into Archie's room, she turned and hugged him again. "I'm so glad you're okay. You had me worried to death."

He stroked her back and gave a tug on her ponytail. "You never have to worry about your old man. I've always got it under control."

She released him and took a steading breath. "Okay, now that we've got that out of the way"—she held up the picture Kelsey had found—"start talking."

Her dad's stiff military posture slipped, and he dropped to the edge of the bed, burying his face in his hands. "Riley, I hate that you had to find out this way. I should have told you about your uncle."

"You should have told me I had an uncle. Preferably before he died." She set her hands on her hips, trying to look stern.

"You're right."

His admission took the wind out of her sails, and she sank down on the bed beside him. "Why was he such a big secret?"

"My brother wasn't like the rest of my family. Growing up, he preferred the arts to sports, he would rather read than go outside—he was in theater, for God's sake." He rose and crossed to a bookcase, where he picked up a photograph of Archie with some white-haired guy. "He would rather meet Andy Warhol than General MacArthur. But his biggest sin, in our father's eyes at least, was that he was a pacifist."

"So, you kicked him out of the family because he didn't want to kill people?" Riley was well aware of the Kirkwood history in the Marines and other branches of the military. Her great-grandfather had been awarded a purple heart for his service. But none of that excused cutting someone out of the family.

"I didn't do anything, Riley." A whoosh of air escaped his lips, and a pained look crossed his face briefly. "I didn't do anything."

She had never heard her dad sound defeated, unsure, sad. He had always been a pillar of strength and confidence that she knew would hold their family up, no matter what.

He joined her on the bed again, took her hand, and ducked his head (in shame?). "Archie and my father had it out when he graduated from high school. I was a kid, maybe nine or ten, although it's no excuse, but people didn't cross my father. And Archie did." He took a deep breath, his whole body shuddering. "He told our father he wasn't joining up, instead he was going to move to New York City and study art. My father told him if he went anywhere other than boot camp, he might as well change his last name, because he was no longer part of our family."

Riley tried to reconcile this response with the grandfather she had known. He was a stooped old man with a stark white buzz cut, but to her and Kelsey, he was Gramps. He was the one who snuck them bowls of ice cream after bed and told them stories about princesses that rescued the prince and didn't need a man to stick up for them.

He squeezed her hand, as if reading her mind. "He softened in his old age, and once you girls came along, he was basically a teddy bear that let you dress him up for a tea party. But he was different when my grandfather was still alive—well, basically as long as he was still in the service. He was hard and unmovable. And proud to a fault. A son who wouldn't fight for his country was the ultimate stain on his record, so he removed him from the record completely."

Her heart ached for Archie, having to choose between his passion and his family. "Gram went along with this?"

"My mother stood by my father's decision, but every year on my birthday, she'd slip a letter from Archie under my pillow." He finally met her eyes. "When I turned eighteen, the letters stopped. I enlisted, and I didn't hear from him for years. Then, one day, my mom forwarded me a letter from him, saying he had settled in Eastport Beach and was fixing up an old house. This house. Once I had an address, I started writing to him when significant things happened—making Captain, meeting your mom and Kelsey, having you. I sent him pictures, asked if we could meet up, even talk on the phone. But he always said he was too busy. I think he was as stubborn as our father."

"You could have just shown up."

He nodded, thoughtful. "Yeah, I guess I could have, but I have some of the Kirkwood stubbornness in me as well." He wrapped an arm around her shoulder and pulled her in for a side hug. "Sometimes people get in the way of their own happiness. I loved my brother, but we were all too proud to get past the trauma of something that happened a long time ago. I missed him terribly and I hate that he never got to meet you, because you are my greatest accomplishment." He kissed her temple. "I hope you can forgive me someday, but it's okay if you need to be mad for a while. I was mad at my father for twenty years. Then I realized that as adults, sometimes we make hard choices, and sometimes we make mistakes."

She digested everything he'd told her, happy to sit in his safe embrace and feel his presence. "I could never be mad at you. But I feel bad for Archie."

He chuckled. "Don't feel too bad for old Archie. He lived a full life. The man had more adventures than I did—with a lot fewer battle scars."

Chapter Forty-Two

Riley slid into bed well after midnight. Her parents were next door, her sister across from them, and her ex-husband at the end of the hall.

"I'm sorry your birthday sucked." And he couldn't even make it better with an orgasm, because he knew from experience that Riley was quite vocal.

She tucked her body under his arm and burrowed into his embrace. "I didn't want it to be a big deal, anyway."

"At least your dad made it." He rested his hand on her hip, trying to keep things from progressing into screaming territory. "Did you get the answers you wanted?"

"I got some answers. Honestly, I'm not sure if there were any excusable answers to be had. But at least I know now." Her voice sounded flat, disappointed.

He wanted to flip her over and kiss away her sadness, but instead he squeezed her tighter, careful to avoid her delectable breasts. Maybe they could go sleep on the boat. Only the herons and gators out there to hear her scream in ecstasy. "If it's any consolation, I think Archie was generally a happy guy. He made his own family out of the people he mentored. Some people aren't close to their family, and that's okay." He couldn't remember the last time he'd seen his parents, although he was certain their faces held expressions of disapproval. Maybe that's why he and Archie had bonded so easily.

"I wish I could have known him."

"Me too. He was a remarkable man."

They were quiet for a while, and he thought she'd fallen asleep when she spoke again. "You said the third floor was used for studio space. Did Sarah ever paint up there?"

He forced himself to breathe—evenly—so she would think he was asleep. Because he was a freaking coward.

***

Ben awoke to an empty bed, sunlight streaming through the windows, and a key with a red tag attached laying on the bedside table. He didn't have to turn the tag over to know what it said.

His dreams had been plagued by both Sarah and Riley. The two women he loved ganging up against him. Forgetting Sarah felt impossible, but if he didn't, how could he love Riley fully? And if he couldn't even unlock a door and face the demons inside, how could he be man enough to be a husband again, and a father?

Dragging into the bathroom, he flicked the light switch out of habit. It took him a full minute to realize the lights came on. If the power was back on, it meant things were getting back to normal and maybe at least some of their visitors would leave.

He and Riley needed alone time to hash things out. He needed to share his insecurities, and hope like hell she trusted him enough to tell him about her miscarriage.

After brushing his teeth and draining his bladder, he pulled on a pair of jeans and an old Cheerwine t-shirt. He needed to do some work outside if he expected their company to be able to drive their cars off the property.

He followed the joyful noise of family into the kitchen. Riley's parents stood hip to hip at the stove, stirring their respective pots and speaking in low tones. The sisters sat at the kitchen table, helping Noel put together a mermaid puzzle. Liam lay in the bassinet, cooing at the ceiling. Larry was nowhere to be seen.

"Morning, all." He bent down and kissed Riley on the cheek, then headed for the coffeepot. "Everyone happy to have the power back on?"

"Praise coffee and hot showers." Kelsey held her mug aloft.

Margaret smiled blissfully at her husband. "Electricity means hollandaise sauce. You're in for a real treat. My Bill here makes the best eggs Benedict you've ever had."

He'd never tried the dish, but from the smells wafting up from the stove, he was on board. "Did you learn to cook in the service, sir?"

"The only thing remotely French you'd eat in the mess is a fry. I learned to cook when I was stationed in France, a long, long time ago."

"He means before he met me." Margaret winked at Ben over her husband's shoulder. "Because it was a lady who taught him this particular recipe."

"Before my life truly began." He bumped his wife's hip with his and she tittered.

Kelsey refilled her mug with coffee. "Ignore our parents. They are disgusting for weeks after Dad gets back."

Ben caught Riley's eye and smiled. He wanted to be standing at a stove with her in thirty years, still this much in love. He could picture it, clear as day, and he didn't feel scared anymore, just hopeful. "Hope you don't mind if I steal Riley for a bit."

"Breakfast will be ready at 0800 hours, son. I suggest you're back by then or you'll have to fight for the scraps."

He resisted the urge to salute the Colonel. "Yes, sir." He grabbed Riley's hand and pulled her up from the table. She followed, but her face showed that she wasn't completely convinced.

In the hallway, she opened her mouth, but he held up his hand. "Just come with me, okay?"

She nodded once and allowed herself to be dragged up the stairs. They sailed right past the door to her bedroom and her look turned into one of confusion.

"I'd like that, but not until your family leaves. These walls are way too thin." He tugged her toward the staircase to the third floor.

"Ben—"

"Riley, please. I'll explain in a minute."

She closed her mouth again.

He took a fortifying breath and started up the narrow stairs. The feel of her hand in his grounded him, and he made it to the top without vomiting. When they stopped in front of the red door, he gave himself a mental pep talk (brow beating—tomato, toemato).

Digging the key out of his pocket, he placed it in her hand. "This was Sarah's studio. I haven't been inside it since a few months before she died. I think I felt like if I locked it up tight, I could store her in here forever, never have to worry about losing her. It was wrong of me not to tell you immediately. This is your house now."

"Ben, I have a million rooms in this house. I don't need this one. It's okay." She tucked the key back into his hand.

He took her hands, the key pressed between their palms. "Ri, if I don't open this door, I might as well keep my heart locked up to you, too. And I want to let you in. I want to cook with you thirty years from now."

The confused look was back.

"I want to be with you, Riley. I love you. So, I have to let Sarah go."

She shook her head fiercely, ponytail whipping back and forth and a tear sliding down her cheek. "I'd never ask you to do that." She placed her hand over his heart. "Just like there are plenty of rooms in this house, there is enough room in your heart for Sarah and anyone else you choose to love."

Chapter Forty-Three

Ben's brow furrowed, pain flashing in his eyes. "What do you mean, anyone I choose to love?"

She didn't want to do this now, not while her family was downstairs, and breakfast was going to be ready in a matter of minutes. Knowing her sister, she'd come looking for them. "Can we talk about this later?'

He staggered back from her, hands dropping to his sides, the key clambering to the floor between them.

They stared at the key, then at each other, then he turned and left.

Riley wasn't much for swearing, but she had some choice words for herself in that moment. Sliding down the red door, she pulled her knees up and stared at the key, which taunted her from the hardwoods. More tears joined the first, and she cried until Kelsey came to find her long after breakfast got cold.

***

"Want me to kick his ass?" Larry tossed his bag in the back seat of his truck.

Riley rolled her eyes. "No, if anyone needs their ass kicked, it's me."

He pulled her into his beefy embrace, and for a split second, she remembered the good times. "You call me anytime, okay?"

She nodded against his chest, refusing to cry in front of her ex—again.

He pulled away and hefted his body into the truck, then powered down the window. "You're the strongest person I know, Riley. Give yourself some credit. And don't write off being a mother. You'll be a damn fine one."

As his truck bumped over the now pond-sized ruts in the driveway, she wondered what the hell alternate universe she was living in that Larry seemed mature and maybe even wise.

The screen door banged, and Kelsey called from the porch. "Buttface hit the road?"

"Yes, Larry's gone."

"Thank goodness. I've been holding my breath for three days."

Riley climbed the steps and linked arms with her sister. "You're gonna miss having someone to verbally abuse."

"Nah, I can always text him."

"I'm so glad you came for my birthday."

"Larry, Ben and you stuck in this house during a hurricane? Someone wouldn't have made it out alive. You were just happy for a buffer."

She leaned her head on Kelsey's shoulder and stared down at where she knew Ben's boat bobbed behind the trees. "Best damn buffer ever. That's why I was hoping you'd go down to the boat with me."

"I am not going to be your break-up buffer! Besides, I think you're a fool for breaking up with him, anyway."

"Break up?" The screen door banged as Margaret joined her daughters on the porch. "Riley, please tell me you aren't breaking up with Ben."

Kelsey elbowed her in the side. "Told you it was a bad idea."

"He's wonderful, Riley. The way he took care of things during the storm, and the way he looks at you…That man is smitten."

It was getting harder to justify her decision with everyone telling her how wrong she was. "I know he's great, that's why he deserves to be with someone who wants the same things he does."

"And what's that?"

Riley bit her lip and shifted her weight from leg to leg. She stared up at the porch ceiling, freshly painted and shining bright white. If only it was that easy to cover up the damage she had done.

"Riley doesn't want to try to have another baby because she's afraid she'll lose it, too." Kelsey patted her back.

"Oh, Riley." Margaret gripped her shoulders with a sympathetic look on her face. "I had no idea you were still worried about that." She tucked a stray hair behind her daughter's ear and Riley came undone.

A flood of tears released like the dam had broken. Her mother pulled her into a tight embrace.

"Baby girl. I'm so sorry you had to go through that. I know how hard it is." She pulled back, wiping her fingers under her daughter's eyes. "Riley, I had two miscarriages before I had Kelsey. Sometimes biology can be cruel, but usually it means the baby wasn't strong enough to survive. For me, it seemed more humane for that baby to pass safe inside me than to have to enter the world and struggle. Our role as mothers is to try to make our children's lives as happy as possible. I would never want one of my children to suffer. I protected those two babies, just like I protected you and your sister when you were young and vulnerable. It was my honor to do that."

Riley took a few steading breaths. "Why didn't you tell me this last year?"

"I didn't realize you were taking it so hard. Obviously, you did too good of a job hiding your pain. Riley, you never have to hide anything from us. We're your family."

She twisted her hands in the hem of her shirt. "I felt so hopeless, but everyone's lives went on like nothing happened, so I thought I needed to be strong." Which meant she only cried when she was alone at night.

"Honey, when you're feeling weak, we'll be strong for you. It's what family does. And I think it's what Ben would do too if you let him in."

Riley stared across the lawn, straining to see the top of his boat. "I don't think I can handle that again."

"If you have to, you can, because you're stronger than you think. But if I never tried again, I wouldn't have you girls, and where would I be then? You are the best thing to ever happen to me. That joy outweighs any pain I've endured."

While she was watching the tree line, Ben emerged, walking their way. The sun was glinting off the water and two herons flew overhead. He stopped, watching the graceful birds until they disappeared. Riley felt her heart swell. She wanted that joy, and she wanted it with this man.

"Thanks, Mom." She gave her mom a quick hug, then raced down the steps and across the lawn.

Ben saw her and quickened his pace.

They met near the dock, where they shared their first (real) kiss.

Silently, he led her down to the water where they stood looking out at the shimmering river, hands latched together.

She closed her eyes, the feel of his hand holding hers giving her such comfort, when she realized something felt different. She peeked between them, rotating her wrist to turn his hand out, and confirmed her suspicions. He had taken off his wedding ring. She rubbed her finger over the groove left in its absence, knowing what a big deal it was for him to let go of that symbol of his love for Sarah. He was opening his heart up to her, and she needed to do the same.

"I had a miscarriage last year." The words tumbled out, raw and painful, but once they were out there, it was a relief, like the feeling after you've thrown up.

He squeezed her hand tighter.

"It was the worst pain I've ever felt, and I don't mean physically, although that was hard too."

"I can imagine."

If any man could, she supposed it was him. He understood loss.

She turned to face him, and he linked their other hands together. "I'm scared to try again."

He nodded. "I know. Me too."

"But I think with you, it might be worth the risk."

He squeezed his eyes shut and pulled her into his arms. "Me too." She couldn't see him, but if she had to guess, he was crying too.

She clung to him, certain she had found her person in this world. She felt safe and loved and excited and scared. "I love you, Ben."

He pulled back, his face wet, and cupped her cheek. "I love you, too, Riley." Then he kissed her. Sweet and slow like the summer afternoon.

He was panting when his lips left hers. "When is your family leaving?"

"Not until tomorrow. How about the boat?"

Grinning, he took her hand again. "It's time we celebrated your birthday properly." Then he pulled her back to shore and through the trees.

Epilogue
One Month Later

Riley held the screen door open as Ben and Trip angled the trunk through it and down the porch steps. They loaded it in the back of the SUV and leaned against the gate exhausted.

"I made lemonade. I'll be right back."

"None for me, Riley," Trip called out. "I've got to get out of here if I'm going to make it to the church before they lock up."

She'd spent the last month sorting through Archie's belongings and now most of them were headed to the annual bazaar down at Eastport Beach Christian Fellowship. There were a few special pieces she held on to and displayed in prominent places throughout Heron House. She always wanted Archie to be a fixture here. "Thanks, Trip, you've been a tremendous help."

"You're saving me from sleeping on Chesnee's couch, so I've got no complaints." He slid behind the wheel and waved his hand out the window as he drove away.

"I'd take a glass of lemonade," Ben spoke up from where he was picking leaves out of the now-working fountain.

She headed back to the kitchen, with its freshly painted green cabinets and new countertops. Taking the pitcher from the new fridge Ben had surprised her with last week—as a reward for all her hard work and the money she saved doing much of it herself—she filled two glasses with ice (from the ice maker!) and fresh-squeezed lemonade and garnished them with a slice of lemon.

She used her hip to push open the screen door, and Ben greeted her on the porch, taking one glass and planting a kiss on her lips.

They settled on the swing, sipping their lemonade, watching the sun sink lower in the sky. Ben's hand idly traced patterns on her thigh as she curled her fingers through the ends of his hair.

"I hope you don't get your hair cut too short. I like playing with it."

"Well, I can't show up in court looking like a hippie, but I won't let Leonard take too much off." Ben had closed the office for a couple weeks and helped her with a lot of the work on the house. They'd spent time getting to know one another and christening every room—and staircase—in the place.

"I sent the invitations to the printer. We can't turn back now."

He turned and grinned at her. "I'm so proud of you, Riley. Heron House is going to be a huge success."

She was planning a grand reopening next month, inviting everyone who had been touched by Archie and this place. The website had been updated with a contact form and she even had Wi-Fi so she could answer the dozens of emails she received on a weekly basis. "I'm pretty proud of myself, too. But I couldn't have done it without your help."

He shrugged. "It just would have taken longer."

"No, without you, we wouldn't have a spider-free secret passageway to delight guests with, and Ansel never would have accepted me as his new owner." She tried to pout, but it twisted into a grin. "But he still likes you better."

"I marked something off my to-do list today, too."

"Oh, yeah? Besides toting all that stuff out to Trip's car?"

"Yup." He stood up and grabbed her hand. "I want to show you something."

Usually, when Ben started a conversation that way, it ended with them having sex in a new spot in the house. Or on the grounds. Or in the river. (Turned out the promise of an orgasm outweighed the fear of alligators.) "Okey dokey." She trailed happily behind him as he led her into the house and up both sets of stairs. When she reached the third floor, she gasped in surprise. The red door at the end of the hall stood wide open, and the setting sun cast a golden glow over the room and spilled out into the hallway.

"You won't believe what I found." He tightened his grip on her hand and pulled her forward.

She was terrified and excited. He'd told her a lot about Sarah in the past month, but she had left the red door up to him. She figured he'd open it when he was ready, but she didn't imagine it would be this soon.

Standing in the doorway, she gazed in marvel at hundreds of paintings covering every inch of the walls, leaning on the floor stacked on a small table. Sarah had clearly been a talented painter.

Riley had also spent the last month studying her uncle's art books and joining internet forums to learn everything she could about art. She recognized that this art was good. Very good. There were paintings of ladybugs, sunflowers, sailboats, and, of course, herons. There were landscapes and abstracts and a few portraits. But one painting drew her attention immediately.

In the center of the room, propped on an easel, as if Sarah had just completed it, was a picture of the river right outside this house. Of the gazebo, of the dock, of a sailboat bobbing in the distance. On that dock sat a family, feet dangling in the water, only their backs visible. There was a brown-headed man with a blond-headed boy next to him. The little boy held a fishing pole. Beside him sat a brown-haired little girl with curls that stretched down her back. And to her right sat a woman with a blonde ponytail.

Never before had Riley felt such empathy for anyone. She ached for Ben, having to see this dream of their family shattered, but mostly, she mourned for Sarah who had envisioned this and never had a chance to see it through.

"It's lovely." Her voice shook, and she fought back tears. Ben was being so brave, and she didn't want to lose it in front of him.

"Ri." He wrapped his arm around her and pulled her to his side, the two of them facing the painting. "Sarah didn't have blonde hair."

Her hand flew to cover her mouth. So much for not losing it.

"At the end, she'd have these dreams. Of my future. I refused to talk about it. Never wanted to hear what she had to say. So damn stubborn." He reached up and swiped at his face. "So, she'd come in here and paint."

"Oh Ben." What could she say? It was too much to process.

He kissed her on the top of her head, then rested his head on hers, looking at the painting. "Sarah was at peace when she died. And I think it was because she knew I'd find you."

The tears really started to flow then. He pulled her to his chest and held her tight. Her favorite place to be.

"I love you so much, Ri. We've both had to lose a lot to get here, but look how much we've gained."

As she breathed in his scent, she was reminded of the hoodie he had loaned her in the cafe after the whipped cream incident. They had come so far—clear across the state—and found what they both needed. "I love you too, Ben."

About the Author

Tara grew up with her nose buried in a book, and not much has changed. She's a serial entrepreneur – doggie daycare owner, quilt shop owner, maker and, of course, author. Currently, she lives in the mountains of North Carolina with her #1 love, a shichon named Agador Spartacus. Her whole family lives nearby, including her two grown sons, who are inspirations for the "cool" things young people say.

Also by

Stay tuned for more books in the Eastport Beach series.

A Heron House Affair (Sept 2025)

Preorder on Amazon

turn the page for an excerpt!

Standalones

Above Average Girl (2022)

This is a sweet romance about a plus-sized girl trying to find her way in the dating world with a little help from her friends.

The Things I Do For Her (2022)

Truly a story of friendship, this sweet romance is about growing up, finding love and moving on.

For signed paperback copies, visit www.dreamingoftheseafabrics.com.

A Heron House Affair
Chapter 1

The invitation was the first thing Ada noticed when she walked into her mother's Soho loft. Not the soot coating the cabinets above the stove or the melted pile of goo that may have been a spatula. She didn't notice the puddles of water remaining on the brushed concrete floors or the lone plate on the counter—a soggy piece of wheat toast as its centerpiece.

Ada's mother didn't believe in displaying photos, or appointment reminder cards, or the A+ her only child got on that American History exam. As far as she knew, her mother didn't even own a magnet.

Yet, there it was. Stark white and black in design, art déco font and trendy tropical leaves centered on the stainless-steel refrigerator door. A magnet advertising a Chinese restaurant offering delivery and a free egg roll with every order held it in place.

So, as Ada took in all the evidence of the kitchen fire, saw Gertrude, her mother's pathos plant, barely clinging to life, and found several paintbrushes left in dirty water next to her work in progress, it was the placement of the invitation that most signaled something was wrong with Charlotte Maddox.

Stepping to the refrigerator, Ada reached out and traced the raised lettering with one finger. Her mother had always been up for a party, but had she really considered traveling to North Carolina? Not that it mattered now, because Charlotte's days of jetting around the world had come to a screeching halt.

They still didn't know exactly how the fire had started, only that her mother, THE Charlotte Maddox, now had second-degree burns to both hands and a brand-new diagnosis of early onset dementia. If that neighbor hadn't heard her screams, if that fire extinguisher wasn't three steps from her door, if Ada hadn't taken that job in Virginia. There were too many what ifs.

She turned and leaned against the counter, suddenly unable to support her own weight. Her mother's New York loft was an open plan with large windows facing the east—for the best light. Her mother's eclectic tastes filled the space—the purple velvet sofa (eggplant, not plum, Charlotte insisted), the rattan chair with a cushion the color of mustard, the textured rug from India, or Burma, or Indonesia. Ada couldn't keep up with her mother's travels.

Now Charlotte would be confined to a 10' x 14' white box. It was unfathomable.

Her eyes settled next on the large canvas propped on an easel. Deep greens and blues signaled water churning. Dark storm clouds towered over the water, threatening and ominous. The piece was unfinished and a departure from Charlotte Maddox's usual work. It was as if the artist was relaying the turmoil in herself as her own mind betrayed her.

Her phone rang and without looking, Ada sensed it was Paul. He always seemed to know when she needed him. Whether it was to attend a dance recital because her mother was out of the country, or to buy her a backpack filled with school supplies because Charlotte was feeling inspired and wouldn't leave the house—she wondered if all managers helped raise the orphans of their artists. Because even when her mother was around, she was never really present.

"Did you make it okay?"

"Yes, I'm here. The whole place just feels, I don't know, off." She opened the refrigerator door. Eggs, fancy water, a few random condiments and a plate of stinky cheese. Ada wasn't sure if it was the kind that was stinky on purpose or if it had come to this refrigerator to die.

"I hate that I can't be there. I've got an opening tonight and this kid is green. He's currently freaking out because the hardware we used to hang his paintings is gold and not nickel. I'm too old for this kind of drama."

Ada smiled, feeling some of the tension drain out of her, just hearing his voice. "You live for that kind of drama. Without it, you'd just shrivel up and die."

"Maybe. All artists have their peculiarities, I know, but this younger generation—I'm not sure it's worth it. I'd take your mother's over-the-top attitude any day."

She closed the refrigerator door, staring again at the invitation. "Paul, what is Heron House?" She slid the card out from the magnet's hold and flipped it over. There was a handwritten note addressed to Charlotte.

"It was a retreat of sorts, your mom went there in the late 90s, gosh, I guess it was right before you came along." His voice got muffled, but she thought she heard him tell someone they could shove the gold hardware up their ass for all he cared.

"Well, apparently, it's reopening, and they wanted Charlotte to come down. And they had a question about one of her pieces."

"If you give me the number, I'll handle it. I haven't had time to put out a press release, but sooner or later, we must let people know."

"Paul, you've already gone above and beyond. You were here when I wasn't. You got her settled in a facility and you're taking care of the financial end. I couldn't do this without you." Her eyes scanned the apartment, mentally cataloguing everything she'd need to do to get it on the market. "I'll give them a call and let them know she won't be attending. You worry about Mr. Green and his nickels. I'll worry about Charlotte."

"And I'll worry about you."

"Guess very little has changed."

"Love ya, kiddo."

"Back at you." Ada disconnected from the call and started assembling boxes.

***

She'd packed up most of the kitchen and living room when her phone rang again. It was after six and she hadn't eaten anything since the bag of salt and vinegar chips she'd bought at a gas station five hours ago.

As soon as she got Miranda off the phone, she'd be putting her mother's magnet to good use. "Hey Randi."

"You were supposed to text me that you got to New York okay. Either you forgot or you took a detour to Canada."

"I'm in the city and before you ask, yes, I've eaten today." *Chips count as a meal, right?*

"And stay hydrated. You're going to be using all your muscles moving boxes and furniture. Do you have some Powerade?"

"How was class, Randi? Did you tell the girls I'll be back soon?" She had only started at the dance school three weeks ago, but she was already getting attached to the students. As scholarship kids, they really appreciated the chance to learn how to dance.

"Yeah, so about that."

"What happened? Did someone get hurt? I bet it was Elsie. She's a little wild." The seven-year-old had spent half of the last class sitting in the corner after she kicked another student in the head while cartwheeling across the room.

"Someone got hurt, but it wasn't a student."

"Are you okay?"

"I'm fine. It's Susan."

The director of the school was a little odd, but she had taken a chance and hired Ada despite her lack of teaching experience. "Oh no, what happened?"

"She was riding her unicycle when a chipmunk ran out in front her. The chipmunk is fine, but Susan has a broken hip."

"That's awful. I can help cover her classes as soon as I'm back." She'd have to dig deep into her memory banks to recall her tap and hip-hop skills, but it was like riding a bike, right? She'd steer clear of unicycles, though.

"Hold your horses, there's more. And please don't shoot the messenger."

It was her worst nightmare. Fired. She knew having to leave so soon after arriving would cause issues. But she couldn't see any way around it. It had always been just her and Charlotte. She held her breath, waiting to hear the dreaded words.

"She's closing down for the semester."

"Closing? What about all the students? What about the grant? If we cancel the program, we'll lose the funding." Ada had worked tirelessly on the application for the arts grant to offer classes to underprivileged kids. She'd assured Susan that she'd take care of everything and that it would be great PR for the school and most of all, would help more little girls gain the confidence that dance had given Ada when she was little, and her mother couldn't be bothered with a child.

"They pulled the funding."

"What the hell? Can they do that?"

"Some uppedity-up in Congress killed the bill that was funding our grant and thousands of other arts projects. So, if you need to get your anger out, stop in DC on your way back."

Ada squeezed her eyes shut, spots spinning behind her lids. She tried to control her breathing, to calm the anger threatening to explode out of her. She had a plan. She had a rental house. She needed a job to pay her bills. She was so proud of the program that she had started at Susie B's Dance Academy. She would not scream at Miranda. It wasn't her fault.

"I guess you can stay in New York a while longer. Hang out with your family, eat great pizza." She laughed awkwardly.

"My mom barely knows who I am. I'm packing up her apartment so her manager can sell it. We need the money to pay for her care."

"What about your father?"

Ada had known Miranda for less than a month and hadn't felt the need to share her dysfunctional family situation with her over tutus and leotards. She let out a sigh and plopped down on the sofa. "I don't know my father." She was tired, pissed off, and hungry. She didn't have time to fill her friend in on her childhood and semi-famous mother. It had never been convenient for Charlotte to have a daughter, and now she'd conveniently forgotten that she had one at all. "I have no reason to stay here."

"Where will you go?"

"I have no idea."

Preorder on Amazon!